"An adult mystery with young adult appeal . . . The second in Curtis's fun new series featuring Geri and Pepe is tailor-made for anyone who can't get enough dog mysteries and those readers who never miss an episode of *Dancing with the Stars*."

—*VOYA (Voice of Youth Advocates)*

DIAL C FOR CHIHUAHUA

"Three woofs and a big bow-wow for *Dial C for Chihuahua*. Pepe is one cool sleuth—just don't call him a dog! I really loved the book."

—**Leslie Meier**, author of the Lucy Stone mysteries

"Readers will sit up and beg for more."

—**Sushi the Shih Tzu**, canine star of the Trash 'n' Treasures mysteries by Barbara Allan

"Writing duo Curtis has created a humorous but deadly serious mystery. Pepe is a delight and more intelligent than most humans in the book. An ex-husband and current love interest keep Geri's life hopping. Crafty plotting will keep you engrossed until the end and have you eagerly awaiting the next book."

—*RT Book Reviews* (four stars)

"Every dog has its day and there'll be plenty of days for Geri Sullivan and Pepe in this fun twist on the typical PI partnership."

—**Simon Wood**, author of *Did Not Finish*

"Waverly Curtis has created a delightful cast of human and canine characters in *Dial C for Chihuahua*. Pepe never loses his essential dogginess, even as he amazes gutsy Geri Sullivan, his partner in crime detection, with his past exploits and keen nose for detail. I look forward to Pepe's next adventure!"

—**Bernadette Pajer**, author of the Professor
　　Bradshaw Mysteries

"Move over, Scooby-Doo, there's a new dog in town! *Dial C for Chihuahua* is a fun and breezy read, with polished writing and charming characters, both human and canine. If you like a little Chihuahua with your mystery, former purse-dog Pepe is a perfect fit!"

—**Jennie Bentley**, author of the Do-It-
　　Yourself Home Renovation mysteries

The Chihuahua Always Sniffs Twice

Waverly Curtis

KENSINGTON PUBLISHING CORP.

http://www.kensingtonbooks.com

KENSINGTON BOOKS are published by

Kensington Publishing Corp.
119 West 40th Street
New York, NY 10018

All Kensington Titles, Imprints, and Distributed Lines are available at special quantity discounts for bulk purchases for sales
promotions, premiums, fund-raising, and educational or insti-
tutional use. Special book excerpts or customized printings can
also be created to fit specific needs. For details, write or phone
the office of the Kensington special sales manager: Kensington
Publishing Corp., 119 West 40th Street, New York, NY 10018,
attn: Special Sales Department, Phone: 1-800-221-2647.

Kensington and the K logo Reg. U.S. Pat & TM Off.

ISBN-13: 978-1-61773-062-7
ISBN-10: 1-61773-062-9
First Kensington Mass Market Edition: December 2014

eISBN-13: 978-1-61773-063-4
eISBN-10: 1-61773-063-7
First Kensington Electronic Edition: December 2014

10 9 8 7 6 5 4 3 2

Printed in the United States of America

Chapter 1

It was a sunny day in July—the kind of beautiful summer day that makes living in rain-soaked Seattle worthwhile. My Chihuahua, Pepe, was lying on the top of the sofa, sprawled in a sunbeam that lit up his short white fur. He's like a cat, the way he likes to perch in the sun—which doesn't go over well with my actual cat, Albert, who used to be able to soak up sunshine anyplace he chose. Instead, Albert now has to share his domain. They were getting along for the moment, anyway, and I'd taken a seat on the front porch with a glass of iced tea and the latest Sparkle Abbey mystery. Then the phone rang.

I jumped up and went back inside, hoping it was Felix, the handsome dog trainer I was dating. We were supposed to get together for dinner, though sometimes he had cancellations in his busy schedule. But when I looked at the caller ID on my phone, I saw the name Gerrard Agency.

"Hi, Jimmy G," I said. Pepe perked up. Jimmy G is our boss; he owns the private detective agency that Pepe and I work for.

"Hey, doll, Jimmy G needs you at the office. Toot sweet!" Jimmy G added. He always talks about himself in the third person.

"What for?" I asked. I was reluctant to give up on my plan for a lazy afternoon. I had signed on with Jimmy G thinking he was going to train me to be a PI. It turned out to be a little bit more involved than just getting hired. Private eyes in Washington State need to complete a training course and take a test. I was registered for an upcoming class at the University of Washington. Meanwhile, Jimmy G called me his girl Friday and kept me busy picking up his dry cleaning and fetching coffee.

"Jimmy G cannot explicate over the horn," he said. "Shake a leg!" And he hung up.

"Do we have a case, Geri?" Pepe asked, standing at my feet and looking up at me.

Yes, my Chihuahua talks. It was a shock to me when he began speaking, a couple of hours after I adopted him from a Seattle shelter, but I've gotten used to it. Unfortunately, no one else can hear him.

"Sounds like it," I said. "The boss wants us to meet him at the office."

"*Vamonos!*" he said. Then he glanced over at Albert the Cat, who'd already jumped up on the sofa and taken Pepe's former spot in the sun. "Enjoy it while you can, *gato*," he told Albert. "If you are still in my place when I return, we will have words."

Jimmy G's office is in an old brick building on the edge of downtown Seattle, near the Greyhound bus station. The building is always deserted even in the middle of the day. Pepe and I strolled down the long hallway, past the frosted-glass windows of offices where the lights were always out. Jimmy G's office is at the end of the hallway.

When I knocked, I heard Jimmy G talking to someone, but when he opened the door, the office was empty.

"Who were you talking to?" I asked, looking around. The place was a mess, as usual. Candy-bar wrappers, crumpled cellophane from cigars, and wadded-up pieces of paper covered the desk and floor. The latest goldfish was floating belly up in the swamp Jimmy G called an aquarium. The air reeked of cigar smoke and tuna salad.

"Client. On the phone," said Jimmy G. He glanced at the old black rotary phone sitting on a corner of his desk. He seemed uncharacteristically jumpy. He actually cleared a place on the small black-leather sofa beside his desk so I could sit down.

"I have seen better dumps at the dump," said Pepe. (The rips in this couch, a thrift-store find, had been "fixed" by our boss with Xs of silver duct tape.) I was longing to do a makeover—before I became a PI, I was a stager, making houses for sale look appealing to prospective buyers—but Jimmy G said he liked his office the way it was.

Jimmy G took a seat behind his desk. He has a rugged face, with a nose that looks like it might once have been broken, and big brown eyes that bulge out more than Pepe's. He was dressed, as usual, like a 1940s private eye, but he'd outdone himself this morning. He had on a blue-and-white-striped shirt with red suspenders. A brown fedora clung to the back of his head. His pencil-thin mous-tache finished off his retro look with perfection.

Pepe headed for the overflowing wastebasket and began rooting around.

"So, I suppose," said the boss, "you're probably wondering why Jimmy G wanted you in the office this morning."

"Yes," I said.

"The thought has crossed our minds," said Pepe, looking up from his scrounging.

"Jimmy G has a case for you!" Those were the words I had been waiting to hear ever since I started working for Jimmy G, private dick, as he likes to call himself. (Sometimes Pepe and I call him a public dick, but only to each other.) "You and your rat-dog." He looked at Pepe, who was sniffing something he had found in a corner.

"Yum!" I heard Pepe say.

"Don't eat anything you find down there," I warned him. "I don't want you getting sick."

"Funny you should say that," Jimmy G said. "That's the case. Someone tried to poison some dogs. They had to be rushed to the vet."

"Oh, my God! That's terrible!" I said. "Who would do such a thing?"

"*Sí!*" said Pepe, coming over to me, quivering with indignation. "A poisoner of *perros!* Lower than a *cucaracha!* Such a person would have to possess a heart of ice-cold stone!" Pepe is given to overly melodramatic statements, possibly derived from the Spanish telenovelas he loves to watch.

Jimmy G spoke up. "Whoever did it obviously wants the old lady's money."

"Tell him to start at the beginning," said Pepe, who has a keen sense of propriety. "What old lady?"

"An old lady hired us?" I asked Jimmy G.

"No. Our client is Barrett Boswell. He's the trustee of the old lady's estate," said Jimmy G. "The old lady died and left her entire fortune to her dogs. The house. The money. Everything. We're talking a whole pile of moola. Millions."

"The senora was someone who truly appreciates and rewards the loyalty of her canine friends," observed Pepe. "Too bad she is no longer around. I think she would enjoy my company."

"So is Boswell meeting us here?" I asked.

"No, you've got an appointment with him at *his* office," said Jimmy G. "Three-thirty this afternoon. He's up in Port Townsend. You better get a move on, doll."

"What about you?" I asked Jimmy G. Technically, I wasn't a private investigator yet.

"Jimmy G has another case," he said in a hurry. Jimmy G always has another case, yet he's always in the office.

"Do not worry, Geri," said Pepe. "We are seasoned detectives. We can handle this on our own." It is true we had managed to solve two murder cases, but more by getting in the way of the murderer than through our detecting skills.

Chapter 2

As soon as Geri and her Chihuahua left the office, Jimmy G picked up the phone again.

"Bickerstaff here," said the voice on the other end.

"Jimmy G reporting in," Jimmy G said. "Just wanted to let you know that Jimmy G has assigned his operatives to the case. They're on their way to meet with Boswell as we speak."

"Excellent," said Bickerstaff. "I want an update immediately as soon as you hear anything from them."

"Will do," said Jimmy G.

"No one would be stupid enough to leave a million dollars to a bunch of dogs," said Bickerstaff. "There has to be something else going on."

"Agreed," said Jimmy G, pouring himself a few fingers of bourbon.

"Can't win a war without intelligence," said Bickerstaff.

"Agreed," said Jimmy G, putting his feet up on his desk. This action tipped his desk chair perilously far back, and his fedora dropped to the floor. He swiveled around to pick it up.

"Have you considered a raid on Boswell's office?" Jimmy G asked, clapping his hat back on top of his head.

There was a long silence on the other end. Jimmy G polished off the bourbon.

"I like the way you think," said Bickerstaff. "Devious means are necessary when there is so much at stake."

"Devious is Jimmy G's middle name," said Jimmy G. Actually, his middle name was Francis, but he never admitted that.

"I'll see what I can do," said Bickerstaff. "Meanwhile, I need you here. How long will it take you to get to Port Townsend?"

Jimmy G straightened up. "Jimmy G doesn't usually handle cases personally."

"I need feet on the ground," said Bickerstaff.

Jimmy G was about to suggest that there must be private detectives in Port Townsend when Bickerstaff added. "I'll double what I offered earlier."

"Ah, now we're talking," said Jimmy G, thinking of the fat retainer he had already deposited in his bank account. He started calculating his course. A short hop on the ferry over to Bremerton, then a drive up the Kitsap Peninsula to Port Townsend. Maybe he'd stop and see an old buddy of his who lived in Bremerton. "Jimmy G can be there in three hours."

"We can't meet at my office," said Bickerstaff. "It's right across the hall from Boswell's office, and your operatives might still be there."

"Doubt it," said Jimmy G.

"Still better to be safe than sorry," said Bickerstaff. "There's a bar on the main street called the Windjammer. Let's meet there."

"Jimmy G is on the way."

Chapter 3

To get to Port Townsend from Seattle, you have to cross the water—the deep waters of Puget Sound that cut a long channel separating Seattle from the Olympic Peninsula, home to one of the last old-growth forests in the Northwest.

You can get there several ways. We chose the scenic route, driving north from Seattle to the little seaside town of Mukilteo, taking the ferry across to Whidbey Island, driving up the highway through the still mostly rural island, and then crossing over to Port Townsend on another ferry.

Since dogs aren't allowed on deck on the Washington State Ferries, we stayed in the car.

"It is nice that you chose to stay with me, Geri," said Pepe.

"Well, I didn't want to leave you all alone in the car."

"That is *bueno. Muy bueno*," he told me. "Perhaps I should entertain you with some sea chanteys."

"Do you know any?" I asked, always amazed at my dog's wide range of experience.

"No, I do not," he said. "But it is the thought that counts, is it not?"

We got into Port Townsend around two. No matter how many times I take a ferry, I always have a moment of panic when I drive off the boat. Because our Washington ferries come into the dock nose first to load and unload, the only thing holding them against the dock is the power of the aft engines. I always have a nagging fear that the ferry will drift back as I drive off the metal gangplank to shore and dump me into the drink. (It actually happened to somebody once at Seattle's downtown ferry dock.)

"You should not have told me about that," said Pepe as our front wheels rolled onto the metal gangplank with a loud clunking sound.

"Sorry," I said. I concentrated on making sure the tires didn't swerve on the metal grate.

"How well do you swim?" he asked me.

"I'm an excellent swimmer," I said. "You're the one who's afraid of water. But neither of us will do much swimming if we go down in the car."

"Is that supposed to be reassuring?" Pepe asked, with some degree of tension in his voice. He stood stiff as a board in the passenger seat as we disembarked.

Well, I thought, if the only thing my fearless pooch feared was getting off a ferryboat, that was pretty good.

"I was *not* afraid," Pepe told me as we drove up the dock toward the main street. "Quite the opposite. It is well known that *perros* and their humans pick up on each other's emotions. I was merely reflecting your vibes—my own vibes were rock steady and *muy* calm."

"Sure," I said.

"Geri?" he asked me. "Just out of curiosity. Is there another way home besides the ferry?"

"Yes, but it would add about an hour to our trip."

"But we are not in a hurry to get home," Pepe pointed out.

"Perhaps you aren't," I said. I was thinking about my plans to have dinner with Felix Navarro. We had met when Pepe tried to attack his Great Dane. Pepe did not approve of the match. He thought Felix was too controlling. Frankly, the way I saw it, Pepe wanted to be the only person bossing me around.

A sandy bluff, about fifty feet tall, ran parallel to the only road into town from the ferry dock. It was topped with huge Victorian mansions. Most were wooden structures that were beautifully preserved; they still displayed the original fish-scale siding and gingerbread embellishments. They were painted in bright colors with complementary trim work: purple and orange, olive green and maroon. These, and many others, had been built by the town's movers and shakers just before the turn of the century, when it was thought that Port Townsend, not Seattle, would become the main shipping terminal for northwest Washington.

"This city is *muy* old, is it not?" said Pepe as we drove into the downtown proper, only six blocks or so from the ferry dock. The ancient brick buildings were similar to those in Seattle's Pioneer Square.

"Yes," I said, thinking that it was like Pioneer Square in another respect—crawling with tourists on a sunny summer day. All the old buildings, most three or four stories tall, had restaurants and shops catering to the tourist trade on the ground floor. It was hard to believe that the majority of these old, red-brick buildings had originally been saloons and cathouses way back when.

"*Gato* houses!" said Pepe in horror. "Which ones? Stay away from them!"

"Not *that* kind of *gato*," I told him, having forgotten about my fearless dog's only other fear—that of cats. "Not real cats, Pepe," I said. "Cathouse is just slang for a whorehouse."

"Oh, that is not so scary," said Pepe. "I spent many happy hours in a whorehouse in Tijuana. Those women have hearts of gold."

"Really?" I said. Pepe is always full of colorful stories, most of which I don't believe.

"Yes, when I worked for the DEA, the agents would leave me there between assignments, and the women would dress me up and feed me treats."

About halfway into town, I spotted the address I'd been looking for. It was a narrow, two-story building on the water side of the street. We found parking half a block away and walked back, Pepe trotting by my side, and both of us enjoying the salty breeze that tempered the heat of the sun.

The double doors were open and led into a small foyer with a white tile floor, dark oak trim, a twelve-foot ceiling, and the same exposed, red-brick walls in the interior as on the building's exterior. A big ceiling fan whirred overhead, providing a little ventilation. A brass plaque by the wide stairwell leading upstairs read, BOSWELL & BICKERSTAFF, ATTORNEYS-AT-LAW—2ND FLOOR.

"I think I will like this attorney," said Pepe as we climbed the stairs.

"Why's that?"

"Because he cares enough for *perros* to represent them."

At the top of the stairs was an oak door with an old-fashioned, smoked-glass window in it. BOSWELL & BICKERSTAFF was stenciled in gold on the glass. I knocked on the door, but no one answered, so I turned the knob and walked in.

We were in a small waiting room, with two chairs and a table. A neat fan of magazines was splayed on the table: *Smithsonian, House and Garden,* and *Sunset.* There were two doors leading off the room. One bore the name BARRETT BOSWELL, the other BERNARD BICKERSTAFF.

Boswell's door was slightly ajar.

"Hello," I called, pushing it most of the way open and giving it another knock. Still no answer. I opened it all the way and took a step inside. It was a luxurious office, with a fine Persian carpet on the floor and a stunning view of the water. I could see the ferry, like a floating white wedding cake, heading back out across the dark blue waters of Puget Sound.

But there was no sign of Mr. Boswell.

"Geri!" said Pepe. He had trotted around the desk. "Geri! There is something you should know—"

"What?" I asked, coming around the desk. And then, "Oh my God!"

A man lay sprawled on the carpet between the desk and the back wall. He was wearing a gray suit. His face was bright red and all contorted like some medieval gargoyle. His eyes were open, staring up at the ceiling. And his hands were curled like claws.

"Not this again," said Pepe. "Why do we keep meeting *muerte* people on our cases?"

"Good lord!" came a man's voice from behind us. I turned and saw a middle-aged man, slightly balding, clutching a briefcase in one hand. He was peering over the desk at the body on the floor.

Then he turned to me. "Who are you?"

"I'm Geri Sullivan," I said. "I was supposed to meet Mr. Boswell, but found him dead."

"I'm Boswell," said the man. "That's Bernie Bickerstaff."

Chapter 4

Boswell set down his briefcase and approached the body. An odd expression flickered over his face—perhaps disgust or revulsion. He knelt down and placed his fingers against Bickerstaff's neck.

"Definitely dead," he said. Having ascertained this to be true, he pulled out his cell phone and dialed 911.

"I want to report a death," he said. "I came into my office—Two Water Street, Suite 201—and found my colleague dead." There was a pause. Then he said, "Yes, we will be here."

Then he clicked off the phone and looked at me.

"Who are you?" he asked again.

"Geri Sullivan," I said, holding out my hand. "I had an appointment at three-thirty with Mr. Boswell—I mean you." I waved my hand at Pepe. "And this is my dog."

"And partner," said Pepe.

"And my partner, Pepe," I said.

"Ah, yes," said Boswell studying him intently. "So

this is the famous dog. Frankly, I expected him to be a bit bigger."

Pepe was actually large for a Chihuahua at seven pounds. And all of that muscle, as Pepe would have said.

"But fully capable of solving any crime," said Pepe, "including this one."

"He's been invaluable to me," I said, and it was true. Together Pepe and I had solved multiple murders, starred on *Dancing with Dogs,* and broken up a dog-napping ring.

"Very well," said Boswell. He did not seem very concerned about the death of his colleague. "Perhaps we can meet in Bernie's office while we wait for the police."

I followed Boswell back into the waiting room. The door that read BERNARD BICKERSTAFF was locked. Boswell rattled it impatiently. Then he pulled out a ring of keys, fitting each one into the lock and rejecting it when it failed to produce the desired results.

"Geri, he is possibly contaminating a crime scene," Pepe pointed out.

"That's right," I said, grateful that no one else can hear my dog since it makes me look so much smarter. "It's just as well," I said to Boswell, "because the police will want to go over his office for clues."

"Yes! And what was he doing in *my* office?" Boswell asked, marching back into it. He went over to the bank of file cabinets against the wall.

"Do you normally lock your office?" I asked, following him back in.

"Yes, but Bernie has a key. We both have keys to each other's offices." He was thumbing through the files, tsking as he went. "If he poked his nose into the Carpenter case, I will be most vexed." He turned his attention to a folder that lay open on his desk.

"Is that the case you were having us investigate?" I asked.

"Yes, and Bernie had no business availing himself of this information," said Boswell, snapping up the folder.

"Geri!" said Pepe.

"Yes, I know, it's evidence," I said.

"It is also my livelihood," said Boswell. "Eighty percent of my current income comes from this trust. I'm not going to let the police interfere with that. At least I have the satisfaction of knowing that whatever Bernie may have learned did not leave this room."

"I'm confused," I said. "Weren't you partners?" I was thinking of the signs downstairs.

"Oh, no," said Boswell. "We simply share an office and an answering service. We are actually on opposite sides in this litigation."

Pepe was sniffing the dead body.

"Do you smell anything, Pepe?" I asked.

Pepe didn't answer, seemed oblivious to my question, and just continued to sniff the corpse from head to toe and side to side. I'd seen him this way before, totally engaged in an olfactory pursuit, as only a dog can be, and figured he was onto some kind of clue.

I stepped closer to the body and repeated my question, "Do you smell anything, Pepe?"

"*Sí*, I smell lemonade, and a faint floral odor. I know what it is. It is lavender. *Sí*, lavender."

"Lavender?" I asked. "And lemonade?"

"Lavender lemonade," said Boswell. "My favorite summer beverage." He pointed to a large glass pitcher on a silver tray near the window and an empty glass on the edge of the desk.

Boswell reached for it, but I rushed over and stopped him before he could put his hands on it.

"There might be fingerprints on it," I pointed out.

"Of course there are," he said. "Bernie was sitting in my office, snooping around my case, and swiping my lemonade. His fingerprints will be all over it."

"Yes, but it's evidence."

He looked at the corpse and frowned. Then he turned to me. "What do you mean evidence?"

"In the murder investigation," I said.

"Murder?" Boswell looked positively frightened. "What makes you think Bernie was murdered?"

I was embarrassed to admit that I automatically assumed all deaths were homicides. Call it the fate of the hardened PI.

"What do *you* think happened to him?" I asked.

"Well, I assume he died of a heart attack or a stroke. He's been taking medication for high blood pressure. Probably popped a blood vessel when he saw how much I'm getting paid by Lucille's trust."

There was a clatter of feet in the hall outside, and two uniformed policemen came into the room. They quickly called for backup and the E.M.T.s, then moved us into separate rooms. Luckily, the police never think to separate me and Pepe, so we did have a chance to get our story straight. And our story was that we had an appointment with Boswell at 3:30 PM and had entered his office to find the body sprawled on the floor.

"What was your business with Mr. Boswell?" the lead detective asked me.

"We're private eyes. Out of Seattle. We're working a case."

"We?" He looked around.

"Down here, *senor*," said Pepe. "I may be small, but I am mighty."

"My dog helps me," I said. "Especially on this case. It involves dogs."

"Oh, Mrs. Carpenter," said the detective. "Very disturbing, that."

"So you know about somebody trying to poison her dogs?"

"No." He frowned. "I know about her leaving five million dollars to four cocker spaniels. Ridiculous. Dogs don't live long enough to spend five million dollars."

"I could easily spend that," said Pepe. "Fresh, organic food, prepared by a private chef." Pepe has discriminating tastes. After all, he was once the pampered pet of movie star Caprice Kennedy. "Trips around the world to visit sites of historic interest to dogs."

"What sites?" I asked Pepe.

"Do you know, Geri," said Pepe, "there is actually a statue of a dog in a Tokyo subway?"

"Yes. The dog named Hachiko," I said. That was a tragic story: about how the Akita waited patiently for his master every night at the train station where he had last seen his master. "So sad."

"It is sad," said the policeman. "People around

here are pretty riled up about it. They'll be even more angry when they find out Bernie's dead."

"Why is that?" I asked.

"Because Bernie was hired by the kids to get back the money Mrs. Carpenter left to the dogs. Most people in town are on their side. Nice kids. Nice family. Been here for decades. Mrs. Carpenter was an outsider. She brought a bunch of money with her, it's true. Helped Mr. Carpenter save his farm. But then she alienated everyone with her high-and-mighty ways and that pack of yapping dogs that went everywhere with her."

I looked at Pepe, figuring he'd have something to say about that, but he just shrugged his shoulders. "It is true. Some dogs yap."

Another policeman poked his head into the room.

"The ME's here," he said. "Got some bad news."

"What's that?"

"Looks like Bernie might have been poisoned."

Chapter 5

When we next saw our client, his composure was shaken. His face was a pasty white, and his hands were shaking.

"They think the poison was meant for me," he said. "I can't believe it."

"Ah! I thought so!" said Pepe.

"What makes you think he was poisoned?" I asked Pepe.

But Boswell misunderstood. "I thought he had a heart attack!"

"Elementary," said Pepe. "You noted the horrible grimace on Senor Bickerstaff's face? And the claw-like clutch of his hands in *muerte*?"

"Yes, but—"

"The same thing happened to Ramon on *Paraíso Perdido*. He was poisoned by his wife, who had learned he was having an affair with her sister. He suffered terrible contractions of all his muscles as he writhed in agony on the floor. He looked much like Mr. Bickerstaff as he expired." Pepe was so excited he was dancing around the room.

"Settle down," I told him.

"Yes. You're right," said Boswell, taking a deep breath. "I do need to settle down. Let's adjourn to the bar downstairs."

"Are you done talking to the police?" I asked. I was surprised. Usually when I got dragged in for questioning, which was happening all too often since I had started working for Jimmy G, I would be stuck at the station for hours.

"No, they want me to come down to the station, but I need a little nip before I head over there."

We headed to the restaurant downstairs, which was packed with tourists. We ended up in the bar section in back, which was nice and bright since it had an outside deck that seemed as large as the bar itself. I thought we'd go out there, but Boswell bellied up to the bar, pulled out one of the green faux-leather stools for me, then took a seat beside me. Most of the seats at the bar were empty, perhaps because they faced away from the water and the view.

The bartender, a thirtyish guy with a chubby, ruddy face, came right over to us.

"Hey, Barry," he said. "What's happening upstairs?"

"Bickerstaff's dead," said Boswell, shuddering.

"You're kidding?"

"No, looks like he was poisoned. They think it was meant for me."

"Damn. That sucks." The bartender shook his head. "The usual?"

Boswell nodded.

"And you, ma'am?" the bartender turned to me.

I don't usually drink while working, but this situation seemed to require some attitude adjustment. "I'll take a glass of your house white," I said.

"And I will have a bowl of water," said Pepe. "No chaser."

"Plus a bowl of water," I said. "For my dog."

I couldn't put Pepe on the floor. He was sure to wander off and someone would trip on him, so I set him up on the bar. He wandered down a ways, sniffing as he went, looking for food, no doubt.

"My boss gave me only the bare details about the case," I said to Boswell as we waited for our drinks. "Can you tell me more about why you hired us?"

"As the executor of Mrs. Carpenter's estate, it's my job to make sure the dogs are well cared for. And, obviously, if somebody is trying to kill them, I'm not doing my job. So I need you to find out who is trying to kill the dogs."

The drinks arrived. Boswell's came in a tall glass full of ice. It looked like lemonade, which shocked me, as that is the last thing I would drink considering the circumstances.

Boswell took a long gulp, then set down the glass and turned to me.

"How do you know someone is trying to kill the dogs?" I asked.

Pepe inspected his bowl of water, then sniffed and turned away from it.

"What's wrong? Do you think it's poisoned?" I asked.

"Well, someone tried to poison them," Boswell said.

"Ask him what kind of poison," Pepe said.

"What kind of poison?"

"I understand it was chocolate," said Boswell.

"Chocolate is very bad for *perros*," Pepe told me.

"So what happened?" I asked.

Boswell took another long gulp of his lemonade. "Hugh will know. You can talk to him about it."

"Who's Hugh?" I asked.

"Mrs. Carpenter's vet. He's the one who cares for the dogs."

"And does he think it was deliberate?"

"Again, you'll have to talk to him," said Boswell. "All I know is my job is to keep those dogs alive." He took another sip and looked at me. "I'm the trustee."

"Wouldn't the job of trustee usually go to a relative?" I asked.

"Not always," said Boswell. "Some people, in an effort to be sure their trust is handled in an objective manner, select a professional, like a lawyer or a banker. In this case, Mrs. Carpenter knew there would be trouble brewing. Lots of bad blood between the kids. So she left each of them a small bequest in her will and put the rest in a trust for the dogs."

"How small a bequest?"

"One hundred dollars each," Boswell said.

"And the entire estate is worth?"

"Several million. Five point seven to be exact."

"Ouch!" I said. "That must have hurt her children."

"But pleased the *perros*," said Pepe. "And for some people, *perros* are more precious than kids." He looked at me wistfully. "Like for you, Geri!"

It was a sore point between us. Pepe dislikes kids. I think I might want to have kids someday. Pepe is worried that he will be pushed aside in my affections if that ever happens.

"Stepchildren," said Mr. Boswell. "There's no love lost there. Although she did have children by a previous marriage. They had already inherited from their father's estate, but they were expecting more when their mother died. So they were insulted, too."

"So they would be the obvious suspects," said Pepe.

"What happens if the dogs die?" I asked.

"When the dogs die," said Boswell, "the remainder passes to the local humane society."

"Not to her children?"

"No. That's the way Lucille wanted it. I wrote the original trust document," said Boswell, "so I do know what I'm talking about."

"Can I see a copy of the trust document?" I asked.

"Certainly," said Boswell. "There's a copy in my office." He frowned. "Unless Bickerstaff got his hands on it." He frowned again. "But I guess he didn't get a chance to remove anything he found." He waved the bartender over to us. "Can I have the bill?"

"I'll just put it on your tab," said the bartender. "Don't worry about it."

As we got up to go out the door, we were stopped at the front door by two policemen in dark uniforms and shiny badges.

"Barrett Boswell?" said one of them, stepping forward, his hand on his belt, right above a pair of handcuffs.

Boswell nodded, a bit annoyed. He tried to brush past them.

The younger of the two put out a hand and blocked his passage. "We need you to come with us, sir."

"First I need to get some papers from my office for this young lady," said Boswell, pointing his finger at me.

"The office is off-limits," the policeman said. "No one's getting in there until we're done analyzing the crime scene."

"But that's ridiculous," said Boswell. He didn't seem to grasp the seriousness of the situation. The other policeman held out the handcuffs. Everyone in the restaurant had stopped eating and was watching the drama.

"I think you should go with them," I said, stepping forward. "I can wait."

"Yes, you should come with us," the policeman repeated to Boswell. Then he turned to me. "It will be a long wait. We've got a lot of questions."

"I'll have to get you the documents later," Boswell told me. He didn't seem fazed by all the attention. Customers were backed up into the lobby, trying to see what was happening in the restaurant. "Meanwhile you should go talk to Hugh. He can tell you more about the attempt to poison the dogs."

"Where do I find this Hugh?"

"At his veterinary clinic. It's just outside of Sequim. I'll give you the address." Boswell pulled a small notepad from his pocket and scribbled something on it before handing it to me. It was an address.

I looked at it.

"Is there a problem?" Boswell asked.

"Well, I've got a date in Seattle tonight, and—"

"Partner," Pepe interrupted, "this is an opportunity to learn more about the situation. We can interrogate this *vet*." He said the last word contemptuously. Pepe did not have a high opinion of vets.

Pepe had a good point. It would be better to question the vet without Boswell present. "Sure, I'll do whatever it takes," I said.

"Good," said Boswell. "I'll be in contact later."

"Come on," said the policeman. "I've got a date myself tonight, and wouldn't mind being able to keep it."

At least somebody would have a date tonight, I thought, as we left.

Chapter 6

Jimmy G sat at the bar of the Windjammer and stared at his empty glass. The damn client had stood him up. At least that's how it appeared. It was true Jimmy G had arrived late, after stopping to have a beer with his buddy in Bremerton, but he had called Bickerstaff and left a message on his phone, telling him about the delay.

It took a while, but Jimmy G finally flagged down the bartender and indicated that he wanted another drink. The restaurant was packed and the outdoor deck was full. The bartender was busy filling orders for the waitresses.

"Sorry, sir," said the bartender, when he finally came over with the glass of bourbon. "It's been a really crazy evening. Lots of excitement in the building today."

Jimmy G rolled his eyes. He meant to indicate that he was not the slightest bit interested in small-town gossip, but apparently it had the opposite effect.

"The police came in here and made an arrest in

a murder investigation," said the bartender. "A very prominent citizen, too," he added.

Jimmy G tipped up his glass and took a swig.

"The murder happened just this afternoon," the bartender went on.

That was disturbing. After all, Jimmy G had operatives in town. He was responsible for their safety.

"Who got murdered?" he asked.

"Lawyer name of Bickerstaff," said the bartender.

Jimmy G almost dropped his glass. Fortunately he did not. He polished off the drink and tapped the rim of the empty glass. He noticed the bartender hesitated. His name tag said his name was Flynn. Jimmy G slid a twenty across the counter toward him.

"Bernie Bickerstaff?" Jimmy G asked, as Flynn pocketed the twenty and poured him another shot.

Flynn nodded. "You know him?"

Jimmy G shrugged. "Mere acquaintance," he said. He wondered about the ethics of this situation. Could he keep the retainer even though he hadn't done any work for the guy?

At least it solved another ethical dilemma. He really didn't feel good about keeping Geri and Pepe in the dark about the true nature of the case. With Bickerstaff dead, any work they did for Boswell would be legitimate.

"So you said they caught the guy who killed him?" Jimmy G asked.

The bartender nodded. "Another lawyer. Shared offices with Bickerstaff. A guy named Boswell."

This time Jimmy G did drop his glass. Flynn was right there to mop it up and pour him another shot.

Jimmy G knocked it back. What was going on? Had Geri and Pepe been with Boswell when he committed the murder? He pulled his cell phone out of his pocket. He hated the newfangled thing, but Geri had insisted on it. In this case it would come in handy.

The phone began ringing as he fumbled to unlock it.

"What's up, doll?" he said, thinking it was Geri.

But the female voice on the other end was not familiar. "Am I speaking to James Gerrard?" she asked.

"Who wants to know?" Jimmy G asked.

"This is Detective Michelle Howard of the Homicide Division of the Port Townsend Police Department," she said. "We need to talk to you."

Chapter 7

The veterinary clinic was halfway between Port Townsend and Sequim, which meant we were getting farther away from Seattle and my date with Felix. It was a long, low, modern building, all concrete, glass, and steel, with a cantilevered roof and large, smoked-glass windows. The front was landscaped with box hedges and feathery white pampas grass. Set among the landscaping was a curved-steel sign engraved with the words WILLIAMS VETERINARY HOSPITAL.

I had called Felix to let him know I probably wouldn't be back in Seattle in time for our dinner. He didn't answer his phone, so I left a voice mail. Meanwhile, Pepe added his scent to what was surely a medley of doggie scents on one of the concrete posts holding up the sign. I looked around the car for his leash, but it seemed he'd hidden it again. Pepe hates the leash. He always fights me when I try to put it on him, but he also likes to pick fights with any large dog he sees. I guess you could call it "small-dog complex."

"Are you coming in with me?" I asked him when he was through with his business. "Or do you prefer to wait in the car?"

"Of course I am coming in with you," Pepe said huffily. "I know this is not our vet—nobody here will prod and poke and foist sundry other indignities on me."

"Whatever you say. But if there are any dogs in there, particularly big dogs," I told him, picking him up as we headed into the clinic, "I don't want you making a scene."

Luckily the waiting room was empty. It was bright and airy, with a stained concrete floor and a desk made of poured green glass, topped with a slab of polished stainless steel. It was furnished with two chrome-accented, black-leather benches and matching chairs that looked as if they'd come from a Scandinavian design store.

There was a bell on the desk. I went over and gave it a ring. After a few moments, a woman came out through a stainless-steel double door behind the desk.

She was quite good-looking, in a Barbie doll sort of way. She wore a pink smock, her blond hair was frosted and piled up on top of her head, and she had long, bubblegum-pink nails that looked like claws. The plastic name tag pinned to her smock said her name was Bonnie.

"Hello," she said in a high, squeaky voice. "Do you have an appointment?"

"We're here to talk to the vet," I said. "Mr. Boswell sent us."

"Oh," she said. "I'll get Hugh. He's in back." She turned and went out through the double door.

A few minutes later, the door opened and a man emerged. He was so good-looking, he took my breath away. He was about my age—somewhere in his midthirties. He was dressed casually, in blue jeans and a white doctor's coat, open over an ice-blue shirt. He had a square jaw and sandy-blond hair, a bit long, that kept falling forward over his startlingly blue eyes.

"Geri, restrain yourself," Pepe told me.

"What are you talking about?" I asked him.

"Do not be offended, Geri," he said. "I recognize the symptoms of heat."

I swear, there's nothing as disconcerting as having your dog be so knowledgeable about your love life. I felt myself blush—I mean, really blush.

"Hello," the vet said, as he extended his hand, "I'm Doctor Hugh Williams."

I took his hand—it was as warm as the flush on my cheeks. "Yes," I managed to say, noting his grip was firm but very gentle. "I'm Geri—Geri Sullivan."

I thought about withdrawing my hand, but Doctor Hugh was giving me little electric tingles. (Either that or I had a pinched nerve, which I very much doubted.)

"You seem flushed," Hugh told me. "Are you hot?"

"*Sí!*" Pepe told him. "She is *muy caliente.*"

"No, I'm fine," I said.

He let go of my hand and turned his attention to Pepe, who was still snuggled in my arms. "Cute little Chihuahua. What's her name?"

Pepe bristled at the suggestion that he was a female dog. "I am Pepe *el Macho*," he declared.

"Pepe," I said. "He's my partner," I added.

"Ah! Of course," said the vet. "You're the private detectives. It was wise of Barry to hire you to protect Mrs. Carpenter's dogs."

"I'd like to ask you some questions about them if I could."

"Yes, of course. My pleasure," Hugh said.

He led us into his office, which was as modern and composed as the rest of the building. A burnished teak desk dominated the room. Bookcases lined one wall, while his diplomas were mounted on the other. The outside wall was all glass and looked out over the bay, glimpsed through a scrim of evergreen trees. Hugh motioned us to sit on a couch covered in buttery black leather and seated himself in a matching swivel chair behind the desk.

"I don't think I've ever met a private detective," he said. "Let alone such an attractive one, if you don't mind my saying so."

I didn't mind one bit, but just said, "Thanks. It's nice of you to take the time to talk to us."

"Get to the point, Geri," Pepe told me. "That is why we are here."

I pulled out my notebook. "Could you tell me more about what happened with the dogs?" I asked.

"Sure," said Hugh. "It didn't amount to much. Someone scattered some chocolate-chip cookies in the yard. Yolanda knew chocolate was poisonous for dogs, so she wanted me to check them out."

"And the dogs were OK?"

Hugh nodded. "There wasn't enough chocolate in those cookies to kill a dog. They'd have to eat dozens to suffer any truly serious effects."

"So if someone wanted to poison the dogs," I said, "they really didn't do a very good job."

"That's correct," said Hugh. "Henry was the only dog we were concerned about. Just because he's older. We decided to keep him overnight for observation."

"And how is he doing?"

"He's fine. Ready to go home."

"Ask him about Mrs. Carpenter," Pepe reminded me.

"What can you tell me about Mrs. Carpenter?" I asked Hugh.

Hugh pointed to a framed photograph on the wall surrounded by his diplomas. It showed an older woman with white hair, styled in the pageboy that was popular among movie stars in the forties. She was draped in white furs, dripping with diamonds, and surrounded by four cocker spaniels.

"That's Lucille Carpenter right there," he said. "A magnificent woman. She was very particular, too. She expected the highest quality of care for her animals."

"Well, she seems to have found it with you," I said. "You've got a very modern clinic here."

"Thanks to Lucille," he said. "This was just a dumpy little small-town clinic before I met her. She tore it down and hired an architect to design this building. She really knew how to get things done. Smart as a whip; learned a lot from her husband— he was a general contractor."

"Oh," I said. "I thought he was a farmer."

"You must mean Chuck Carpenter. He was

her second husband. I'm talking about her first husband, Fred. He built several large shopping malls in Seattle."

"I see," I said.

"After he died, she moved here to Sequim. Said she wanted a little more sun in her life."

"I heard there are three hundred days of sunshine in Sequim," I said.

"You heard right," said Hugh. "That's why we are able to grow lavender here.

And speaking of lavender, are you staying for the lavender festival? It's this weekend."

"I wasn't planning on it," I said. "Tell me about it."

"There are booths in town selling lavender products, and more booths at the fairgrounds serving lavender-themed food and products, and musical groups playing all day long. Then there are buses that take people around to tour the various lavender farms."

"Sounds fascinating," I said.

"If you're interested, I could arrange a special, private dinner with a focus on lavender," Hugh said. "I know quite a few restaurant owners." He paused. "If you decide to stay around."

"I think we'll be back in Seattle by the weekend," I said, "but I appreciate the invitation."

"Well, if you change your mind, just give me a call," he said, standing up. He scribbled a number on the back of one of his professional cards. When he handed it to me, he pressed it into my palm. I swear I blushed again.

His attractive receptionist appeared in the

doorway. "Hugh," she said in a high-pitched scolding tone. "Jean just called to remind you to bring the financials to the meeting."

"Oh!" He glanced down at his appointment book. "You're right. Why don't you print them up for me?"

After she left, Hugh explained, "I'm the treasurer for the local humane society. We're trying to develop a no-kill shelter here. Far too many dogs, and other pets, are needlessly killed every year. We've got a major investor who is going to give us a large sum of money if we can raise enough money to match his grant."

"That sounds like an amazing cause," I said.

"But, unfortunately, going to the meeting means I can't take Henry back home, as I intended. Would you be willing to take him up to the Carpenter mansion for me?"

When you get a request like that from a handsome vet with a heart of gold, it's hard to resist. I looked at Pepe.

"A good chance to do more investigating, partner," he said.

"Sure," I said.

"And be sure to tell Yolanda that I've scheduled Henry for dental surgery on Tuesday. I think he has a few teeth that need to come out."

Pepe shuddered.

Hugh looked at him. "Has your little dog had his teeth checked recently?"

I shook my head. Pepe started shivering.

"It's one of my favorite exams to conduct," said

Hugh with hearty good humor, his own perfectly white, perfectly straight teeth gleaming. "It can make such a difference in terms of how comfortable they feel."

Pepe turned and ran out of the room.

"Thanks. I'll keep that in mind," I said.

Chapter 8

"So, how do you explain that?" the detective asked Jimmy G. She leaned down, her face only inches from Jimmy G's nose.

He took his time, looked around the small room. Some sort of weird foam padding on the walls. A big mirror he knew was a one-way window. Jimmy G was no stranger to police stations. He knew how to handle an interrogation.

"Can't explain it," he said. No way he was going to give her what she wanted. Detectives and police—they were natural enemies, like cats and dogs.

"According to the preliminary tests, he died less than ten minutes after he called you and about three hours before you left a message on his phone," the detective said.

Jimmy G lifted his eyebrows. He felt like he was winning this round. She was giving away more information than she was getting.

"So I'm going to ask you again," she said. "What was the subject of your conversation?"

"Confidential," said Jimmy G.

"You realize this is a murder investigation?"

"I thought you had a suspect in custody," he replied.

She frowned, then shook her head. "Boswell? No, he was the intended victim." She must have realized she had made a mistake. She squinted her eyes. "How do you know about that?"

"Small town," Jimmy G said. He held out his hands in an attempt to look hapless, which was easy, as Jimmy G usually was hapless. "Heard about it at the bar."

She shook that off by dismissing it with her hand. She tried a new tack. "If you were working for Mr. Bickerstaff, you are no longer obligated by client privilege. Just think about that."

Jimmy G did think about it. How would the police react if they knew Jimmy G was working both sides? Maybe they knew already.

The door opened, and an older man entered the room. He was stocky and square, with graying hair. He introduced himself as a homicide detective by the name of Rick Moore. The female detective stood back against the closed door with her arms crossed.

Moore threw a piece of paper on the table in front of Jimmy G. It made his head spin. It was covered with numbers. He couldn't made heads or tails out of it.

"We know that a call was placed to your office by Barrett Boswell earlier in the day," Moore said. He leaned over the table.

"So?" said Jimmy G. "Lots of people call Jimmy G."

"Why was Boswell calling you?"

Jimmy G shrugged his shoulders again. "Don't know. Didn't talk to him." A glimmer of an idea appeared in his brain. "Probably he talked to my girl Friday. Her name is Geri Sullivan. I can give you her number, if you want it."

He could see that was effective. The two detectives looked at each other. Jimmy G pulled out his brand-new cell phone and started poking buttons. He found the call log, then realized that it recorded his calls to and from Bickerstaff, then realized they already knew about that. He was getting confused.

"I think I need a lawyer," he said. He shoved the cell phone back into his pocket.

"We've already made contact with Miss Sullivan," said Moore.

That surprised Jimmy G, but he tried not to show it.

"Am I under arrest?" he asked.

"No, you're free to go," said Moore, stepping aside. "We'll be in touch if we have more questions."

Jimmy G got up, nodding to both detectives. He ambled out of the room, found his way through the warren of little hallways, and emerged in the lobby. Outside, the sun was just setting.

As he went through the lobby, a tall, fair-haired man in a tight gray T-shirt got up from one of the benches where he had been studying a newspaper.

"Ah, Mr. Gerrard," he said, stepping in front of Jimmy G. He opened the front door with a flourish and waved Jimmy G through. There was a long black limousine idling outside.

"My boss wants to speak to you," the man said.

Chapter 9

The light was beginning to fade out of the sky as we drove off with the snoozing Henry in the backseat. I followed the directions Hugh had given me, heading west, then pulling off the highway about ten miles down the road and following a two-lane road that angled off toward the foothills on the outskirts of Sequim. We passed farmhouses, surrounded by rows of cottonwoods, and manufactured homes that overlooked gardens studded with gnomes.

Then we went over a rise and entered a valley full of lavender, long rows of rounded purple bushes, slanting across the countryside in the golden light of the sunset. The sweet scent permeated the car.

A sign on the left read CARPENTER MANOR. I turned and proceeded up a long driveway. At the top was a sprawling Tudor-style mansion. The walls were made of white plaster and crisscrossed with dark beams. The windows were mullioned, and the roof was covered in gray slate.

The house was perfectly positioned at the top of

a low rise. As we rolled to a stop, next to a silver Mercedes, we got a magnificent view of the lavender fields. The sweet scent became even stronger, almost cloying, as it drifted in through the open car window and surrounded us.

And so did the dogs. Two cocker spaniels, one chocolate colored and one black, came tearing out of the open front door and surrounded the car, yapping and turning in circles.

"*Hola,* fellow *perros!*" said Pepe, greeting the dogs through the window. "I am called Pepe. Perhaps you have heard of my exploits."

Hearing the familiar sounds of his pack, Henry, with some effort, got to his feet and also looked out the car window. "Woof!" he said with a small wag of his tail. "Woof! Woof!"

It wasn't a very big bark, but it seemed to be a happy one. Both dogs turned and looked at me as if waiting for me to open the door and let them out. Henry, at least, was polite about it. Pepe, on the other hand, was Pepe.

"*Vamonos,* Geri!" he commanded, hopping up and down.

"OK, OK," I told him, taking off my seat belt. "When I let you out, you're not going to cause trouble with these other dogs, are you?"

"Far be it from me," he said. "I wish only to investigate, identify, and apprehend the evil miscreant who so vilely attempted their demise."

It was clear that my dog watched *too* many telenovelas. It was affecting his vocabulary. Pepe jumped down, but Henry waited for me to lift him out of the car.

My pooch's idea of investigation turned out to be

some butt sniffing and cavorting with the friendly cockers as they barked greetings to their returning pal, Henry, whom I was still carrying.

A winding stone path led from the driveway to the house through an English cottage garden overflowing with peonies and snapdragons, hollyhocks and foxgloves, and edged with neatly trimmed box hedges.

As we got closer to the door, we saw a golden cocker spaniel sitting on the stoop. She was different than the others. For one thing, she had a certain regal presence. For another, she was calm. I don't know how I knew it, but I was sure this beautiful animal was female.

Pepe realized the same thing. He swaggered up to her, stopped just a few feet away from her, and said, "Ah, nymph, in thy orisons be all my sins remembered."

I'd forgotten that my dog knew some Shakespeare. He'd quoted something from the bard when he first met his Pomeranian love, Siren Song. And it had gone pretty well for him with her after that.

But there the similarity ended. After uttering his come-on line to the cocker spaniel, he sauntered up to give her a friendly butt sniff and got a growling snap at his shoulder for his efforts.

He jumped away from her faster than I'd ever seen him move.

"Pepe!" I called.

"Do not worry, Geri," he said, returning to my side. "She is just playing hard to get, that is all." He said this nonchalantly, as if it was no big deal, but I did notice that his tail was between his legs.

A woman in her fifties stepped out onto the stoop.

She had dark hair, pulled back from her face, with just a few hints of silver around the edges. Her neck was long and swan-like, her eyes dark. She wore a dark, rather understated dress that set off the caramel color of her skin.

"I see that someone has just met the Queen," she said, looking at Pepe, then at the cocker spaniel who was still sitting at the bottom of the steps. She had a faint accent, but I couldn't quite place it.

"The Queen?" I said.

"Yes," said Boswell. He stepped out onto the porch beside the woman. "Her name is Mary," he continued, giving a nod toward the golden cocker. "We call her Queen Mary."

"Because she doesn't stand for any monkey business," said the woman on the stoop. "Like what your dog just tried, for example."

"I am no monkey," Pepe told me, sounding offended.

"How did you get here?" I asked Boswell, puzzled.

Boswell put a protective arm around the woman's shoulder. "I wanted to apprise Yolanda of recent developments in person, rather than over the phone."

"What is she talking about, Barry?" Yolanda turned to him.

"Let's go inside," he said.

We followed Yolanda through a dark-paneled vestibule and into a large room with a low-beamed ceiling. There was a massive stone fireplace with a beam for a mantel and a fire lit within it, despite the heat of the day. All the windows were open, admitting the scent of hot dust and lavender. The floor was dark, polished oak. The dogs' nails made little clicking sounds as they raced around in circles.

All except Queen Mary, who padded over to a wicker basket near the hearth and settled down in it, her golden head lifted, surveying the scene. Eventually the two other dogs settled down as well: one jumped up on a sofa, while the other curled up in a basket placed along the wall.

I set Henry down, and he wobbled over to another basket, circled around, and lay down, as if he had just been on a long, weary journey. I noticed that each of the baskets bore a silver nameplate above it; there was one for each dog: Mary, Henry, Victoria and James.

"Lucille always named her dogs after English royalty," Boswell explained.

The sofas and armchairs in the room were covered in purple and pink floral chintz. We all found our places, just like the dogs, and then Yolanda sent her niece, Clara, to fetch tea.

"Hugh says that he wants to see Henry again on Tuesday for some oral surgery," I said.

Boswell frowned. "I think he's taking advantage of the trust," he said.

"What do you mean?"

"Well, under the terms of the trust, he gets paid every time he provides any veterinary services for the dogs," Boswell said, "but I'm beginning to think he's scheduling unnecessary procedures just to make a little extra money."

"How would we know, Barry?" Yolanda asked.

"We're not veterinarians. We have to trust his judgment."

"There is another vet in town," Boswell pointed out. "Maybe we need to get a second opinion."

Just then the tea arrived on a fancy silver tray, complete with delicate bone china cups, painted with floral designs and rimmed with gold. We each had our own cup and saucer, plus Yolanda poured a little bit of tea out into saucers for each of the dogs. There were also tiny bits of toast for the dogs, cut into diamonds and smeared with some kind of liver pâté.

Boswell noticed my raised eyebrows.

"It's one of the terms of the trust," he said. "The caretaker of the dogs is to provide them with high tea every day."

"Do they like it?" I asked. I didn't think tea would be good for dogs.

But Pepe seemed to be enjoying it. He was polishing off his toast when the doorbell rang. The melody was familiar. I think it was "God Save the Queen."

Clara came into the room and had a whispered conversation in Spanish with Yolanda. Yolanda looked frightened and hurried out into the hall.

"What's going on, Pepe?" I asked. But before he could answer, Yolanda returned, clutching a fat envelope.

"It's an envelope from Bernard Bickerstaff," she said. "It came certified. I had to sign for it." She handed the envelope to Boswell. "Will you tell me what it says? You know I'm not comfortable with legal documents."

"Hmmm," said Boswell, setting down his teacup. He examined the postmark. "It appears he mailed this yesterday. How unfortunate!" He pried open the flap and pulled out a sheaf of papers, stapled at one corner. As he read them, his brow furrowed, and the color drained from his face.

"What is it?" Yolanda asked.

"Calm down, my dear," Boswell told her. "This has infinitely more to do with me than with you."

"Just tell her what it is, will you?" said Clara, crossing to Yolanda and putting a hand on her shoulder. "You know how my aunt worries."

Boswell cleared his throat, then spoke in a somber tone. "You know Lucille's children hired Bickerstaff to represent them?"

She nodded.

"Well, this is notification that they have filed a lawsuit against the trust. And me, personally, I might add."

"Oh, no," said Yolanda. "How can they do that? And why would they send this to me?"

"Because, according to the terms of the trust, you are the legal caretaker of the dogs. As such, you are naturally included," he told her. "There might be a letter waiting for me back at my office." He looked thoughtful. "I wonder if that was what Bernie was looking for."

"What's the basis of the lawsuit?" I asked.

"They are claiming that Lucille was not of sound mind when she established the trust." He sighed. "And that those who profited from it"—he glanced up at Yolanda—"somehow coerced her into setting it up for our own monetary gain."

Chapter 10

Jimmy G stared at the limousine. Nothing was visible behind the smoked glass. He looked at the man at his side, noting the width of his shoulders and the size of his biceps. He knew better than to get into a limousine with a stranger. He had seen too many films in which people got taken for one-way rides.

Stalling for time, he pulled a cigar out of his pocket. Smoking a cigar always helped him think. He unwrapped the stogie and fired it up with his Zippo.

"You don't want to keep my boss waiting," said the man, pointing at the idling limo. "Get in."

"Don't think so. Why would Jimmy G do that?"

The rear window of the limo rolled down a bit, and a hand came out, waving what looked like a bunch of hundred-dollar bills.

"Does that work for you?" the man asked Jimmy G.

Sure did. Jimmy G approached the car, and the man at his side opened the door. In a minute, Jimmy G was sliding into the dark leather seat facing the limo's sole occupant. He was no kind of dope, though. He kept one hand near the .45 in his shoulder holster as he studied the occupant of the car.

The guy was midforties, had dark brown hair, wore a well-tailored, summer-weight tan suit. His lips were large and fleshy. There were dark circles under his eyes.

"If you must smoke," the stranger said, "at least smoke something good."

"White Owl," said Jimmy G, holding up his cigar. "It is good."

"This is better." The man reached into his coat pocket, withdrew a leather cigar case, took out a large, Churchill-style cigar, and handed it to Jimmy G.

One look at it told Jimmy G it was a Cohiba. Cuban. Illegal in the US.

"Little expensive for Jimmy G's blood," he told him.

"We can pay you enough so you can afford these from now on."

Jimmy G tossed his White Owl out the window and fired up the Cuban. It was so rich and smooth, it was almost intoxicating.

"Who are you?" he asked the man.

"I'm a Superior Court judge," he said, carefully lighting a cigar of his own. "My name is Julian Valentine. Let's just say I have an interest in the disposition of the late Lucille Carpenter's fortune."

"A judge, huh?"

"Clallam County Superior Court."

"What do you want?"

"We want you to finish the job you started for Bernie Bickerstaff."

"You know about that?"

"Yes, and we know how much he paid you and how little you delivered."

"Hey, the guy was dead!" Jimmy G was quick to point out.

"Exactly," said Valentine, sucking at his cigar. He paused for a moment, then released a curl of smoke from his pursed-up mouth. "So now you work for us."

"Who's us?" Jimmy G asked cautiously.

"Those who have an interest in seeing that the Carpenter fortune goes to the rightful heirs."

"And what do you expect Jimmy G to do?" Jimmy G asked.

"We need a copy of the trust document. You should be able to get one from Boswell. Here's his address." He handed him a sheet of paper.

"What if he doesn't want to share it with Jimmy G?"

"Use whatever means you consider necessary," said the judge. "We can't proceed until we see that document."

Jimmy G folded the piece of paper and stuffed it into his pocket.

"In addition," said the judge, "we need statements from witnesses who can prove that my mother was crazy when she signed that trust document. Here's a list of people who should be helpful." And he passed Jimmy G another sheet of paper.

Jimmy G was confused. "Your mother? I thought we were talking about some rich old lady name of Carpenter."

"Hey!" said the judge. "Show some respect. That's my mother you're talking about. She was a Valentine before she was a Carpenter."

"Oh," said Jimmy G, thinking he understood. "How will Jimmy G get in contact with you?" he asked.

Valentine frowned, pulled his cigar out of his mouth, and squashed it in the large crystal ashtray to his right. "You'll be staying here." He handed Jimmy G a card that advertised FLORAL FANTASY B&B, with an address in Port Townsend. "That way we'll know how to find you. You don't contact us. We contact you."

Chapter 11

"That's ridiculous!" snapped Clara. "My aunt has given up her life for those dogs. She deserves every penny she gets for their upkeep."

Yolanda fired off a string of rapid Spanish directed at her niece. Clara pouted but began picking up the dog's saucers.

"What do we do next, Barry?" Yolanda asked.

"Well, they've set a court date for a hearing, about three weeks away. We'll just have to show up with evidence that Lucille was of sane mind. I don't think that will be any problem." He picked up his teacup and took a sip.

"I know what they will say," said Clara, pausing in her task. "That anyone who would leave five million dollars to dogs has to be crazy." Her voice was belligerent. It sounded like she agreed with this.

"That is absurd," said Pepe. "Anyone who said such a thing would themselves have to be loco."

"How do you prove that someone is sane?" I asked.

"A good question," said Boswell, setting down his

teacup. He turned to me. "We should expand the scope of your work. Besides investigating the attempt on the dogs, I need you to collect statements from people who can testify as to Lucille's state of mind."

"Anyone who ever met her will say she was crazy," said Clara. She loaded the used saucers on the tea tray, making a lot of noise as she did. Yolanda frowned at her. "It's true," she said defiantly, "she acted like her dogs talked to her."

"Did she really?" I asked. I turned to Pepe. "Do the cockers talk?"

"Of course they don't talk!" said Clara, who left the room, carrying the tray of saucers.

"Not all dogs talk," said Pepe, looking at the sleeping dogs.

Boswell ignored our conversation. "Of course, *you* could testify, Yolanda, but we really need testimony from people who did not personally benefit from Lucille's trust. And I can't think of any, can you?"

"No," Yolanda said with a shrug of her shoulders. "Everyone who got left out of her trust is angry at her and would be happy to testify for Mr. Bickerstaff."

"About that," said Boswell, "there is something I need to tell you."

"What is it?" Yolanda poured herself another cup of tea from the teapot.

"Bernie's dead."

"What? How?" Yolanda looked rattled. "But the letter . . ."

"He must have sent it yesterday. He died sometime today. The police think he was poisoned."

"Oh no!" Yolanda shrieked. "No, no, no, no, no!"

Her niece came running back in. "What did you do now?" she asked Barrett, as she cradled her aunt's head in her arms. Yolanda rocked back and forth, sobbing. She seemed to have completely fallen apart.

"I just told her that Bickerstaff was dead," Boswell said. He had gotten up and was hovering around Yolanda, as if he wanted to comfort her but was afraid to touch her. "Murdered, actually."

"Who killed him?" asked Clara.

"We don't know," Boswell said. "The police think I might have been the target."

"Who's next?" Yolanda asked. "First, the dogs. Then you, Barrett. What if they come after us?" She was shaking. "I don't feel safe."

"That's why I hired these two," said Boswell, waving his hand at me and Pepe.

"Them?" That was Clara. Her tone was scornful or amazed. Maybe both.

"Yes, they're private investigators," said Boswell.

"Really?" Clara perked up. "Like on TV?"

"Yes, we are as good as Shawn Spencer and Burton Guster," said Pepe, who was a big fan of the TV show *Psych*.

"I'm not sure that's a good comparison," I said. "And besides, which one are you?"

"Let me put it this way," said Pepe. "I am not the sidekick."

"What do you mean?" asked Clara, clearly confused.

"Yes, they need to interview you," Boswell said to Yolanda, shaking his head. "I will leave you in their capable hands. I must return to Port Townsend. I've already talked to the police once, but they want me to provide them with some papers I was not able to find. Do you mind if I take this with me?"

"Please, take it away! I don't want to see it!" said Yolanda. When Boswell got up to leave, she got up, too.

"Do not worry, Yolanda," he said. "I will clear this up." He took her hand and gave the back of it a kiss.

"Please check in with me in the morning," he said, turning to me and Pepe. "I can give you a copy of the trust document and a list of people to interview. Until the police release the crime scene, I'll be working out of my home office." He handed me a card with an address scribbled across the back.

"I was planning to head back to Seattle tonight," I said.

"Surely you have some questions for Yolanda," Boswell said.

"Yes, you should be our guests," said Yolanda. "We can talk after dinner. And I will feel so much safer with you on the premises." She turned to Clara. "Go tell Caroline to set two extra places for dinner."

After Boswell left, Yolanda took us on a tour of the house. Mrs. Carpenter had obviously been a fan of English décor. The house was full of sturdy oak pieces, four-poster beds, heavy velvet curtains, and lots of English bric-a-brac. The tour ended in the kitchen, which was a bit more modern, and the domain of Caroline, the cook, who, as Yolanda explained, did not "live in." She drove in from town every day to prepare breakfast, lunch, and dinner, for humans and dogs, but left as soon as dinner was served.

Caroline had prepared a feast of vegetarian lasagna, a salad of tossed greens (which she said came straight from the garden), and zucchini muffins, all of which were laid out on the island in the kitchen. There was a choice of fresh lemonade (I couldn't handle that, remembering Bickerstaff's contorted visage), locally pressed cider, or red wine. I chose the wine, a blend of Washington reds, which went well with the lasagna.

The dogs had their own meal of fresh raw meat that had been mixed with vegetables and rice. They padded into the dining room, and the cook set out their dishes along the wall, in order, according to their age. Pepe was given a small plate at the end of the line. He gobbled down his dinner, then prowled along the line to see if any of the other dogs' dishes held leftovers.

The humans sat at one end of a long oak table that had places for twelve guests. A large silver candelabra occupied the center. On one end of the room, a china closet with glass doors displayed stacks of gold-rimmed porcelain. The wallpaper was a William Morris design: a greenish background with pink and yellow flowers. Paintings of cocker spaniels hung on the walls.

"How long have you known Mrs. Carpenter?" I asked Yolanda, after taking a few bites of my lasagna.

She was just toying with her food. "I've been with her for thirty years."

"Since my aunt first came to the United States," Clara observed. She was attacking her meal with gusto.

"That's right. I wouldn't be here if it wasn't for Mrs. Carpenter. There was a civil war going on in my country, but I couldn't leave without a sponsor. She sponsored me. It was so generous of her."

"You mean so cunning," Clara said. "She just wanted a slave."

Yolanda rebuked her with a glance. "Hush, I was not a slave!"

"Then why did you never leave?" Clara asked.

"Mrs. Carpenter was very good to me," Yolanda said.

"She was not! She was rude and demanding and disrespectful!" Clara said.

"You never saw the good side of her," Yolanda remarked mildly. "Besides, the kids needed me. Especially after their father died."

"The Carpenter kids?" I was confused.

"Oh, no! I'm talking about the Valentine kids. They were only teenagers when their father died. I helped raise them until they went off to college. Then Lucille moved to Sequim and met Mr. Carpenter. He had his own set of kids. Lucille needed me more than ever. And the kids did, too!"

Clara rolled her eyes.

"You don't think much of that?"

"You'd have to know the kids."

"I brought Clara up to help me three years ago, when Lucille got sick," Yolanda said.

"What did she die of?"

"Meanness," said Clara.

Yolanda glared at her. "Congestive heart failure. Her poor heart broke when all the kids refused to speak to her. First her own, then Mr. C's, whom she helped raise."

"Why did they hate her so much?"

"Because she killed their father," said Clara.

Chapter 12

"What?" I almost dropped my wineglass. "Mrs. Carpenter killed her husband?"

"Oh no!" said Yolanda, giving her niece a sharp look. "That's not true!"

"Then what?"

"He tripped over one of her yappy little dogs and fell down the stairs and broke his neck," said Clara. She said it with great satisfaction.

Pepe jumped into my lap. "Who killed who?" he asked me.

"Shhh!" I told him. "Just listen."

"I was trying to," he said. "But licking all those plates clean took precedence."

"Spoiled, isn't he?" said Clara, referring to Pepe. All the other dogs had stayed on the floor.

"Sorry," I told Clara. "I think he's still a little hungry."

"I'm sure Caroline gave him the correct portion for a dog his size. Lucille was very strict about the dogs' meals," Yolanda explained. "She didn't want them getting fat."

"I do not have to worry about that," said Pepe, "since I burn off my energy through investigating."

"So," I said, trying to get us back on track, "one of Mrs. Carpenter's dogs was responsible for her husband's death? She must have felt terrible about it."

"Oh, she did," said Yolanda. "Lucille felt just awful."

"Sure she did," said Clara, her voice dripping with sarcasm. "She felt so bad that she rushed her precious dog off to the vet while her husband's body lay at the bottom of the stairs."

"Clara!" said Yolanda. "You weren't here! You don't know what happened."

"Well, it's true," said Clara. "You've told me the story enough times. Mr. Carpenter fell on top of Henry, and Mrs. C was worried that the dog was hurt." She turned to us. "Turns out Henry had a sprained shoulder. Nothing compared to her husband's broken neck."

"Please don't think too badly of Lucille," Yolanda told me. "She was a realist, that's all. Her husband was obviously dead, and her dog was injured. What else could she do?"

"Yes, what else could she do?" asked Clara.

I was wondering the same thing—what would I do if Felix tripped over Pepe and Pepe was hurt?—when Pepe said, "There is an uneaten piece of lasagna on your plate, Geri. May I have it, *por favor*?"

"It'll give you a tummy ache," I told him.

"Just because tomato sauce gave me pains in my stomach *uno* time, does not mean it will do so again," he said, putting one paw on the tablecloth and pulling it and the plate toward him.

"Oh, all right." I took my plate and put it on the floor for him. Yolanda gave me a disapproving look. Pepe slurped it down quickly as the other dogs gathered around him.

We finished our meal with a rich and fragrant lavender ice cream for dessert. Yolanda told me it came from the lavender farm next door, which was run by Colleen Carpenter. It was one of her specialties—homemade lavender-infused ice cream, always a popular item during the upcoming lavender festival.

"How did Colleen end up with the farm?" I asked, as I polished off the last creamy bite of my ice cream.

"She was the only one of the kids interested in going into the family business," Yolanda said.

"Mr. Carpenter was a lavender farmer?" I asked.

"Not until he met Lucille. Before that he ran a dairy farm, but the business was failing. It was her idea to switch over to growing lavender."

"It seems like that worked out well," I commented.

"Actually, Colleen told me that if she doesn't make enough during this year's lavender festival, she's going to have to declare bankruptcy," said Clara.

"What are you doing over there?" said Yolanda. "I told you to stay away from them! They're not our friends."

"Whatever!" Clara got up from the table and left the room.

"Why do you disapprove of her going over there?" I asked.

"For all I know," said Yolanda, getting up herself, "Colleen is the one who tried to poison the dogs. She never liked them, and if they died, it would solve all her financial problems." She began gathering up the plates.

"I thought the money went to the local humane society if the dogs died," I said.

"Oh, does it?" said Yolanda. "I've never really looked at the trust document. I let Barrett handle all the legal and financial issues."

I got up to help her, and the dogs, who had been lounging around the room, all got up too. We crowded into the kitchen, where Clara was putting her dirty dishes into the dishwasher. The dogs swirled around us, barking and whining and yipping.

Clara opened the back door, and the canine multitude poured out into the yard. The spaniels ran up and down the yard, bumping into and tumbling over each other. They looked like a bunch of clowns.

A long chain-link fence separated the yard of Carpenter Manor from the back of the neighboring property. Bamboo that had been planted along its length screened our view of the farm outbuildings, although I could glimpse a reddish-brown barn and the roof of a farmhouse.

The scent of fresh lavender was everywhere, especially as the light breeze was blowing our way across the rolling fields of lavender that stretched out for a hundred yards or so behind the backyard. That wonderful scent and the sky, which was turning a gorgeous shade of orange-red around the setting sun, made the pastoral surroundings seem almost magical.

"So, tell me about the day someone tried to poison the dogs," I said when we were all back inside. Clara had gone off to study. According to her aunt, she was taking classes at the local community college. Caroline had gone home. Yolanda and I sat with the dogs in the living room. I pulled out my notebook.

"It was an ordinary day," said Yolanda. "The dog walker came to take them out for their morning walk."

"And who is the dog walker?"

"A high school student from town."

"Do the dogs get walked every day?"

"Yes, she comes around seven in the morning and takes them out in groups. She's always done by eight."

"She noticed them getting sick?"

"No, she found the cookies scattered along the side of the driveway. She didn't think any of the dogs had managed to eat any, but she wasn't sure. And it wasn't just the chocolate she was worried about. She thought maybe the cookies were poisoned."

"Why would she think that?"

"We had received several threatening phone calls, someone calling to say the dogs were doomed."

"Did you report them to the police?"

"Yes, but they didn't seem very sympathetic. Most people in town are on the side of the kids."

"What did you do?"

"I called Barry, and he said to take them to the vet. I don't drive, so the dog walker took them."

"And what did the vet say?"

"Hugh said there wasn't enough chocolate in the cookies to harm any of the dogs. But he kept Henry overnight for observation, just because of Henry's age. Poor Henry." She dabbed at her eyes with her knuckles.

"Do you know if the vet ever tested the cookies?" I asked.

Yolanda shook her head. "I have heard nothing."

I made a note. We would have to return to talk to Hugh the Handsome.

"So who could have left the cookies there?" I asked. "Is it possible someone just dropped a bag of cookies?"

Yolanda gave me a chiding look, like the one she had given Clara. "People don't just walk by out here in the country," she said. "But anyone in a car could have stopped on the road and thrown the cookies out of the window."

"Again, making it seem deliberate," I said.

"Of course, it was deliberate!" Yolanda declared.

An hour later, Pepe and I were in bed, in the room that had once belonged to Colleen Carpenter. It was a sparsely furnished room: just a single bed and a maple chest of drawers. A warm breeze blew through the lace curtains around the window that I'd opened slightly for ventilation. The sheets were soft and warm and smelled like lavender.

At home, Albert the Cat has claimed the bedroom as his territory, so Pepe rarely sleeps with me. Instead, he sleeps in the living room on the couch in front of the TV. He dozes off while watching his favorite shows, which is where he gets his ridiculous

ideas about human nature and forensic science.
But here there was no TV. No yellow glow from
streetlights. No swish of traffic. No rumble of air-
planes overhead. Just darkness and quiet.

As I turned off the small lamp on the bedside
table, Pepe snuggled up close to me, warm and cozy
as the bed itself. I patted his soft head and reflected
on the silence, so very relaxing.

Until Pepe's stomach began to rumble.

He denied it, of course. "Those were just frogs
you heard, Geri. Listen! There they go again, a
whole chorus of them just outside our window."

Chapter 13

Jimmy G proceeded slowly up the flagstone walk that led to Boswell's front door. He still wasn't sure what was going on, and who he was working for, and what he was looking for. So how the hell was he supposed to question the guy?

Boswell's house sat high on a hill above Port Townsend. It was three stories tall and had a turret with a conical roof like a witch's hat. The front door was one of those old-fashioned oak jobs with an oval, etched-glass window. Seemed to be original, as old as the house. And the doorbell sure was— mounted on the door itself, it was a small, square box, made of dark metal, with a twister-type gizmo that you wound up like a watch. So Jimmy G did just that. When he let it go, the thing set off a loud mechanical bell that rang half a dozen times or so.

No one answered, which was fine by Jimmy G. He could report to his mysterious new boss that Boswell was not home and be done with it. He turned to go, but just then the door opened. Standing on the other side was a short, balding man with a round red face.

"Mr. Boswell, I presume," said Jimmy G.

Boswell frowned. "Yes, and you are?"

Jimmy G had a momentary flash of brilliance. "Jimmy G of the Gerrard Agency," he said, holding out his hand. "Here to check on my operatives."

Boswell shook his hand, but stared oddly at his chest for a moment.

Must be the tie, Jimmy G thought. He was wearing his favorite—extrawide, a combination of bright red, green, blue, and orange swirls so loud it could be heard over the cries of the crowd when a long shot came in at the racetrack. It was always a good icebreaker.

Finally meeting his gaze again, Boswell said, "Your operatives are at Carpenter Manor, talking to the caretaker and her niece."

"Ah, good," said Jimmy G. "Better to talk about them when they're not here. Jimmy G is conducting an evaluation, you know, assessing their performance." Boswell was still frowning. "Mind if Jimmy G comes in?"

"I guess," said Boswell. "But we must be quick. I'm rather busy."

"This will only take a minute," said Jimmy G.

"Well, come into my study." Boswell led Jimmy G down a hallway that was crowded with furniture and through a door at the end of the hall.

"Forgive the mess," he said, waving his hand at a desk that was heaped with papers. A very large and tall violet-colored cat with a fluffy, fanlike tail sat on the corner of the desk and directed a baleful look at Jimmy G. "I've just realized there are some irregularities in the trust document."

Jimmy G wondered if this was the document the judge wanted him to steal—or obtain, as the judge would have phrased it.

"Perhaps Jimmy G can help," he said, reaching out his hand for the paper.

The cat snarled, and Jimmy G drew back his hand quickly.

Boswell frowned. "Are you a lawyer, sir?"

"A private dick has to know a little about a lot of things."

Boswell did not hand over the paper. Instead, he waved Jimmy G to a seat in a wing-back chair and took a seat himself in a similar chair behind the desk. Only Boswell's chair swiveled. "You wanted to ask me about your employees."

"Ah, yes, what have they done so far?"

Boswell's eyes narrowed. "Well, you should know, shouldn't you?"

"Of course, but Jimmy G is trying to verify if they are making a full report," said Jimmy G. When he saw that Boswell still hesitated, he added, "Customer satisfaction is the most important thing at the Gerrard Agency."

Boswell sighed. "We actually have not had much of a chance to talk. They were the ones who discovered the body of my colleague, Bickerstaff, in my office." He narrowed his eyes and peered at Jimmy G. "You do know about that, right?"

"Of course," said Jimmy G, nodding.

"I sent them off to talk to the vet who treated the dogs, while I spoke to the police."

"What did they ask you?" Jimmy G wanted to know.

"The police? Or your operatives?"

"The police."

"Routine questions. Where was I? At what times? What was my relationship to Bickerstaff like? Did I kill him?"

"Did you?"

"I say!" said Boswell, standing up abruptly. The cat stood up. too, with back arched and tail bristling. "That is outrageous, sir! I had nothing to do with Bickerstaff's unfortunate death. I hired your agency to find out if someone is trying to harm the dogs. And unless your questions are relevant to that purpose, I refuse to answer them."

"Hey! Just making sure," said Jimmy G. "Would not want to involve the Gerrard Agency in anything unsavory." He had to get his hands on that piece of paper. How to do so?

"This conversation is over," said Boswell, coming out from behind the desk.

Jimmy G had a brilliant idea. It did involve some personal risk. He reached for the cat, thinking he would be able pick it up and drop it on the desk, creating a distraction. "Nice cat!" he said.

The cat did not appreciate the compliment. It reared up and swiped at him, managing to leave claw marks down the back of his hand. At the same time, it lost its footing on the slippery papers and went sliding over the edge of the desk. He heard the cat hit the floor with a thud. On its feet, he presumed. After all, they say cats always land on their feet.

"Oh, good heavens!" said Boswell, dropping to his knees beside the cat. "Did that awful man hurt you, Precious?" As he bent over the cat, checking the animal for injuries, Jimmy G scooped up the papers on the top of the pile and stuffed them into his jacket.

"I'll see myself out," he said, strolling out the door. When he stopped at the threshold to look back, Boswell was cradling the cat in his arms. He did not seem to have noticed Jimmy G's theft. He was kissing the cat on the top of its head. And Jimmy G could hear the cat purring, from yards away.

Chapter 14

I awoke to the realization that something was wrong. Very wrong. It took me a moment to figure out where I was: the guest bedroom at Carpenter Manor. The door to the hall was open. The breeze had turned chilly. The rising sun was painting the sky a pale pink in the distance.

Then I realized what was wrong. Pepe was gone.

Almost simultaneously, I heard a screech. Ouch! A muffled curse. Then a thud.

That woke up the dogs in the locked bedroom down the hall. They started barking furiously and scratching at the door.

Where was Pepe? I slipped out of bed and pulled on the bathrobe Yolanda had loaned me. I thought the sounds had come from downstairs, but I couldn't be sure. I tiptoed down the stairs, moving as fast as I dared in the darkness. I could hear doors opening upstairs. Must be Yolanda and Clara coming to see what was happening.

There was no sign of Pepe in the living room or the dining room, but as I pushed into the kitchen,

I saw that the back door was open wide. And I saw a dark figure outlined against the pink sky—a tall figure dressed all in black with a mask over its face and my little white dog tucked into its arm.

"Let go of my dog!" I shouted, not really sure how I was going to enforce that command.

The figure turned and looked at me with soulless, glittering eyes. And at the same time, Pepe wrestled his head free and chomped down on the arm that confined him.

"Ow!" The intruder dropped Pepe on the ground and took off running. Pepe landed with an undignified grunt, but scrambled to his feet and took off after the intruder, who dashed through the garden and vaulted the fence that separated Carpenter Manor from the adjoining lavender farm. Within seconds there was no sign of the dark figure, which blended into the shadows created by the clutter of outbuildings and farm machinery.

Pepe danced up and down at the base of the fence, furious!

"Geri, pick me up and put me over there!" he said.

"I don't want you getting hurt!" I said.

"*No problema!*" he said, panting with fury. "It is that miscreant who will be feeling my wrath."

At that moment, the four cocker spaniels came pouring out into the yard, followed by Yolanda, shivering in a cotton nightgown, and Clara, in a fluffy pink bathrobe.

I tried to explain what had happened, with constant interruptions from Pepe.

"I heard Pepe barking," I said. "That woke me up."

"I heard the sound of footsteps downstairs,"

Pepe said. "That woke me up. Naturally I went to investigate."

"Naturally I got up to see what was going on," I said.

"As soon as I saw the villain, clothed all in black, I rushed at him, telling him to halt!"

"What happened next?" I asked.

"We heard the dogs barking," said Yolanda, thinking I was speaking to her.

"He kicked me!" said Pepe indignantly.

"The intruder kicked my dog!" I declared.

"But I was not going to let violence stop me!" said Pepe. "I knew my duty was to protect the dogs." He looked at me. "And you, of course."

"Thanks!"

"So I rushed at him again, threatening him with bodily harm. That was when he snatched me up and headed for the door."

"Perhaps he mistook you for one of the dogs?" I suggested.

"Only a fool would mistake a Chihuahua for a cocker spaniel!" said Pepe.

"Do we know what he wanted?" asked Clara. "Do we know it was a man? Do we know anything?"

"Hush! I have not yet finished my tale," said Pepe, who was inclined to go on whenever anything cast him in a flattering light. The cocker spaniels had gathered around him as children do around a librarian during story hour.

"I sank my fangs into his arm and he let go." He paused for effect. "Then he ran off, and Geri prevented me from pursuing him, fearing for her own safety and wishing to keep me by her side."

* * *

We looked at the door but couldn't see any signs of forced entry. Pepe told us he had first seen the intruder in the hall between the office and the kitchen. Yolanda looked around but could find no sign that anything had been disturbed. I have to admit that I don't know how she would have known. The whole office looked like it had been trashed, with file cabinets so full they didn't shut and papers in drifts on the floor as well as the desk.

But Yolanda claimed it always looked that way. "No one has been in here since Lucille died," she said. "She called this her headquarters. She was in here every day: making lists, making phone calls. But when she got sick, it became just a general storage room."

Yolanda called the police, and Clara made a pot of coffee. Caroline arrived and fixed us breakfast (bacon and scrambled eggs) while we waited for the police. Yolanda was very distressed. She kept muttering to herself in Spanish. Pepe said she was raining down curses on anyone who would be so evil as to threaten innocent dogs.

The police arrived just as the dogs were finishing their own breakfast: a medley of kale, rice, and lamb. Pepe took one look at the police and jumped up into my lap. Pepe has a thing about the police. I think he confuses them with animal control. He did his time in several shelters before I adopted him. He was shivering as only an agitated Chihuahua can shiver.

"Kind of timid, isn't he?" asked the cop with sergeant's stripes on his sleeve.

"Timid-shmimid!" exclaimed Pepe. "I learned all

about your bribe-taking, donut-eating ways south of the border!"

"I don't think they eat donuts south of the border," I said. "Maybe churros."

"Donuts?" said the sergeant's partner, a young man with a freckled face and flaming red hair in a buzz cut.

"No donuts," said Caroline, bringing the coffeepot over to the table. "But I do have coffee."

"Thanks," said the sergeant. "I'll take a cup." While Yolanda poured him a cup, using one of the pretty flowered china teacups, he went on: "Dispatch radioed that you had an intruder in the house, Yolanda. That correct?"

"Yes," she said.

"Anybody hurt?" asked the young cop.

"No, but someone is trying to kill the dogs," Yolanda said.

"Didn't your dogs set up a ruckus?" the sergeant asked Yolanda. "Start barking when he broke in, or go after the guy when he ran out?"

"They were locked up in their room," she said. When he raised his eyebrows at her, she said, "We lock them in at night. For their own protection."

"I went after him!" said Pepe.

"My dog was the one who chased him off!" I said.

"Really?" The sergeant looked surprised.

"I may be small, but I am fearless," declared Pepe.

"So did you get a look at this intruder?"

"Yes, he was dressed all in black and wearing a black ski mask," I said.

"Any other distinguishing characteristics?"

"Tell him the *hombre* smelled strongly of lavender," Pepe told me.

"So does everything around here," I said. "That's a big help."

"What's a big help?" the sergeant asked me.

"The guy smelled very strongly of lavender," I told him.

"Well, that's a big help," he said. "So do half the people around here this time of year."

The young cop chuckled.

"You getting all this down?" the sergeant asked him.

"Yeah, Sarge, I think so." He read from the small notebook in his hands. "The guy was dressed all in black and smelled like lavender."

The sergeant shook his head slowly side to side. "Yeah," he told his partner. "That's about what we've got to work with."

"And the dog bite!" said Pepe.

"Yes, and my dog bit him," I said.

The sergeant sighed. "Yes, we can put out a BOLO to the local ERs to watch out for a guy who's been bitten by a Chihuahua."

"Do you think that will work?" I asked, excited. It was just like a crime show on TV.

The sergeant sighed. "No! Seems unlikely that a Chihuahua could inflict any serious harm."

"*Caramba!*" said Pepe. "That is libelous."

"Anyway," said the sergeant, "I think we've got what we need. Thanks for the coffee, Yolanda. If you think of anything else that might help, don't hesitate to call us."

We all followed them to the front door, where the sergeant turned to me. "Crime is rare in Sequim," he said. "And this kind of crime is particularly rare. Most likely it was a neighborhood kid out on a dare."

"Do they usually dress in all black and wear ski masks?" I asked, indignant.

"Well, you know the idea of being a ninja and sneaking into houses—it appeals to some kids." The cop seemed blasé. "Anyway, let's keep this quiet. We wouldn't want to give anyone the wrong impression about crime in Sequim. Especially since we're expecting so many visitors to our fair town over the next few days."

I watched them depart with a frown. "I think they're blowing me off," I said.

"I know," said Yolanda. "No one really takes the threat to the dogs seriously. That's why I'm so glad that Boswell hired you."

Speaking of Boswell, it was time for us to pick up the trust document from his office and head back to Seattle to make a report to Jimmy G.

Chapter 15

Jimmy G fought his way out of a fog of bizarre dreams full of swirling patterns and attacking cats and opened his eyes, then shut them again. Surely he was still dreaming. He popped one eyelid open. Nope, not dreaming.

He lay very still as the fragments of the night before settled around him. After leaving Boswell's house, he had headed for the Floral Fantasy B&B, where the judge said he had a room waiting. The owner, a slim young man who introduced himself as Lionel, ushered him upstairs and into what he called the Lavender Room.

The whole place reeked of lavender. The walls were covered with wide stripes of lilac and purple. There was no TV, just a vase filled with dried lavender flowers on top of the looming chest of drawers. "We don't believe in mass entertainment," Lionel said. "Our guests come here to relax and get away from it all."

Not Jimmy G. He left to hang out at the nearest bar and staggered back to the B&B after last call,

waking up his disgruntled host by leaning on the
bell. His key had disappeared somewhere during
the evening.

Jimmy G struggled out of the bed, throwing off
the purple floral bedspread and gathering up his
scattered belongings. Something was missing, but
he couldn't quite put his finger on what. His head
was still spinning, and he figured getting out of the
lavender stink would help clear it.

As he clattered down the narrow stairs, Lionel
popped out of a doorway: "Mr. Gerrard," he said. His
forehead wrinkled slightly as he took in Jimmy G's
attire: the wrinkled jacket, the stained tie, the un-
combed hair. "We've been holding breakfast for you."
Oh, yeah, Jimmy G remembered something about
breakfast being served at certain ungodly hours.

Lionel held open the door, which led into a
sunny, glassed-in porch, lined with green plants.
One place was set at a glass table in the middle of
the room. "The other guests have already break-
fasted and taken off for the day," Lionel said.
"Coffee or tea, Mr. Gerrard?"

"Coffee," said Jimmy G, then remembered to
add, "black."

"Very well." Lionel disappeared, reappearing a
few minutes later with a plate heaped with food.
Behind him was another young man, with a freckled face and strawberry blond hair, who was carrying a silver urn and a china cup.

"Here we have our special frittata made with kale
and egg whites," said Lionel, setting down the plate
with a flourish, "served with potatoes à la greque."

"And this is our special blend, roasted just for us
by our friends at PT Roasters, totally shade-free,

organic coffee," said the other man, pouring coffee from the urn into the china cup. "And when you're ready, I'll be happy to sit down and answer your questions."

"And you are?"

"Kevin Carpenter. Didn't Julian tell you?"

"Who's Julian?"

"Judge Valentine!" The young man seemed amazed that Jimmy G would not recognize Julian by name.

"Oh, yeah." Jimmy G tried to remember if the judge had told him anything about Kevin Carpenter. All he remembered was something about a paper. He patted around in his pockets. Not there, but maybe he had left it up in the room.

He did find his flask and poured a little swig into his coffee. That helped settle his stomach, and he was able to polish off the rather peculiar breakfast.

Just as he was finishing up, Kevin appeared, carrying a cup of his own. Jimmy G thought it was only polite to offer him a swig of bourbon.

Kevin looked alarmed. "It would totally spoil the flavor of the Darjeeling," he said. "This is first flush."

Whatever that meant. Jimmy G poked around in his pockets and found a pen and a relatively clean napkin from the Anchor Tavern.

Kevin sat across from him expectantly. "So what do you need to know?'

Jimmy G tried to remember what he was supposed to ask. Better to fake it.

"Why don't you tell me in your own words," he suggested.

"Well, obviously the whole thing is a ghastly

mistake. I mean my father would have turned over in his grave, if he had known Lucille was going to leave all his hard-earned money to her dogs. He hated those dogs."

"So your father is?"

"Charles Carpenter." Kevin studied him. "Shouldn't you know this already?"

"Best to start from the beginning," said Jimmy G. Kevin sighed.

"And what were your feelings about your mother?"

"My mother?" Kevin seemed puzzled. "My mother died when I was twelve."

"The lady who left her money to the dogs was not your mother?"

"No, Lucille was my stepmother." Kevin's voice got louder. "She married my father when I was sixteen and sent me and my sister away to boarding schools." The door opened and Lionel appeared, whisked away the empty plate, gave Kevin a disapproving look, and disappeared again.

"So you probably feel the money should belong to you," Jimmy G said.

Kevin shrugged. "We get by with the income from our business."

"Business?"

"Floral Fantasy," said Kevin. "Our bed-and-breakfast. We're usually completely booked from May through September. Then there's another busy period around the holidays."

Jimmy G scribbled that down, though he wasn't sure that was relevant.

"It's really my sister I worry about."

"Sister?"

"Colleen. She runs the farm: Lost Lakes Lavender. She's got a bit of a chip on her shoulder. My dad didn't think girls could be farmers. So she's always trying to prove herself. She would be OK if it wasn't for the constant fighting."

"Fighting with her stepmother?"

"No, the other lavender farmers! They're ruthless—each one trying to compete for the attention of the tourists. Poor Colleen! I don't think she's going to make it. She's just not cut out for that kind of conflict."

Jimmy G wrote that down, too, though he didn't see how it was relevant. He tried to think of something else to ask.

"So who do you think killed Bickerstaff?"

"If I had to guess, I'd say Boswell," Kevin replied quickly. "They hated each other."

"But the police questioned Boswell and let him go."

Kevin raised his eyebrows. "You know how they do that. They can't make an arrest until they get enough evidence. But I'll bet they're closing in on him even as we speak."

Jimmy G gulped, thinking of his late-night visit. Maybe he had been alone with a murderer. He was lucky to be alive.

"Well, thanks for talking to Jimmy G," he said, crumpling the napkin and putting it back into his pocket. Then he remembered the missing document, the one he had lifted from Boswell's desk. "I left something in my room. I'll just head up to collect it."

"The maid just finished cleaning your room,"

Kevin said. "Let me ask her if she found anything. What was it?"

"Some legal papers," Jimmy G said quickly. "Relating to the case."

Out in the hall, Kevin approached a dark-haired young woman who was putting towels into a closet. "Helen, did you find any papers in the Lavender Room?"

Helen shook her head.

"Are you sure?' Jimmy G asked.

"Positive."

Jimmy G swallowed hard. The judge was not going to like this at all.

Chapter 16

As I opened the door to my car, Pepe turned his attention to the chain-link fence that ran along the driveway that led up to the Carpenter mansion.

"Let's go!" I said. I was eager to get back to Seattle.

"I would, but I have something more important to do," was his reply. He moved along the base of the fence, sniffing furiously.

"Are you finding clues?" I asked, curious. I didn't see how anyone could get over that fence to get into the yard. It ran down the whole length of the driveway out to the road, a good half mile.

"No, I am investigating," he said. "Something that no one else is doing."

"What do you expect me to do?" I asked.

"We should question Colleen Carpenter," he said. "After all, the intruder ran over here. Perhaps he lives on the property."

"Hmmm," I said, "that's an excellent idea. But what would I say? 'Did you attack my dog last night?'"

"I had something more clever in mind," Pepe

said in a mild tone that still managed to convey his superiority. "It is a ploy we have employed many times before."

"And that is?"

"My dog got loose!" He squeaked a little, trying to imitate the hysterical tones of a female human.

"Oh!" It's true we had used this technique successfully to gain access to yards on previous cases. "But the fence!" I pointed out.

"*Sí,*" said Pepe. "But the fence was designed to keep out cocker spaniels, not Chihuahuas. I can simply slip through it."

"But what about me? I can't chase after you."

"*Es verdad,*" said Pepe, eyeing me up and down. I was afraid he was going to say something about the few pounds I had gained. Felix didn't seem to mind. In fact, he was responsible for some of them as he almost always showed up at my house with a pint of chocolate-chip cookie-dough ice cream, my favorite.

"You will have to go around," Pepe said at last, gesturing down the road. "You can drive up the driveway on the other side."

"OK!" I wasn't so sure this would work. "But, Pepe, I don't think you can fit through there!"

"Watch me, Geri!" he said. And he dove at the bottom of the fence, scraping away with his little paws, shoveling dirt as fast as a gopher. Pretty soon he had a nice trench dug out, and he scrunched down to get through it, pushing with his hind legs, scrabbling at the dirt with his front legs, his little white torso completely filling the gap.

After a few minutes I said, "Pepe, you're stuck!"

"I am not!" he declared. He scrabbled some more with his front paws.

"Decidedly not," he said after a brief struggle, during which he used his hind legs to wriggle forward about half an inch.

"Perhaps," he admitted with a gasp.

I studied him. "You remind me of Pooh Bear when he got stuck in Rabbit's hole after eating all of Rabbit's honey," I said, studying his little white butt, "though you look more like Piglet."

"Did this bear manage to get unstuck?" Pepe asked.

"Yes, he did," I said.

"Was it because his friends pushed or pulled him through?" he asked.

"No, they tried that, but it didn't work," I said. "But just to be sure, let's give it a try." I tried pulling him by his hind legs, then tried pushing on his butt. Back and forth we went, with Pepe making the most heart-breaking little squeaks. Finally I gave up.

"So how did this Pooh character get free?" Pepe asked.

"I don't think you're going to like it."

"Just tell me, Geri. This is a most undignified position to be in."

"They left him there without food for several days, and he lost enough weight so he could slip through."

"Unacceptable!" said Pepe.

"Here!" I said. "Maybe I can make the opening larger." I grasped the wires of the fence with both hands and pulled up a little. With a gasp, Pepe wriggled free. He trotted out into the driveway and shook himself off.

"I will reconnoiter," he said, turning to face me. "You meet me!"

"OK!" I climbed into my car and drove down the gravel drive. The turn was too tight at the bottom for me to make a U-turn. It was obvious the two driveways had been one long drive before they were divided by the fence. So I had to go down the road to the driveway of another farm, pull in, back up, and reapproach the entrance to the farm.

This driveway was also paved with gravel. I could hear my tires crunching as I drove up toward the red barn. Off to my right, in the lavender fields, I could see hunched figures. Workers were out there with baskets, picking lavender.

I was about twenty yards from the big red barn when suddenly I heard gunfire. Pow! Pow! Pow! The gravel rattled. And I saw a little white streak heading down the driveway. Pepe was heading straight for my car, running so fast he was almost a blur.

I slammed on my brakes and jumped out of the car, leaving the driver's-side door open so I could duck down behind it if necessary. Pow! Another shot rattled the fence at my side. Right behind Pepe, stepping out from behind the barn, was a woman, dressed in overalls. Her strawberry-blond hair was swept back by a blue bandanna. And she carried a rifle. She stopped to pull back the lever on the gun.

"Hey!" I shouted and waved my hands in the air. "Don't shoot! That's my dog!"

Meanwhile, Pepe darted into the car through the open driver's-side door. I saw him heading for the tiny space under the passenger seat.

"Well, keep him out of my yard!" she said, advancing on me, the gun at her side. A black-and-white spaniel-sized dog was at her side. "He was chasing my chickens. If I ever see him here again, I swear I'll kill him. I have every right to do so."

"Look," I said, slamming my door shut so Pepe would be safe. But, come to think of it, he might just put the car in gear and take off down the road. I wouldn't put it past him. He had learned to operate a TV remote control, a telephone, and my laptop. I reached in through the open window and yanked the key out of the ignition. All I could see of Pepe was his little white tail sticking out from under the seat. "He got away from me and ran over here. I'm sure he didn't mean any harm."

I walked up to her, keeping my eye on the rifle, and held out my hand. "I'm Geri Sullivan. You must be Colleen Carpenter?"

She didn't take my hand, just stared at me with icy-blue eyes. Her skin was weathered by the sun, so the contrast was striking. "I know who you are," she said. "You're a private detective out of Seattle."

"Who told you that?" I asked, thinking maybe Clara had conveyed the information across the property line. And how did she get to the farm? Was there a gate somewhere along that imposing fence? Or did she walk all the way around when she visited?

"We're protecting our interests," Colleen said.

"We have people working for us. We know all about what you're up to."

'Can I talk to you about Mrs. Carpenter?" I asked.

"No. Now get off my property."

"Are you aware that someone broke into Carpenter Manor last night and escaped by jumping the fence and running into your yard."

She seemed surprised by that, although she tried to hide it.

"If you don't leave," she said, "I'll call the police."

"Don't bother," I said. I got back in my car and began backing up the drive. Little clouds of dust spewed out from under my wheels, obscuring my view. I just hoped I didn't run into the fence or the lavender field while Colleen stood there at the end of driveway, the rifle at her side, watching.

Pepe crawled out from under the seat about ten minutes later.

"Are you OK?" I asked, as he plunked himself down in the passenger seat.

"Of course," he said, casually, taking the time to nibble on his hind leg. "That was quite an adventure. I have not been shot at in a long time."

"Oh, really?"

"*Sí.*"

"When was the last time?"

"When I was hunting at the big rancho in Texas with the vice president of the United States."

"What?" I was incredulous. "No way!"

"Sadly, it is true, Geri," he said. "It was my job to retrieve the birds the vice president and his companions were hunting."

"That's ridiculous! Chihuahuas aren't bird dogs."

"Oh, I will agree that the various spaniel and retriever breeds have their merits, but these good old boys were hunting very small birds, and for that sort of job, a Chihuahua is supreme. That is why I was given the honor of being the *numero uno* retriever for the hunting party," he told me.

"Of course," Pepe continued, "once trained to retrieve, it is hard to resist when one spots a bird. Thus when I saw the chickens, well, instinct just kicked in."

"What an excuse!" I said. "You can't possibly expect me to believe you were there when Dick Cheney accidently shot his lawyer friend."

"Believe what you will," said Pepe. "When his shotgun went off, some of the pellets missed me only by inches." He shuddered and grew thoughtful. "Luckily that other fellow threw himself in front of me, thus taking the bullets meant for me into his own hide."

"Pepe, that's the most outlandish tale you've ever told!" I started laughing. He looked insulted. "OK," I said, "I'll play along. So what did you do after that?"

"I ran, of course," he said, perking back up. "Self-preservation kicked in, and I ran and ran—and that is how I ended up in California."

"I don't believe you," I told him. "That business with the vice president happened years ago. You're not old enough to have been there."

"I beg to differ," he said. "I am a dog of my word. And anyway, just as you should not ask a senorita her true age, neither should you ask a Chihuahua *his* true age."

I couldn't think of a response to that, so I changed the subject. "You told me you were going to investigate. Did you actually do that, or were you just chasing chickens?"

"I only chased *uno*—well, maybe *dos* chickens," said Pepe. "But that was just to impress the most beautiful bitch in the universe."

"What?" It took me a minute to realize what he meant. I always forget how dogs use that word. "I thought Siren Song was the most beautiful dog in the world." Siren Song is a fluffy golden Pomeranian whom Pepe met in Seattle during our first case. "And what about Queen Mary?"

"Merely moons revolving around a dazzling planet," sighed Pepe. "A dazzling planet by the name of Phoebe."

"Describe this Phoebe," I said.

"Black-and-white, with beautiful, big, brown eyes," said Pepe in a dreamy voice.

Hmmm! I didn't tell him that I had seen his new crush standing beside Colleen Carpenter, and I doubted she was impressed by his hasty retreat.

Chapter 17

"Are you sure this is the right address?" asked Pepe, as we pulled to a stop in front of an enormous, three-story Victorian. It was bigger than any of the Victorians around it and had an incredible view of Port Townsend's harbor.

The house was painted in a bright fuchsia tone, with teal-green trim. A rounded turret with tall narrow windows rose from ground level to just above the second floor. The steep roof was crowned with a widow's walk, the railing painted apple green.

I double-checked the message on my cell phone. "Yes, this is the address Boswell gave me."

We went up the front steps to the wide porch, which was full of rattan chairs with floral fabric seats. Pots of fuchsias hung from the rafters, creating a sense of an enclosed garden space. The door had a frosted glass window and an old-fashioned doorbell that you had to turn, like the key of a music box. It made a scratchy, tinkly sound.

I could see vague shapes through the frosted glass, but I didn't see any sign of movement.

"I do not hear anyone inside," said Pepe, sniffing around the edges of the door. "Perhaps Boswell has gone out."

"He told us to meet him here in the morning," I said impatiently. I was eager to get home.

"Wait, that is not true," said Pepe. "Do you hear that?"

I put my ear close to the door and heard what Pepe was hearing. It was a terrible sound, a cross between a mournful wail and a baby on a crying jag.

"What is that?"

"A *gato*," my dog told me, his hackles rising.

"A cat?"

"*Sí*," Pepe told me, cocking his head toward the door. "A *gato* in *mucho* distress."

"Really? Since when did you start speaking cat?"

"Distress is a universal language," said Pepe.

He sniffed around the door while I rang the doorbell. The awful sound continued. If the cat was distressed, I was even more distressed. Surely if Boswell was home, he would hear the ruckus his cat was making and do something about it.

"There is something most definitely wrong," Pepe told me when we got no response. "We must get inside."

I rattled the doorknob, but it was locked.

"This way," said Pepe, racing down the porch stairs. I followed him as he circled around the side of the house. Lacy curtains shrouded the windows, so I couldn't see inside. A flight of stairs led up to a redwood deck, which was crowded with garden furniture: wrought-iron chairs, glass tables with umbrellas, a fancy grill and tall palm trees in ceramic pots. Pepe was scratching at the screen that covered the back door.

The terrible caterwauling was even louder, so I wasted no time pulling open the screen and trying the back door. It was locked.

"Can you see anything?" Pepe asked me.

I peered through the small window at the top of the door and said, "It looks like the kitchen. What should we do?"

"Try a credit card," Pepe told me. "This is an old door; it probably has one of those angled locks you can slip with a stiff credit card. I have seen this done many times on *Paraíso Perdido*."

Just because he saw it on his favorite telenovela didn't mean it would work for us. But I tried it anyway. I put one of my cards between the wooden door and the doorjamb, found the lock's position, and pushed the angled bolt back. To my surprise, it worked!

As the door opened inward, Pepe said, "Told you so."

Just then we heard a very loud thud, immediately followed by a softer thunk. The caterwauling suddenly stopped.

"This is not good," said Pepe. "Proceed with caution, Geri."

He didn't have to tell me twice. I was scared out of my wits. The crashing sound had come from my right. I pushed the door open slowly, glad that it was between me and whatever had made the sound.

"I will protect you!" cried Pepe, rushing past me and around the door.

"Pepe!" I started to push my way inside when my

dog came running back and hid behind one of the ceramic pots.

"What is it, Pepe?" I said.

He was shaking, and his big brown eyes were bulging out. "The horror!" he said. "The horror!"

I peered around the door carefully to see what I could see, still keeping the door between me and any danger. All I saw was a huge, fluffy, almost lilac-colored cat. He was at least three times bigger than Pepe, maybe four. And he was crouched next to a huge bag of dry cat food that had split open. The cat was chowing down on the crunchy nuggets that had spilled out and onto the floor. The cat looked up from its meal, fixing me with its golden eyes, then went back to his task.

"Ha!" I said. "It's just a cat!"

"Just a cat!" said Pepe, from behind me. He had crept up close to my heels. "That is a brute! *Monstruo!*"

"Don't worry. I'll protect you from the evil kitty." I said it jokingly, but it was no joke to Pepe, who had been bested in his one confrontation with my cat Albert.

I tiptoed into the kitchen. I couldn't help noticing its design. It's something that comes naturally when you have been trained in interior design. Boswell (or his decorator) was obviously going for a French country look, with a wood-block island, copper pans hanging above it, and cabinets painted a creamy white. A big bouquet of sunflowers sat on the island, next to a pitcher of lemonade. Pepe followed me, staying close.

To the right was a pantry area, like a walk-in closet for food, with every surface full: tins of tea, cans of soup, cereal boxes, cracker boxes, cookies galore, and lots of chocolate. On the floor, I saw two china dishes set out for the cat. Both were empty.

"Aha!" said Pepe. "The *gato* must have been crying to be fed, and when nobody came to feed him, he pushed over his bag of food. That is what we heard."

"I'm glad," I said. "Let's get out of here before someone calls the cops and charges us with breaking and entering."

"I am with you," Pepe told me. "This beast will doubtless turn on us when he is through concentrating on his feast."

"I do wonder why Boswell did not feed his cat," I said, as I turned to go.

Pepe had tiptoed past the cat and was looking down the dim corridor. He was sniffing away, his head lifted.

"I think I know why," he said, moving a few feet into the hall, still sniffing. "I smell *muerte!*"

"What?"

"*Sí,*" he said. "The scent of death. It is strong."

"Oh, no." I passed the cat and peered down the hall and saw nothing except for a lot of furniture and boxes lining the walls, leaving only a narrow path. "Are you sure?"

"My nose does not lie," said Pepe. He wagged his head toward an open door on the right. "The scent comes from this room."

He disappeared through the door, so I had to follow. It was obviously Boswell's home office. Multiple bookcases lined the walls; the hardwood floor was covered with a Persian rug; and a couple of leather wing-back chairs faced a vintage oak desk at the far end the room.

Pepe had disappeared behind the desk, and that's where we found Boswell. He was sprawled on the floor, his face a bright red, and his features contorted like a gargoyle's.

"Oh my God!" I said. "He looks just like Bicker-staff." He was still wearing the dark blue suit we had last seen him in. Apparently he had died sometime after he left the Carpenter mansion.

Pepe was at work, sniffing the papers surrounding the body, apparently searching for clues. I choked back my immediate desire to flee and forced myself to examine the scene carefully: the jumble of papers on Boswell's desk, the empty glass on the carpet, and the two large file cabinets behind the desk, all their drawers open, half their files pulled out and scattered about all willy-nilly.

"It looks as though somebody was searching for something," I said.

"*Sí*, it does," Pepe responded. I examined the papers on the desk, trying to read them without touching anything. They looked like documents that had been filed in various court cases.

"What did you find?"

"It is very odd," said Pepe, "but the papers smell like Jimmy G."

"Our boss?"

"Yes. They smell like cigar smoke and bourbon. But there is one small detail that troubles me. The cigar is a Cohiba."

"Jimmy G smokes cigars."

"Yes, but he smokes White Owls. The Cohiba comes from Cuba. It is illegal in the United States."

I stared at my dog. He always amazed me. "You mean to tell me you can distinguish one cigar from another?"

"Certainly, my dear Sullivan," said Pepe. "Like my role model, Sherlock Holmes, I have made an extensive study of the variety of tobacco products."

"Give me a break," I said, dismissing his ridiculous story as I dialed Jimmy G. It would be good to get his opinion on what to do next. Besides, if he did have anything to do with Boswell's death, I wanted to warn him before I called the police.

"Hey, doll," he said. "What's shakin'?"

"Boswell's dead."

"What?"

"Yes. We found him dead in his home office. I think he was poisoned just like Bickerstaff."

There was a long silence on the other end of the line.

"When did this happen?" he asked.

"How should I know?" I asked. "The last time we saw him was yesterday late afternoon at the Carpenter mansion. He told us to drop by his house in the morning to pick up a copy of the trust document. But when we got here, we found him dead. And it looks like someone was going through his papers."

"Can you tell if anything is missing?" Jimmy G asked.

"How would I know that?" I asked.

There was another long silence.

"Yeah, how would you know that!" he said, with a harsh laugh.

"Is something wrong, boss?" He was acting really strange.

"Yeah, just having a few problems with the reception. Jimmy G does not like this cell phone. So did you call the police?"

"I'm just about to, but, boss, there's one more thing."

"Yeah?"

"Pepe says the papers smell like you."

"Yeah, right! The dog is talking. You must be hallucinating, doll!"

I figured I might as well be direct. "Were you here?"

"Ha! Jimmy G in Port Townsend. That's a laugh."

"Well, where are you?"

"Where hasn't Jimmy G been? Last night he was in Tacoma. Right now he's at Emerald Downs."

"Emerald Downs?"

"Got a lotta money riding on a long shot," he said.

"OK," I said. "I guess Pepe made a mistake. He wasn't sure it was you because he said the cigar was a Cohiba, whatever that is."

Jimmy G gave a weak laugh. "Crazy dog you got there," he said. "Those are imported cigars. From Cuba. Black-market stuff. Jimmy G could never afford one."

Chapter 18

Jimmy G was sweating by the time he arrived at the farm. It wasn't just the temperature—which was hovering around ninety at noon—but the call from Geri telling him they had found Boswell dead in his office. An office that appeared to have been rifled. Geri even claimed her rat-dog could put Jimmy G on the scene.

Of course, he quickly convinced her that was ridiculous. Where would Jimmy G get a Cohiba? And how would the rat-dog know about that?

As soon as he stepped out of the car, a dog came running up and circled around Jimmy G in a menacing manner, barking and wagging its big, fluffy tail. Then a woman appeared, dressed in mud-spattered overalls and cowboy boots. She clomped down the road toward the car, calling to the dog, whose name was apparently Phoebe.

"Hello, Jimmy G is looking for the owner of this farm," he said.

"That's me," she said, peeling a heavy leather glove off her hand and shaking his. She had a hearty grip. "Colleen Carpenter. What can I do for you?"

"Jimmy G needs to ask you a couple of questions, ma'am," Jimmy G said.

"Well, where is this Jimmy G?" she asked, looking at the car to see if someone else was inside.

"Uh, Jimmy G stands here before you," Jimmy G said, pointing at his tie.

"OK, Jimmy G," said Colleen. "And what's this about?"

"The judge hired Jimmy G to ask pertinent questions about the Carpenter trust."

"Well, you can ask me questions, but I need to watch the still."

"Still?" That got Jimmy G's interest.

"Come on, I'll show you!" she said, turning on her heel and striding off toward the barn. Jimmy G followed her, thinking he was in luck. Been a long time since he had any moonshine.

The still was located in an opening in the barn. It was made of brass and shaped like a giant onion turned on its head. A series of pipes and valves led away from the central chamber to a plastic bucket on the floor. And into the bucket was running a pale brown liquid. Jimmy G stuck his finger into the liquid, put it in his mouth, and started to swish it around. Gah! It was awful. He spit it out onto the straw-covered dirt floor.

Colleen frowned at him. "That's lavender essential oil. You're not supposed to drink it!"

Jimmy G nodded. "Absolutely." He winked. "Do you ever use this apparatus to make something more potable?"

Colleen frowned at him. "We're a lavender farm,"

she said. Aha! Jimmy G noted that she had avoided his question.

"So what do you want to know? Make it snappy. I've already had one interruption today. A private detective from Seattle and her little dog."

"Jimmy G knows those two," said Jimmy G "A nice-looking gal, with dark curly hair, and a white rat-dog."

"Yes," Colleen gave him a sharp look. "That's right." She seemed impressed. "She sent her dog to snoop around, but Phoebe ran them off. Right, Phoebe?" Phoebe, who had followed them into the barn, whined softly.

"Did she get any information?"

"Are you kidding? I have nothing to say to anyone on that side."

"Did you know that Bickerstaff is dead?" Jimmy G asked, watching her face carefully for any sign of surprise.

She wasn't surprised. "Yeah, I just heard about it. I guess Julian will have to hire a new lawyer to prove that Mrs. C was crazy."

That was news to Jimmy G, but he decided to go with it. "Was she?"

Colleen laughed, a short, sharp bark of a laugh. "Certainly was!"

"Aha!" Now Jimmy G was getting somewhere.

"Crazy like a fox," Colleen went on. "She knew exactly what she was doing, from day one. She wanted a piece of land with a nice view. She found a lonely man who was heading for bankruptcy. She swooped in and rescued him with an infusion of cash."

"What did she get out of it?" Jimmy G wanted to know.

"She liked to be seen as Lady Bountiful, I guess. Made her feel important."

Jimmy G was confused.

"That was her MO," Colleen said. "She was always trying to buy love."

Jimmy G was confused. "Then why leave money to a bunch of dogs?"

Colleen smiled, a rueful smile. "In the end, those dogs were the only ones who loved her." She thought for a moment. "Except for those parasites who hung around her for the money: her housekeeper and that lawyer of hers."

Jimmy G flinched, remembering his late-night trip to Boswell's house. "So you think Boswell took advantage of her?" he asked.

"Totally," she said. "Julian says it was unprofessional for him to serve as trustee. And I have it on good authority from my brother that he is skimming off the top."

"*Was* skimming off the top," Jimmy G said.

"What do you mean 'was'?"

"Apparently he's dead."

"Oh my God!" That did surprise her. All the color drained from her face. "What has he done now?"

Chapter 19

Once again, Pepe and I were being questioned about the death of a lawyer, this time in an interrogation room in the police station in Port Townsend.

"So how do you explain that?" The policewoman leaned over the table. She had introduced herself as Michelle Howard. She was a black woman in her midthirties with a broad face and high cheekbones.

"He called my boss to hire us," I said. I didn't think I had anything to hide.

"He heard about our success in many cases involving dogs," said Pepe.

"That's why we're here, working for him."

"Not any longer," she said.

"Well, that's a good point." Did we still have a client? I wasn't sure. I would have to check with Jimmy G.

"Your boss says he didn't talk to Mr. Boswell. That you did."

"That's absurd," I said.

"Someone is lying."

"Tell them to check the phone records," Pepe

suggested. He watches a lot of crime TV shows and knows how the police work.

"Well, I'm sure you can check phone records," I said.

"We did," she said. Her eyebrows went up.

"Then you know the call was made to the Gerrard Agency," I pointed out. "I never answer the phone there."

"But Mr. Gerrard said," she looked down at her notes, "that you are his secretary. Actually the term he used was girl Friday."

"Well, yes, I am, or at least he thinks I am, but I didn't take the initial call. I was at my house, reading a novel and sitting in the sun when he called me and told me to come down to the office because we had a case." It seemed so long ago since that carefree morning.

"And what was the case?"

"Confidential, *amiga!*" said Pepe.

"I'm not sure I can talk about that," I said. I really didn't know what the rules were about client privilege.

"You don't *think* you can talk about that? Or you *refuse* to talk about that?" she asked.

"If you let me call my boss, I'll check with him," I said.

Jimmy G answered after five rings. "What's up, doll?"

"I'm at the police station. They want information about the case. Do we still have one?"

"Of course we do!" His voice sounded thin and far away. "In fact, it means we have more work."

"So what do I tell them?"

"Nothing. We aren't obligated to share any of our information with them. We keep it close to our vests. You know that. Very hush-hush." And he hung up.

"Thanks a lot, Jimmy G," I said, looking at my phone.

"You know, Geri, that the police can hear every word you are saying," Pepe said.

"Just as long as they can't hear you, I'm good," I said, looking down at him.

Michelle never came back. Instead a middle-aged man in a tweed coat entered the room. He introduced himself as Rick Moore, head homicide detective. He had a bushy moustache, perhaps to compensate for the shiny bald patch on the top of his head.

"Would you like some coffee?" he asked. I guess he was going to be the good cop.

"Yes," I said. "With cream, please."

"I would like some bacon," said Pepe.

"You just had breakfast," I told him.

Rick looked confused. "Are you telling me or asking me?"

"Actually I was talking to my dog," I said.

"You do a lot of that," he said, as he left the room.

"I told you they were listening to us," Pepe said.

"I guess they can't hear you," I said.

"*Muy bien!*" he said. "So listen very carefully. We give nothing away. We extract the information we need!"

"*Sí, amigo!*" I said, just as Rick returned, bearing a paper cup that he set down on the table in front of me. The coffee was watery, and flecks of instant creamer were still swirling around on the top. The detective sat down himself and opened up a folder.

"We've been wanting to talk to you, Miss . . ." He looked at the papers in the folder. "Miss Sullivan."

"Here I am!" I said trying to be cheerful.

"Tell us again about how you came to be in the home of Mr. Boswell."

I repeated the story I had told the responding officers, the story Pepe and I had cooked up while we waited for them on the front porch. I had come for an appointment, he didn't answer the door, we went around back and noticed the door was ajar, we entered and found the body.

"And you didn't notice anything unusual?"

"Besides the fact that he was dead?"

"About the room?"

I wasn't sure what he was trying to get at.

"It looked messy," I said cautiously.

"As if someone were searching for something," Rick prompted.

"Yes, like that."

"And you didn't?"

"Search for anything?"

"We know better," said Pepe.

"We know better," I repeated.

"Interesting," said Pepe. "Perhaps the villain who invaded Carpenter Manor had first killed Mr. Boswell but did not find what he sought there."

"How well did you know Mr. Boswell?" the detective asked.

"Not well. We just met him yesterday." I said. "Briefly."

"Look," he said, "we know from Boswell himself that you were hired to help him with the Carpenter case. We know he believes someone tried to poison the dogs."

"And someone tried to attack them last night!" I said. "Maybe the same person who killed Boswell."

"Oh, that's interesting," said the detective. "Tell me more about that!"

"Tell him about how I marked the miscreant!" said Pepe.

"My dog attacked the intruder. He will have a dog bite on his wrist."

"That little guy?" said Detective Moore, with a sneer.

"I am a fierce warrior!" said Pepe.

"He can be pretty scary when he wants to be," I said. To prove the point, Pepe lifted his lip and delivered a tiny growl.

Detective Moore laughed.

"We reported the attack to the Sequim police," I said, wanting to make it clear that I was willing to cooperate. "I can give you the name of the officer." I found the card and handed it to Mr. Moore.

"All this fuss over a bunch of mangy mutts," Moore said, shaking his head as he returned the card to me. "And now we're looking at two homicides."

"The dogs are neither mangy nor mutts," Pepe pointed out.

"My suggestion to you, Miss . . ."—he looked at his papers again—"Miss Sullivan, would be to return to Seattle and tell your employer"—he looked at his papers again—"this Mr. Gerrard, that the police advised you to stay out of this. It's a murder investigation, and we don't need any private eyes wandering around interfering with our investigation or tampering with witnesses."

"I will certainly consider that advice," I said.

"We certainly will not quit!" said Pepe indignantly. "What do you think we are? Cats?"

Chapter 20

We did go back to Seattle. I had an appointment with my counselor, and I thought it might help me sort out all the different theories and thoughts that were whirling through my mind. Plus I would finally get a chance to catch up with Felix. I had called him as soon as we left the police station, and he said he would meet me at my house after his meeting with his last client. I promised him a good dinner and some other things I won't share with you.

My counselor, Suzanna, leases space in a two-story building on the shores of Lake Union, almost directly across from my condo in Eastlake, if you could fly directly across the waters of the lake. Or row across. There is a dock right below the building, and I sometimes like to sit down there and watch the water lapping against the pilings when I have time. But not today. I was already five minutes late.

"What are we doing here?" Pepe asked, waking up. He had been asleep ever since we got off the ferry.

"I've got a counseling appointment," I said.

"You know I am a therapy dog," said Pepe, jumping out of the car when I opened the door.

"So you say," I replied, heading across the parking lot.

"I will listen to your troubles and comfort you," Pepe said, trotting to keep up with me.

"That's true," I said, giving him a sideways look. "You always make me feel better when you listen to me." The problem is he almost never listens to me. He's the opposite of Suzanna, who is a good listener.

Suzanna's office is on the second floor. There's a small waiting room with a bottled water dispenser and copies of lifestyle magazines. But I didn't have to wait. The door to the room was open, and Suzanna was sitting at the desk, making notes, probably about her last client. The décor is designed to soothe: dark gray walls, dim lighting, a lit candle perfuming the air with a vanilla scent.

Suzanna waved me to a seat on the corduroy sofa, while she took a seat in the armchair near the bookshelf. Suzanna has been my counselor since my divorce. And although she doesn't believe my dog talks, I still count on her to let me know if I am going too far off the deep end.

"So, Geri, tell me what's going on?" she asked, looking at me with her piercing dark eyes. Her bright red hair glowed like a flame. She was wearing amethyst earrings and a light-gray tunic over velvety leggings.

I told her everything, although Pepe kept interrupting me and embellishing the story as we went along. I told her about finding the body of Bickerstaff, about meeting the vet (I left out my attraction to him, though Pepe insisted I should explain I was in heat), about our visit to Carpenter Manor, about Pepe scaring off the intruder (Pepe wanted me to emphasize his heroic actions), and about finding Boswell's body in his study. I left out the part about our breaking and entering, but I did tell her about Pepe being frightened by the cat, just to tease him a little since he was being so bossy. He looked disgusted and crawled under the forest-green afghan to take a nap. He loves burrowing under blankets.

"Geri, that sounds like a lot," Suzanna said.

"I know," I said. I realized I was shaking. "I didn't expect it to be so dangerous."

"Are you reconsidering taking this job?" Suzanna asked. She had never said anything outright, but I got the idea she thought being a private detective was not good for me.

"Yes," I said.

Pepe poked his head out from under the blanket.

"No way, Jose," he said.

"I just don't think I can put myself, or my dog, in danger anymore. I mean, what's the point? We hardly make any money."

"And what about your boss?" Suzanna asked.

"He's no help," said Pepe.

I had to agree. "He's no help," I said. "While we're running around and doing all the work, he's at the racetrack."

Suzanna shook her head. "What do you plan to do?" she asked.

"I don't know. I guess I could quit." I felt a huge relief as I said that. I could go home, make dinner, have a glass of wine, and retire early with Felix. The police would investigate the murders. That was their job. No need for us to get involved. We had already provided them with everything we knew.

"What about the dogs?" asked Pepe. "They need us."

"But if the trustee is dead—"

"Then we must find out who is the new trustee," insisted Pepe. He leaped up and ran to the door.

"We don't have a copy of the trust document," I said.

Suzanna looked perturbed. "Are you talking to your dog?"

"Yes," I said. "He wants us to continue to investigate."

"So there is a part of you that believes you should keep on investigating." Suzanna tends to think that Pepe represents my alter ego, an aspect of my character that is more daring, more confident than my usual personality.

"No, it's Pepe who wants to keep on investigating," I said. "I would be happy to give up."

"That is not true, Geri!" said Pepe, looking at me with dismay. "You would not leave any dogs to suffer."

"Why should they suffer?" I asked. "They've got plenty of money."

"Money does not necessarily make people happy," said Pepe.

That was true. I thought about how lonely Boswell seemed, even though he had a fancy house full of stuff. And Yolanda, who despite her millions lived in a plain little room and took orders from a bunch of spoiled dogs.

"Who?" That was Suzanna.

"The dogs," I said. "They inherited a fortune. Several million dollars."

"And how do you feel about that?"

"You know, it does seem excessive," I said. "Four dogs can't possibly need millions of dollars to keep them happy. Dogs are happy . . ." I looked at Pepe.

"Oh no, you are not!" he said. "You are not going to say that just being around people makes dogs happy!"

"They've done experiments," I told him. "Dogs evolved differently from wolves because they care for us. When given a choice between food and taking care of us, wolves choose food, but dogs choose people."

"Most dogs," said Pepe. "I myself prefer a nice juicy steak."

"You know that's not true," I said.

"OK. A crisp piece of bacon," he conceded.

Suzanna smiled. "Your dog does not agree with you," she said.

I brightened up. "You can hear him?"

She shook her head impatiently. "Geri, you know he doesn't talk. Maybe you are exceptionally good at intuiting what he wants, but he can't talk. Dogs don't talk."

I stared at her. If I couldn't convince my counselor, then who could I convince? And if I was crazy because I thought my dog talked, then maybe Mrs. Carpenter was crazy, too.

"I guess we do have to go back," I said to Pepe.

"Yes, so I can woo the beautiful Phoebe," said

Pepe. "But first we must stop for bacon. Now that you have mentioned it, I must have some."

"I didn't mention it," I said, then stopped. No point in arguing with a dog.

Suzanna looked worried. "I don't like the idea of you going back into such a dangerous situation," she said.

"It's not dangerous for us," I said. "No one is trying to poison us. Just the dogs."

"And the lawyers," pointed out Pepe.

"Can you call your boss and ask him to go with you?" Suzanna asked.

"That's a good idea. I'll try that," I said.

"Geri, we do not need his help!" said Pepe.

I glanced at the clock. The session was almost over. "Well, thanks," I said, getting up. "I feel a lot better."

Suzanna got up, too. She took my hands in hers and fixed me with concern in her eyes. "Geri, I am worried about you. I would feel much better about this if you would keep in touch with me. Can you call me once a day and just leave a message on my answering machine? I'll check it regularly. If something comes up and you need to talk, I'll try to be available, but I'm going away for the weekend with my girlfriends, so it might take me a little while to get back to you."

"Oh, really, where are you going?" I asked.

"To Sequim for the lavender festival," she said. "One of my girlfriends has a vacation home in Discovery Bay, so we go every year. We love it. Good food, music, and lavender ice cream!" She closed her eyes and sighed. "It's so peaceful."

"Well, that's where the dogs live," I said. "Right next to a lavender farm. Maybe we'll see you there."

Suzanna laughed. "Geri, thousands of people attend the lavender festival. We're not likely to run into each other. But do call if you need me."

Chapter 21

Jimmy G was heading back to Seattle. Seemed the best choice by far. He could swing by Emerald Downs and catch the last race of the day. So far he wasn't making much progress with the case. Time for Jimmy G to make a fast getaway before the judge got on his case.

He was snoozing in his car in the ferry line, his fedora pulled down over his eyes and nose, when he heard a rapping at his window. Startled awake, he looked out to see the face of the judge's bodyguard. It wasn't a good-looking face. The guy's nose had obviously been broken at some time. He also had tape wrapped around one of his wrists.

"What's up?" he said, rolling down his window, wondering how the guy had found him.

"That's what my boss wants to know," the guy said.

"Uh, going fine," said Jimmy G.

"Did you get the trust document?"

Jimmy G pondered that for a moment. It would

mean that he had been in Boswell's house, and Boswell was now (according to Geri) dead.

"Have you heard about Boswell?" he asked.

"He died," the guy said. He didn't seem perturbed. That disturbed Jimmy G.

"What about the document?"

"It's in a safe place," said Jimmy G. He figured that would get him off the hook.

"The boss wants it."

"Tell the boss Jimmy G will deliver it."

"When?" The guy had a faint accent. Maybe Russian. That was disturbing, too.

"Jimmy G just needs to get back to Seattle—"

"The boss wants it now!" The guy leaned into the window. His jacket fell back, exposing the outlines of his shoulder holster and pistol. Jimmy G thought about his own pistol, wondered if he could pull it out of his shoulder holster faster than this joe could if things got dicey.

"What's the hurry?' he asked.

"Boss doesn't like to wait."

"Might take a while. Might even miss the last boat."

"Then stay at the B&B again. The judge keeps a room reserved in his name there."

"OK. Will do. Jimmy G has to contact his operatives. They've got the document."

"Fine," said the guy. "Just make sure you get it. And call us as soon as you have it in hand."

He looked sideways down the line of cars. Jimmy G saw a flicker of fear in his pale-blue eyes.

Checking his rearview mirror, Jimmy G saw a man in uniform coming down the line of cars with a German shepherd. Pretty standard policy on the ferry system. The dog would be sniffing for drugs. Or explosives.

"Meanwhile, we'll be watching you," the guy said. And he disappeared.

Chapter 22

"Ah, it is good to be back to our own *casa*," said Pepe as we got out of the car in front of my condo in the Eastlake neighborhood. Although the word *condo* might conjure up something sleek and modern, mine is a one-bedroom apartment in a brick courtyard built in the 1940s. It's perched on the edge of a hill with just a tiny view of Lake Union from the front porch.

"It certainly is," I told him as we started up the stairs to the porch.

We both saw the small package sitting on the porch at the same time.

"What's this?" I picked up the package and noted that it had been sent from Amazon. "I didn't order anything from Amazon."

"Perhaps a present!" said Pepe. "Sent by a secret admirer!"

Albert the Cat greeted us with a great display of affection—that is, he wound around my legs, making loud meowing sounds. Pepe he ignored. That was OK with Pepe, who also ignored him.

"*Andale,* Geri!" Pepe said, circling around the dining room table, where I had placed the package. He was so excited he hadn't even looked at his food dish. "Open it! Open it!"

I gave Albert a generous portion of wet cat food, a bribe since I had left him with only dry food overnight. Then I grabbed my kitchen scissors and attacked the package. Pepe jumped onto a chair and peered over the tabletop. That was unusual. He's not usually so invested in the packages I receive.

"Oh my God," I said, prying open the top of the box and gazing down at the object inside, swaddled in plastic and cellophane, "it's an iPad!"

"*Si!*" said Pepe. He hopped onto the table and poked his nose in the box.

"There must be some mistake," I said. "I didn't order an iPad."

"I did!" Pepe said, taking his nose out of the box.

"You what?"

"Take it out of the box!" Pepe told me.

"Wait a minute. How could you have ordered this?"

"Simple, Geri. I got on the Internet, selected the item at Amazon, then hit the button for one-click ordering."

I stared at my dog in disbelief. "And you did this when?"

"I believe it was Wednesday night," he said. "You were getting busy in the bedroom with Felix."

My pooch always surprises me, but this was too much. "These things cost over five hundred dollars, Pepe."

"Plus shipping," he told me.

"You should have asked me," I told him. "I'm sending it back."

He hung his head and looked as sad as only a sad Chihuahua can look. Which is pretty darn sad.

"You do not understand," he said.

"What don't I understand?"

"I was only trying to help."

"Ordering an expensive item without my permission is helping?"

"Yes," said Pepe. "I will use it to do research for our cases. We will solve twice as many cases with both of us having access to a computer."

I didn't know how to respond to that.

"It has a touch screen—easy for me to manipulate with a simple swipe of a paw," he said. "Plus, it has a virtual keypad—also much simpler for me to use since I am always getting my toenails stuck in the laptop keyboard."

"Pepe—"

"I will also let you use it when I am not using it, *partner*."

The way he emphasized the word *partner* brought me up short. Perhaps I was being a little selfish. After all, he had been instrumental in saving my life on several occasions. Of course, he had also gotten me into those sticky situations in the first place.

"OK," I said, giving him a pat on his velvety head. "You can keep it."

"*Muy bien!* I want to start using it right now!" He stood over it and began running his right forepaw over the iPad's screen. "Hey!" he said. "It is not working!"

"Silly pup," I told him. "It's not charged yet. It

will take a while. We have to use this white cord and plug it in to charge the battery."

He shook his head sadly. "It is most cruel to get something you most dearly want and then not be able to use it."

"Don't worry, Pepe," I told him. "I can plug it in to charge, and you can use it while it's charging. How does that sound?"

"Better than *bueno!*" he said, doing another dance on the tabletop.

I got it plugged in for him, and he immediately began toying with it as the screen came on.

"It has a different operating system than Microsoft," I told him. "Perhaps I should—"

"I will figure it out. Go make us something to eat," said Pepe. "I shall google our deceased attorney, Boswell, and see what I can learn about his background."

I opened up the refrigerator and inspected the contents, trying to figure out what I could make for Felix. I had some heirloom tomatoes and fresh basil I had purchased at the farmers market. I thought if I cooked some angel-hair pasta, I could toss them together, along with some parmesan.

I got the water boiling and was chopping up the tomatoes when I heard Pepe call out from the next room.

"Geri, come quick!" he said. I hurried into the dining room, only to find him mooning over a photo of Phoebe, the farm dog. She was sitting next to the sign that advertised Lost Lakes Lavender Farm, with the big silly grin typical of a Labrador on her furry face.

"I thought you were doing research for our case," I said.

"I was!" said Pepe proudly. "I was looking up the farm. And see what I found? Is she not the most beautiful being you have ever seen?"

At that moment the front doorbell rang, and I hurried to answer it. It was Felix, and he was actually the most beautiful being I have ever seen. His dark hair was combed back, and his dark eyes were shining with pleasure, and the bright white of his ironed shirt contrasted beautifully with his caramel-colored skin. Plus he was carrying a pint of my favorite chocolate-chip cookie-dough ice cream and a bouquet of sweet peas.

He was accompanied by his new furry companion, the little cream-colored poodle-terrier mix we all called Fuzzy. She went charging into the dining room. Albert hissed at her and vanished into the bedroom, while Fuzzy started barking at Pepe.

I took the time for a long, lingering kiss with Felix, then went to see what was happening.

"What's this?" Felix asked, at the sight of Pepe perched on a chair, with his paws on the table, staring down at the screen. "You bought an iPad?"

"It was Pepe," I said.

Felix just smiled. "Sure, it was."

"No, really it was—" I started to say.

"It's so cute how you blame everything on your dog," said Felix, circling me with his arm. "And look, he has a new girlfriend!" He pointed at the photo of the black-and-white dog on the screen.

"Yes, that's Phoebe. We met her while working on our latest case."

"And how is that going?" Felix asked.

"I'll tell you; just follow me into the kitchen. I've got to get the pasta into the water."

"A little early for dinner, isn't it?" Felix asked.

"I'm starving," I said. "It's been a while since breakfast."

Fuzzy followed us into the kitchen, since Pepe was ignoring her. She polished off the food Pepe had left in his dish, so eager was he to use his new toy. To my surprise, the sound of the kibble crunching did not distract him.

Meanwhile, I told Felix about the royal cocker spaniels who had inherited a fortune. He looked as worried as Suzanna when he heard about the two dead lawyers.

"I don't want to tell you what to do," he started to say, but just then my cell phone started ringing. I had left it on the little table in the hallway. I looked at the screen and saw it was Jimmy G.

"Who is it?" Pepe asked. He had come running.

"Jimmy G!" I said.

"Don't answer it!" said Felix.

"Answer it!" said Pepe.

"I have to answer it," I said to Felix. "He's my boss and we're on a case."

Felix just shook his head. "It's a mistake," he said.

"Where are you?" That was Jimmy G.

"At home. Why?"

"Jimmy G needs you here."

"At the office?"

"No, in the field."

"But why?"

"Jimmy G needs to find a copy of the trust document, and Jimmy G expects you to help."

"But with our client dead, who's paying us?" I asked.

"Do not worry your pretty little head about that. Jimmy G's got that under control. Just get your butt over to Whidbey Island and talk to Jillian Valentine. She runs an art gallery on Main Street in Langley. She's one of the parties in the suit against the trust and thus a suspect. Plus, maybe she has a copy of the trust document."

"It's kind of late to be heading over there today," I said, giving Felix a smile. He was leaning against the wall with his arms crossed. "How about I get there first thing tomorrow morning?"

"Traffic's supposed to be horrible tomorrow," Jimmy G said. "First day of the lavender festival. Besides Jimmy G has reserved a room for you at a place in Port Townsend called the Floral Fantasy B&B."

"What?" That did not sound like the kind of place Jimmy would recommend.

"Yes, it's run by Kevin Carpenter. Another one of the suspects in this case."

"Do you think they would let me bring a friend?" I asked, with a meaningful look at Felix.

"What kind of friend?"

"My boyfriend, Felix," I said, then wondered if that was the right term for Felix. We had not really defined our relationship. But it seemed OK with him. He looked intrigued.

Jimmy G snorted. He had met Felix only a couple of times. "Yeah, if he's the kind of guy who likes scented candles and bubble bath."

"Great!" I said. I hung up and turned to Felix. "Want to go stay in a B&B in Port Townsend?"

"When?"

"Tonight!"

Felix looked sad. "I can't. I've got three clients in the morning."

"Can you cancel them?" I asked hopefully.

"No more than you can say no to your boss," he said. He looked downcast.

"Tell you what," I said, "Pepe and I will go over there tonight and scope it out. If it looks good, maybe you could come tomorrow? For a romantic weekend getaway? Apparently there's a big lavender festival. We can see what that's like."

Felix looked mollified but still unhappy. "I just hate it that you keep canceling on me," he said. "I don't think you should be putting your job first."

"You put your job first," I pointed out.

Pepe had run off again, but Fuzzy was hovering around us. She hates it when we fight. She used to belong to a couple who fought a lot, and it makes her nervous.

Felix shook his head. "Look, I don't really feel like talking about this anymore. Why don't you call me when you find out what's happening, and meanwhile I'll think about it. Come on, Fuzzy!"

And the next thing I knew he had walked out the door.

Chapter 23

Jillian Valentine lived in the small town of Langley on Whidbey Island. Taking a ferry was the only way to get to the island without driving miles to the north, crossing a narrow bridge to the north side of the island, and then driving down its length. So I told Pepe there was no choice but to take a ferry ride.

We caught the boat from Mukilteo, and it was only a fifteen-minute voyage to the island. Pepe kept his mouth shut as we boarded (which was unusual for my chatterbox dog), but I knew he wasn't happy about taking another boat ride. Neither was I.

I was still thinking about my unhappy encounter with Felix. And how I had to eat all the pasta by myself. The ice cream, too. All I could hope was that the B&B that Jimmy G had mentioned would be the perfect place for a romantic weekend. Although Felix had spent a couple of weekends at my place, and I had spent one weekend at his place (Pepe complained bitterly the whole time since

Felix doesn't have a TV), we had never gone on a trip together. It might take us to the next level. But to get there, I would have to finish up this case. I could only hope that this Jillian would have the document Jimmy G thought we needed.

Langley is a quaint little town on the water just a few miles from the Clinton ferry dock. Main Street, only six or seven blocks long, is composed of old, but brightly painted, false-fronted wooden buildings. Many of them are small shops selling items to tourists. There are some restaurants, too, including a turn-of-the-century, two-story building that housed a large pub.

It wasn't hard to find the art gallery. It was a nondescript, baby-blue wooden building on the water side of the street. Only a single story fronted the street, but there were two more floors that extended down the small hillside to the water in a terrace-like fashion. The stairs at the side were somewhat rickety.

"Is this it?" Pepe asked. "It does not look like much."

"This is the place," I told him, looking at the newspaper-covered picture window at the front of the building. There was a sign over the door saying VALENTINE GALLERY. There was also a big sign in the window that read FOR LEASE.

"We came all this way, and there is no one here," said Pepe.

Just then, a woman came up the side stairs with a stack of matted art prints in her arms. She was tall and thin, with long hair pulled back off her narrow face and held with a gauzy scarf. She wore a long purple skirt and a dark-purple vest cinched tight over a loose, lilac-colored Indian blouse, along with big hoop earrings and an armful of glittering crystal bracelets. The whole effect was fairy/gypsy.

She dumped the prints into an empty plastic carton on the back of a baby-blue scooter parked in front of the building.

"Hi," I said. "I'm Geri Sullivan. I'm looking for JillianValentine."

"That's me!" She pushed away a stray hair with her forearm and looked at me puzzled. "So?" Her tone said, "Why should I care?"

I hesitated. According to Jimmy G, I was supposed to be assessing the motives of all the potential heirs. Should I tell her that?

Pepe was sniffing around her ankles, and she flinched. A few of the prints slipped from her fingers and scattered on the asphalt. Luckily they were all wrapped in plastic.

"Can you control your dog?" she asked.

"Pepe! *Aqui!*" I said, snapping my fingers. Of course, this had absolutely no effect on Pepe, who simply began sniffing the prints she had dropped.

I bent to help her pick them up and saw that they were landscapes. One showed a Tudor mansion at sunset with the windows just beginning to glow yellow and behind it a smear of purple that I took to be a lavender field.

"Why, this looks like Carpenter Manor," I said, surprised.

She jumped at that. "How do you know that?" she asked.

"Well, we were just there . . ." I gestured at Pepe.

She gave me a sharp look. "Whatever for?"

"A good chance to find out what she knows," Pepe pointed out. "If I were conducting this interrogation I would imply we worked for her side."

Easy for him to say. I hate lying. So I settled for ambiguity. "We were hired to investigate the situation with the dogs."

"Oh, yeah." She seemed relieved. "Julian said he had hired someone to figure out how to break the trust!" She stuffed the prints into the plastic crate. "So what do you want to know?"

"Do you have a copy of the trust document?" I asked.

"Are you kidding?" she asked. "Julian would never confide in me. He keeps treating me like his idiot little sister, just like he did when we were young."

"So were you and your brother annoyed when your mother left all her money to the dogs?"

"Hey, who expected anything else?" she said bitterly.

"She always preferred dogs?"

"She was always a selfish bitch," said Jillian firmly.

"Hey!" said Pepe. "I object to the use of that word in a pejorative way. A bitch is one of the loveliest creatures on the face of the earth."

"Can you tell me more about your relationship with your mother?" I asked Jillian.

She blinked. "Look, I'm in kind of a hurry. Got to get this stuff over to Sequim tonight."

"You're going to Sequim?"

"Yeah, I've got a booth at the lavender festival. I can make a big chunk of change in just a few days if I get my stuff over there. Maybe even enough to pay my back taxes. If you want to keep asking me questions, you need to give me a hand."

"Sure," I said.

"I can lend a paw," said Pepe.

Jillian headed down the steps, and Pepe followed at her heels. I paused on the landing to admire the view: sparkling blue water, mist-cloaked islands, foggy mountain peaks layered one on top of another, suggesting infinity.

Pepe came racing out of the room. "Geri, quick! You must see this!"

I followed as he scampered through the door. The room was huge, just a big open space, with windows at the front looking out on the view. The old wooden floor was peppered with blotches of dried paint. I almost tripped over a big tarp on the way in. All around the room were paintings sitting on easels, paintings stacked against the wall, paintings spread out on tables.

Pepe stood in the middle of the room, his eyes bugging out and his whole body shivering.

And no wonder. The paintings were all of dogs. Dogs of all shapes and sizes, all breeds and colors. All the dogs were dressed in human clothing. I saw a Renaissance princess, a policeman, a Rastafarian, a Victorian gentleman. And all the dogs had the faces of human babies. Did I mention they were all painted on black velvet?

It was the most disturbing thing I had ever seen. It was bad enough seeing dogs dressed like people. Pepe and I had often talked about William Wegman's photos of his Weimaraners. Pepe thought dressing them up was animal abuse. I thought

Wegman was making a comment about the way we tend to treat our animals as if they are human.

But the baby faces made the paintings really disturbing. Most of the dogs appeared to be crying or drooling. None of them were appealing.

"Do you like them?" asked Jillian, watching me.

"They're really unique," I said.

"I know," she said, beaming with pride. "The weird thing is no one wants to buy one. I think I'm just ahead of my time. Instead I have to sell this tripe!"

She gestured at a small card table that contained more plastic-covered prints and the machine she used to wrap them. "For now. To keep afloat. But someday I'll be recognized for my true talent."

"Good luck," said Pepe. "You will need it."

"Oh," was all I could think of to say.

"Here! We've got to get moving!" Jillian dumped a load of plastic-wrapped prints into my arms. One slipped to the floor, and Pepe trotted over and was about to scoop it up when he stopped and stared at it, transfixed.

"What is it, Pepe?" I asked.

"It is the sun around which I revolve," he said. "The divine Phoebe."

I snatched it up.

The picture depicted an old red barn standing in the midst of lavender fields and, in the foreground, a black-and-white dog. It could have been the farm dog. It could have been any black-and-white dog.

"What makes you think this is Phoebe?" I asked.

"Phoebe?" Jillian asked. "I didn't say that."

"You think I would not recognize my love," Pepe asked indignantly. "Would you not recognize Felix if he stood in front of that barn?"

"It would depend," I started to say.

"Geri, you must buy this print," said Pepe. "I cannot afford to let some other Lothario get his paws on this image."

"Very well."

Jillian looked at me quizzically.

"You talk to your dog?"

"Yes!" I said. I was tired of explaining. I was tired of hiding it. "He wants me to buy this print."

"You're as crazy as my mother," said Jillian. "Anyway, that one's thirty dollars."

Thirty dollars seemed steep for a color print wrapped in plastic, but I dug out the money from my bag and handed it over to her. She tucked it into her pocket and handed me the print. I handed it to Pepe, who carried it proudly to the door.

"So your mother thought her dogs talked to her?" I asked.

Jillian nodded impatiently. She scooped up a handful of prints and dumped them into my arms.

"What did they say?" I wanted to know.

"Who knows?" she asked. "Whatever it was, it was more interesting than anything I said." Jillian grabbed her own armful of prints and headed for stairs.

"Mrrrmph," said Pepe. He was trying to tell me something, but his mouth was full. He nodded his head toward a big canvas half hidden by the door. I bumped the door open with my hip so I could see it more clearly and promptly dropped all my prints.

It was a portrait in the tradition of a Madonna and Child. But the Madonna was a giant, golden-blond cocker spaniel wearing blue robes and the face of Lucille Carpenter. And she was looking away from the child in her paws: a tiny, fluffy, silver Yorkshire with the red face of a squalling baby.

Chapter 24

Jimmy G sat in his '62 Thunderbird half a block down the street from the Valentine Gallery. He was on a stakeout, surreptitiously watching his own operative to make sure she followed through on his instructions. Stakeouts were usually boring affairs, but he didn't mind this one: Jimmy G thought this Jillian Valentine was a pretty hot number, easy on the eyes, even liked her retro-hippie style of dress. Of course, he wouldn't include that in his next report to the judge. He knew that older brothers could get kind of wacko-overprotective of their little sisters, something he'd found out the hard way when he was dating Kimberly Haney back in high school and her brother, Chad, big linebacker on the Roosevelt Roughriders football team, had taken exception and boffed him upside the head.

Anyway, he could see Geri talking to Jillian on the sidewalk outside the art gallery and wanted to know what they were saying. So he took out the directional mike that had cost him plenty, took off his fedora and put on the headset, then pointed the mike at them.

All he got was static—snap, crackle, and pop!— like he'd put his ear next to a bowl of Rice Krispies. Blasted thing! It was supposed to pick up sound from exactly where you pointed it, with a range of a hundred yards or more, not make him listen to his breakfast. Jimmy G tried to adjust the mike's receiver, but all he got when he tried it again was louder static.

He shut the thing off and tossed it on the seat beside him. Never should have bought it used, he thought, especially from those bums at Liberty Pawn & Loan.

Jimmy G lit up a stogie and puffed on it hard. He had to do something. He needed to get his mitts on a copy of the trust document. Somebody had to have another one besides the one he'd lost.

Just then, Jillian came up the stairs at the side of the gallery with another bunch of what looked like art prints in her hands. She said something else to Geri, then loaded the prints into the carrier on the back of a little baby-blue motor scooter and putted off down the street. Where was she going?

Jimmy G grabbed his cell phone and called Geri.

When she answered, he said, "What's shakin', doll?"

"Not much," Geri said. Then she asked. "Where are you calling from?"

Jimmy G hesitated. Could she see his car? "At the office. Why do you ask?"

"The call is so clear. You could be right across the street."

Jimmy G almost dropped the phone. Was she messing with him? He refocused. "Did you get a copy of the trust document?"

"No. I talked to Jillian, but she said she never saw it."

"That's what they all say."

"What?"

"Jimmy G means that's a sure sign of guilt."

"We just finished talking to her. She's heading off to Sequim."

"Good. See if you can look around and find it. I bet she has a copy squirreled away."

"You want me to break and enter?"

"Do what you have to do. Take the initiative."

He hung up before she could say another word. While Geri was looking through the building, he needed to follow Jillian, just in case she could lead him to someone else who did have a copy of the trust document.

He could still hear the buzz of her little scooter (probably needed a tune-up) and caught up quickly, just as she pulled onto the only high-speed highway on the island, heading north. Jimmy G made sure to keep several cars between him and her, so she wouldn't suspect she was being tailed.

She pulled off the highway at the exit for the Keystone Ferry. There was a long line of cars when he reached the ferry dock. Looked like they would have to wait for the next boat, which was an hour away. But what Jimmy G had forgotten was that motorcycles and bicycles got waved onto the ferry first. Jillian on her little blue scooter just breezed past the long line of cars and onto the ferry.

All Jimmy G could do was sit there and watch, tapping his fingers on the steering wheel, as the ferry sailed away.

Chapter 25

"Clearly she has some issues," said Pepe, as we watched Jillian zip away on her little blue scooter.

"Yes, and we didn't learn much," I said, mournfully.

"At least, we know where to find her," Pepe said. "And I have the portrait of my love."

The phone rang. It was Jimmy G.

"What's shakin', doll?" he asked.

"Not much," I said. The call was so clear, it sounded like he was across the street. "Where are you calling from?"

There was a long pause. "At the office. Why do you ask?"

"The call is so clear. You could be right across the street."

There was a clunk. Maybe he dropped the phone. Then I heard him ask: "Did you get a copy of the trust document?"

"No, I talked to Jillian, but she said she never saw it."

"That's what they all say," he muttered.

"What?"

"Jimmy G means that's a sure sign of guilt."

"We just finished talking to her. She's heading off to Sequim."

"Good. See if you can look around and find it. I bet she has a copy squirreled away."

"You want me to break and enter?"

"Do what you have to do. Take the initiative."

But it turned out we didn't have to. Jillian had left the door unlocked. I guess there are some advantages to living in a small town. Still, there wasn't much to see in the studio, except for those disturbing paintings. A narrow flight of stairs led up to the gallery, which was pretty spooky with the dim light filtering through the yellowing newspaper on the windows. It was hot as blazes up there.

Pepe trotted around, sniffing in the corners. I studied the paintings she considered salable: the same disturbing mix of pastel seascapes and dogs with human faces.

A small gray metal desk sat in one corner of the room. The surface was bare except for a white plastic phone. The screen read 12 missed calls. I pushed the button to see who they were from. Several from J Valentine. One from the Floral Fantasy B&B. And the last was from my boss, Jimmy Gerrard.

"Odd," I said, noting the phone numbers in my notebook.

"What is odd," said Pepe, "is that she has no food fit for a dog."

He was sniffing around the bottom drawer, which contained a stash of M&Ms. In a top drawer was a telephone book. Both Boswell and Bickerstaff were listed under the Bs, I noted. Beneath the phone book was a recent bank statement, which showed a negative balance and a sheaf of eviction notices. Also a collection of bar napkins, with male names and phone numbers scribbled on them.

"Nothing here," I said to Pepe.

There was only one place left to look: the building had a lower floor. So we headed back down to the studio, past the creepy paintings of dogs, and down another set of narrow stairs to what appeared to be Jillian's living quarters.

There was a gorgeous view out the windows of the dark waters of the bay and the distant islands, swathed in mist. But that was all that was picturesque. The room was covered with trash.

"Has it been tossed?" I asked. The bed was just a mattress on the floor. It was covered with clothes. Drawers were open. Beer cans and a few empty vodka bottles had been flung about. An ashtray sitting on the floor was full and spilling onto the carpet. A bong sat on top of the chest of drawers. The whole room reeked of tobacco, incense, and the somewhat sweet smell of marijuana.

The walls were hung with paintings of naked men. One thing I will say, Jillian seemed to have eclectic taste. There were bulked-up black men with gleaming abs. And tattooed biker types with long silver beards and big bellies. There was a large man with a hairy chest and a slim man with golden skin and a dancer's physique. But the weird thing was that they all had the heads of dogs.

"The Egyptian god Anubis had the head of a jackal," said Pepe, studying the paintings. "And Saint Christopher is sometimes depicted with the head of a dog."

"How do you know that?" I asked.

"I watched a very interesting show on the Discovery channel about cynocephaly," Pepe said. "Do you realize that the Greeks believed there was a race of dog-headed people who lived in India?"

"And did they ever find any of these people?" I asked.

"Fortunately, no," said Pepe. He trotted through an adjoining door. "Geri, I think I have found something interesting."

I walked into a narrow kitchen with a dusty window at one end. The counters were as cluttered and messy as the bedroom, with unwashed bowls and empty glasses and pans full of caked-on food lying about.

"What is it, Pepe?" I asked.

"I believe this pan was last used to cook chocolate-chip cookies," Pepe said, standing on his little feet and sniffing a baking sheet on the yellow linoleum table under the window.

I came closer, but it was hard to see in the dim light. Still, I trust my dog.

"Do you suppose there are any more cookies around?" I said. I didn't see any plates full of cookies or ceramic cookie containers. Perhaps in the refrigerator. I opened the door and immediately slammed it shut again. It was full of takeout containers, and it smelled like something had died in there.

"I believe there is a cookie under here," said Pepe, scratching at a stack of newspaper that had been piled on the table.

Sure enough, I found a cookie—rather dried up,

rather crumbly—under the edge of an overhanging paper.

"Yum!" said Pepe, licking his lips.

"No way!" I said. "Don't you realize this is evidence? This could be one of the cookies used to poison the cocker spaniels." I looked around to see if I could find a plastic bag to slide the cookie into and finally found a box of zip-top bags in a lower drawer. I slipped the cookie into the plastic and zipped the seal.

Just then we both heard it. Footsteps on the rickety stairs that led down the side of the building. They descended rapidly. Thud, thud, thud. Luckily there were three flights of stairs.

"*Rapido!*" said Pepe. "Out onto the deck!"

There was a flimsy sliding-glass door that that led onto a narrow deck, which hung out over the water. I yanked it open, and Pepe and I squeezed through the tiny crack, he a little more easily than I. Then I shoved the door shut, and we inched our way to a position at the end of the deck where we could not be seen from the inside. The deck was crowded with furniture: some flimsy canvas chairs, one of those loungers that looks like it's made out of rubber bands, and a few crates being used as tables.

The footsteps reached the bottom floor, and we heard the rattle of the doorknob. I had a moment of relief when I realized that Jillian did keep the door to her personal space locked, but that quickly disappeared when we heard a loud thud and the slam of the door against the wall. Whoever it was had kicked in the door.

I had another moment of relief when I thought maybe it was the police. Maybe they were raiding the place, looking for marijuana. Of course, it would be hard to explain what we were doing crouched on the deck. And they had not identified themselves, which I thought was usually part of police procedure.

My hope vanished when Pepe whispered.

"Geri, I recognize his smell."

"What smell?"

"The smell of the intruder," he said.

"What about it?" I was getting impatient.

"This is the same person who broke into Carpenter Manor," he said.

"Oh!" That wasn't good.

"Should we not see who it is?" asked Pepe.

"I think not," I said. "What we should do is get off this deck somehow."

I looked around for an exit. The deck hung out over the water, which was about twelve feet below us. I could imagine jumping in, but what about Pepe? He's afraid of water. Maybe I should throw him in, then dive in after him.

From inside the room, we could hear the sound of a room being tossed. Thumps as drawers hit the ground. A grunt as someone heaved the mattress up. The clatter of glass breaking.

A pile of rocks were ranged up along the side of the building, heaped against the foundations. They were huge and jagged. I knew I couldn't land safely on them, certainly not with Pepe. But my purse, containing the cookie evidence and my cell phone, could not go into the water. I threw it down onto the rocks. It landed, perched precariously on a boulder.

Maybe it was the flash of the purse flying by the windows inside that caught the eye of the intruder. The next moment I heard the rattle of the sliding-glass door in the track.

"Time to go!" I said to Pepe. I picked him up and tossed him into the water below. He made a little splash. I heard a little yelp.

Then I dove in after him.

Chapter 26

We got out of the water almost as fast as we got in, as soon as the footsteps that came out on the deck went back into the house. I grabbed Pepe and paddled to the rocky shore. We heard a door slam on the other side of the building and then the sound of a motorcycle taking off.

I grabbed my purse from the rock, and we squelched our way up to my car.

"Was that really necessary?" Pepe asked, as he stood in the passenger seat and shook himself off, spraying water all over me and the interior of the car.

"Was that really necessary?" I asked him, using tissues from my purse to wipe off the dashboard and interior passenger window on his side.

"Certainly it was," he said. Pepe gave himself another brisk shake. "And I repeat my question. Was that really necessary?"

"What are you talking about?" I asked, though I knew very well what he meant.

"Throwing me into the water?"

"It was necessary to protect you."

"I see," he said. "And following your same logic, it was necessary for me to dry myself off. You should not be upset about that."

"Oh, come on." I hated it when my dog was sarcastic.

"*Sí*. You humans can change your wet clothes," he told me. "We *perros* cannot change our fur."

My dog always has an answer for everything. But in this case he was right. My dress was still wet as we pulled away from the curb, and I knew the dunking was going to coil my hair into tight ringlets. Still I thought I would dry out pretty fast as the temperature gauge on the dashboard indicated that it was eighty degrees outside. I had slipped out of my soggy sandals and was driving barefoot.

"Where are we going, Geri?" Pepe asked.

"To Port Townsend," I said. "I want to check in at the B&B and change clothes. So we're heading for the Keystone ferry."

"Is there any way to get there without taking a ferry?" Pepe asked in a forlorn voice.

I had to laugh at the contrast between his earlier ferocity and his fear of ferries.

"Pepe, we're on an island," I said. "there's no way off unless we take a ferry." Technically, that wasn't true. Whidbey Island is connected to the mainland by a long, narrow, high bridge over Deception Pass. But if we went that way we would have to drive east to Mount Vernon, then south to Seattle and farther south to Tacoma, then head west to the coast, and finally drive north up the Olympic Peninsula. All to avoid the Puget Sound, which gets in the way. And it would add about six hours to our trip, maybe seven, given that rush hour was approaching, whereas my current itinerary would get us there in half an hour. As long as there wasn't a lot of traffic.

We were lucky! Reservations are recommended for that particular ferry, but we managed to get on at the very back of the line. Pepe shuddered when he saw that a metal chain was the only thing that kept my little Toyota from sliding across the deck into the choppy, gray-blue waters of the sound. That and the blocks the attendants slid under my back tires. I was tempted to open up the trunk and dig out some clean clothes, but we were too exposed on the ferry dock for me to change in the car, and I didn't want to leave Pepe alone to go change in one of the restrooms. Anyway, the trip is so short. We were in Port Townsend in thirty minutes.

Jimmy G called while we were waiting in the ferry line. He sounded confused. At first he called me Boris. I hoped he wasn't off on another one of his benders. He didn't sound very interested in the news about the chocolate-chip cookies, but he did suggest that when I took them to Hugh, I should ask him about the trust. So I was heading to the vet clinic as soon as I changed my clothes.

The Floral Fantasy B&B was a Victorian-style mansion, similar to Boswell's house, but in the heart of downtown: surrounded by a white picket fence, painted in a soft green with pale pink trim, and decorated with window boxes full of orange nasturtiums and white daisies. I parked in the driveway, behind a silver SUV, and headed up to the front porch, where a white wicker sofa was plumped with purple and orange floral pillows. A cheerful doorbell summoned a young man with fair hair and gray eyes. He looked me over with a worried frown.

I had dried off to some extent, but I knew my curls were wild and my sundress was wrinkled.

"Hello, I'm Lionel," he said. "Can I help you?" he asked in a tone that made it clear he doubted that he could.

"I'm Geri Sullivan," I said, extending my hand. "My boss, Jimmy G, told me he had arranged for me to stay here."

Lionel looked alarmed.

"Do you mean the Lavender Room?"

"I guess. He didn't say which room." That sounded nice.

"Well, I'll have to check with Julian," he said. "You can come on in, while I call him." He started to wave me into the hall. I could see that it was painted in a charming shade of olive green and hung with watercolor paintings of flowers.

"Come on, Pepe!" I said, turning to call my dog, who was sniffing around the edge of the fence.

Lionel looked horrified. "Oh, dear, you can't bring a dog in here!" he said. He clapped his hand over his nose. "We don't allow animal guests. I'm terribly allergic to dogs."

Pepe came running up. "I am not an animal," he said. "I am her partner."

"What is it, Lionel?" Another young man came out from an adjoining room. This young man had strawberry-blond hair and a freckled face. His eyes lit up when he saw Pepe. "Oh, what an adorable little dog," he said, falling to his knees and taking Pepe's snout into his hands. "Look at those lovely long ears!"

"You must be Kevin Carpenter," I said, holding out my hand.

He looked puzzled but gave me a big smile.

"My boss gave me your name. He was the one who suggested I could stay here," I said. "But if it's a problem—"

"Just this one time I think we could make an exception," said Kevin to Lionel.

Lionel frowned. "You know I'm allergic to dogs. Just like you're allergic to cats. Would you ever be OK with letting a cat stay here?"

"If I keep him in my room?" I suggested.

"Yes!" Kevin turned to Lionel. "You'll never have to be near him."

"Pet dander floating around through the air!" Lionel rolled his eyes. "And what about our other guests? They might have allergies!"

"What about the Rose Room? It has a hardwood floor and can be easily swept. I'll personally clean the room."

"Oh, fine! Just make decisions to suit yourself. You always do!" Lionel flounced off down the hall.

Kevin sighed. "He's always so dramatic. I think the allergy to dogs is all in his head. May I?" He bent down and held out his knuckles so Pepe could sniff them.

"He won't bite," I said.

"Not unless you are a *malvado*," said Pepe, giving him a good sniff, starting with his shoes. Kevin scratched his head. "I've always loved dogs," he said.

"Despite the fact that one killed your father?" I asked.

He straightened up.

"I'm doing research for Boswell," I said.

He winced.

"Or rather I was doing research for Boswell. Until he died."

Kevin reeled back. "What?"

"Yes, he was poisoned late last night."

"That can't be!" said Kevin, shaking his head. He looked troubled. "Let me show you to your room. It's just this way." He ushered us down the hall and into a room at the back of the house with a view of a fantastic rose garden. "You can see why we call it the Rose Room," he said, waving his hand at the view.

"Yes," I said, looking at the rest of the furnishings: a rose-red damask spread on the four-poster bed, which was also dotted with small green pillows, a chaise longue covered in a pink fabric, and pale-yellow silk curtains. A vase of roses on top of the dresser was reflected in the mirror on the wall. The flowers scented the air and dropped petals onto the polished surface of the wood.

"I hope you'll be comfortable here," said Kevin. "Now you must excuse me," and he went scurrying off.

"The news about Mr. Boswell frightened him," said Pepe.

"I know," I said, as I went out to the car to fetch my suitcase. "Obviously either he feels he is in danger or he thinks someone else is."

"I do not believe he is a murderer," said Pepe. "On the other hand, it was most peculiar, but I did

not smell any other person on the body of Boswell.
Just as I did not smell another person on the body
of Bickerstaff."

"Well, that's because they were poisoned," I
pointed out. "The murderer did not have to be on
the scene."

"One of the advantages of poison," said Pepe.
"But we must find out how it was administered."

While we were talking, I changed into a linen
skirt, a navy dotted-swiss blouse, and a pair of es-
padrilles. Not my most professional outfit, as Pepe
was quick to point out (he likes to give me fashion
advice), but all the other clothes I had brought
were for my romantic weekend with Felix.

"Partner, we must make haste," said Pepe. "Although the sun remains high in the sky until late on
these summer nights, we have miles to go before
we sleep."

"Robert Frost again," I murmured. Pepe seems
quite fond of Robert Frost.

As we tiptoed past the office of the Floral Fantasy
B&B, I could hear Lionel and Kevin arguing.

"I told you not to steal that paper," Lionel said.

"It's too late now." That was Kevin.

"What are we going to do with it?" Lionel again.

"I don't know. I think I should call my sister."

Chapter 27

As soon as Jimmy G left the ferry, he realized he was being followed. A guy on a motorcycle pulled out right behind him and kept behind him as he drove through Port Townsend. The bad thing about a motorcycle is that you can't get a good look at the person under all that black leather and the shiny helmet and dark sunglasses. The good thing is that a motorcycle is fairly obvious. Jimmy G made a few evasive maneuvers driving through town and lost the tail easily. Pretty soon he was motoring along on the highway to Sequim, wondering what was next.

He had called his operatives while waiting for the ferry, and Geri told him that they had found some chocolate-chip cookies but not the trust document. It bugged him a little that they thought their job was still to protect the dogs when he knew the real job was to prove Mrs. Carpenter was crazy. Maybe that's what he should focus on. Maybe that would get the judge off his back. And where better to do such research than in a bar: Jimmy G's natural ecosystem.

The main street of Sequim was lined with restaurants, bars, and little boutique shops that sold all sorts of lavender gimcracks: pillows and wreaths, painted pots and plastic key chains. One block off the main road, he spotted a line of booths being constructed out of canvas and piping, apparently part of the lavender festival.

Jimmy G found a bar that looked like his sort of place. No windows in the front. Dark inside, with the bar lit mostly by neon lights. Some booths in the back that were mostly empty. But the black-leather stools at the bar were well populated. Jimmy G found a place he could perch between an old man with a wrinkled, hang-dog face and an even older woman who had dyed black hair and bright-red lipstick smeared across her lips.

He ordered his usual shot of bourbon and waited until he had fortified himself with it before he turned to the man on his left.

"Jimmy G is new in town," he said to the guy.

All the response he got was a grunt.

"Doing some research on a woman who used to live here," he said.

Again a grunt.

"Name of Lucille Carpenter," he said.

No response to that.

"Know her?" he asked in desperation.

The old woman took pity on him. "You asking about that snooty bitch who left all her money to her dogs?" she asked.

Jimmy G nodded, turning away from the taciturn old man.

"Folks here think she was crazy," the old woman confided. "Say, are you buying?"

"Sure!" Jimmy G signaled the bartender and asked for a second shot of bourbon and another drink for his new friend.

"So tell me more," he said.

"That's about it," said the old woman, happily sipping at her Manhattan.

"What do you mean?"

"Isn't it obvious?" she said, with a cackle. "She left all her money to a pack of dogs."

And that was it. The bartender kept him supplied with drinks. The silent old man on his left got up and ambled out. And the old woman babbled on about anything and everything except Lucille Carpenter. She gossiped about all the bad feeling in town between the newer growers and the older farms. She complained vociferously about the rude tourists and the terrible traffic. Jimmy G was getting nowhere fast.

"No one who lives here goes into downtown during the festival," she said. "That's why I'm here tonight. Got to get my drinking in while the drinking is good. Next thing you know, all the tourists will be showing up here."

As if to prove her point, the door opened and a young woman walked in. She was younger by about two decades than most of the people in the bar. To Jimmy G's surprise, it was Jillian. She bellied up to the bar and ordered a gin and tonic.

"Can Jimmy G buy that for you?" Jimmy G asked.

She gave him a startled look. He could see that her hands were shaking.

"Who's this Jimmy G?" she asked.

"Right here," he said, pointing at himself.

She looked startled.

"Sure," she said. Her voice was shaky. "I really need one."

She took the gin and tonic when it was poured and went over to a booth in the corner. Jimmy G gave her a moment, while he ordered a second gin and tonic.

Then he sauntered over and set it down in front of her, sliding into the booth at the same time.

"Want to talk about what's bothering you?" he asked.

Chapter 28

To my surprise, Hugh was still at work when Pepe and I arrived at the vet clinic, shortly after 7:00 PM. So was his assistant, Bonnie. And once again the waiting room was completely empty.

"To what do I owe the pleasure of your company?" asked Hugh when Bonnie ushered me and Pepe into his office.

"Well, it's not such a pleasure for us," I said.

"Oh, I'm sorry to hear that," said Hugh. "I hoped I had made a better impression on you."

"It's not you," I said, blushing. "It's just that we found some evidence, or something we think might be evidence."

Hugh smiled. "Before we talk about that, let's discuss something more pleasant. Since you're still in town, I'd like to repeat my offer of dinner."

I felt my heart flutter a little. "Well, I'm actually staying in Port Townsend tonight," I said. "At the Floral Fantasy B&B."

"Even better," he said. He looked at Bonnie. "Call and make a reservation for 10:00 PM at the

chef's table at Chez Pierre in Port Townsend."
When she left the room he said, "The chef is a
personal friend of mine. He'll put together a fabulous feast for the two of us."

"I don't know if I should . . ." I murmured.

"It will be my treat," Hugh insisted. Then he
asked, "So what's this about evidence?"

"I think I may have found the source of the cookies," I said. I rummaged around in my purse for the
plastic bag. "Did you keep any of them?"

"What cookies?"

"The ones that someone tried to feed to the Carpenter cocker spaniels," I said, finally getting my
finger on the plastic bag. "If you did, we can test
these to see if they have the same composition. So
do you still have them?"

"I don't know. Maybe." He pushed a button on
his desk, and Bonnie came back into the room.

"I made the reservation you wanted," she said in
a pouty voice.

"Thanks," said Hugh. "Now the question is what
happened to the cookies?"

"I saw some cookies in a plastic bag in one of the
exam rooms," she said. "But they're not there now.
Maybe they got thrown out by the cleaning crew."

I was frustrated. "So you never had them tested?"

"What for?" Hugh asked.

"For poison. Someone is poisoning lawyers. So
maybe they tried to poison the dogs as well."

"It is cyanide, for sure," said Pepe.

"What lawyers?"

"Boswell is dead."

"Really, Boswell?" Hugh looked dismayed at first.
"When did this happen?"

"Last night," I said.

"So, who's the new trustee?" Hugh asked. He seemed brighter.

"What a good question!" said Pepe.

I thought it was rather odd, myself. Surely Hugh should be asking how Boswell died. But I responded to his question. "No one has a copy of the trust document. Do you, by any chance?"

"I should have one right here," said Hugh, springing up and going over to a lateral file cabinet along the wall. He pulled the drawer open and pawed through the hanging files. He stopped. He gasped.

"What is it?" I asked.

"The trust folder is empty!" said Hugh. He plucked the gray-green folder out of the hanging file cabinet and threw it on the desk. I could read the tab, which said "Carpenter Trust." He turned to Bonnie. "That must have been what they were after!"

"What are you talking about?" I asked.

"Someone broke in last night and set off the alarm. By the time the police got here there was no one on the premises. They called me and I came to check."

"They called me first," said Bonnie.

"It's true," said Hugh. "They couldn't reach me at first. I had my cell switched off." He gave a little laugh. "Can't work all the time." He turned to Bonnie. "I'm glad you didn't respond. It might have been dangerous."

Pepe's little nose began twitching. He started sniffing around the edges of the furniture.

"I looked around and didn't see anything

missing," Hugh continued. "I thought maybe it was someone looking for drugs who got scared off by the alarm."

"I knew I smelled a familiar smell," said Pepe. "It is just so hard to concentrate when the room is full of other delightful smells, like the scent of a bitch in heat, and the pee of a Rottweiler, and the stench of a frightened cat."

"Forget all that!" I said.

Hugh looked hurt. "Not you," I said.

"What is it you smell?" I asked Pepe.

"It is the smell of the intruder, the one I bit!"

"Can he identify the perpetrator?" asked Hugh with a short laugh.

"Probably," I said, although I doubted that Pepe could produce evidence the police could use. "He should be sporting a Chihuahua bite," I said.

Hugh and Bonnie looked at each other.

"My dog thinks it's the same person who broke into Carpenter Manor last night. He bit the intruder."

"What was he looking for at Carpenter Manor?"

"Well, at the time we assumed someone wanted to hurt the dogs." I saw the horrified look on Hugh's face and hurried to add. "They were safe. They were all locked up in their room."

"Oh, that's great!" said Hugh with a sigh of relief.

"Now I wonder if they were looking for a copy of the trust document."

Hugh looked thoughtful. "Yolanda should have one," he said. "All of the interested parties got copies."

"I wonder if the intruder took it?" I said. "I guess

we should head over to Carpenter Manor and ask. Now that Boswell is dead, we need to find out who will take over as trustee."

"Great! I'll look forward to hearing what you find out over dinner," said Hugh.

Chapter 29

As we headed toward Carpenter Manor, Pepe insisted we first stop at Lost Lakes Lavender Farm.

"So you can flirt with Phoebe?" I teased. "What about Siren Song?"

"You should not talk about ears at the donkey's house," said Pepe. "What would Felix have to say about your date with the vet?"

"It's not a date," I said. "He's merely showing someone who's new in town some of the customs associated with the lavender festival."

"Right, and I just want to question Phoebe about what she saw or smelled in the light of the intrusion," Pepe said.

"That's a good idea!" I said, ignoring his sarcasm. "But will she talk to you?"

I was thinking she wouldn't say anything that would reflect badly on Colleen, but Pepe saw things differently.

"She's a highly intelligent being, one who I sense has hidden depths," Pepe said. "She is not like those ditzy cocker spaniels."

"Well, I like your idea," I said, especially since it sounded like Kevin was going to call his sister for advice. We had speculated on the nature of the mysterious document on our way to the vet's. Could it be a copy of the elusive trust document?

But all of our plans changed the moment we got in sight of Carpenter Manor and saw the driveway was full of police cars, their lights flashing.

"Oh, no!" I said. "Are we too late?"

Pepe hopped up, putting his paws on the rim of the window and peering out.

"Do you think someone got to the dogs?" he asked. "If so, we have failed in our duties."

Just then we saw them roll a gurney out the front door and into the back of an aide car There was a human form belted onto the gurney .

"Oh, no! What if it's Yolanda! Or Clara," I said. "Poisoned, like the lawyers!"

The attendants slammed the doors and hopped into the cab, and the aide car pulled out of the driveway, its red lights flashing, and raced off toward town.

I pulled my car over onto the edge of the highway, narrowly avoiding tumbling into a ditch, and Pepe and I raced up the driveway. A policeman barred my further progress by holding his arm across my path as Pepe bombed on up the slate path and into the house.

Luckily the policeman was one of the two who had come to the house on the previous day.

"What is it?" I asked. "What happened?"

"Someone got shot," he said.

"Yolanda? Clara?"

He shook his head. "They're fine. Just a bit shook up."

"Then who? Caroline, the cook?"

He shook his head. "A guy named Jay who worked over there—" He pointed at the farm property, where I saw several people gathered in groups, talking. I thought I recognized Colleen, with a blue bandanna over her hair and Phoebe at her side. There were also a lot more structures set up: a broad tent over a stage at one end of the lawn in front of the farmhouse and a line of booths along the edge of the lavender fields.

"Can I go in? I asked. "You know who I am, and you know I'm here to protect the dogs."

"That's who they were shooting at. Jay just got in the way."

I couldn't help but feel guilty. What were we doing, rummaging around for a trust document when we were supposed to be protecting the dogs?

Yolanda appeared in the doorway, talking to the sergeant. She motioned me over, and he nodded to the officer, who released me. I hurried up the path toward Yolanda.

"Are you OK?" I asked, but I saw as I got near that she wasn't. She was shaking, and her face was almost gray. "It was horrible," she said. "Horrible."

"Tell me what happened," I said, taking her by the elbow and steering her toward a sofa in the living room. To my surprise, Clara was in even worse shape. She was sitting on the floor, wrapped in a blanket, sobbing.

"It's all my fault," she kept saying over and over again. "It's all my fault." The dogs milled around her.

"Who is this Jay, and why is he usurping my role?" Pepe asked.

"Who is Jay?" I asked.

Yolanda looked at Clara. "He's a migrant farmworker. He works on the farm next door."

Clara glared at Yolanda. "He's not a migrant farmworker. He's got a degree in agriculture. He's doing an internship to learn as much as he can before buying his own farm."

Yolanda said, "He's a peasant."

Clara said, "He's a WOOF."

"Woof!" said Pepe.

"Woof?" I repeated.

"He's part of a network called Worldwide Opportunities on Organic Farms," said Clara. "He's learning more about how to be a farmer by working for Colleen."

Yolanda rolled her eyes. "He's a loser. How is that any better than a farmworker?"

"What do you want from me?" Clara cried. "You tell me I'm too good for him. Yet you want to keep me here taking care of a pack of spoiled dogs. Don't you think that's a waste of my life?"

"Do you think it's a waste of mine?" Yolanda asked.

Clara looked defiant. "I do! You've been taking care of other people all your life. Now you take care of dogs. You should be taking care of yourself."

Yolanda shook her head. "By the terms of the trust, that is impossible. Mrs. C left me an allowance and a place to live for as long as I care for the dogs. Without that, I would have no place to live, no money to buy food."

"Speaking of the trust," I said, finding a way to

break into this heated conversation. "Do you have a copy of the trust document?"

"I thought you were getting a copy from Barry," Yolanda said.

"That's what I thought, too," I said. "But it didn't work out that way."

Yolanda looked at Clara and Clara looked at Yolanda.

"Haven't the police called you?" I asked.

"No, I called them," Yolanda was clearly confused.

Darn, what was I supposed to do? Weren't the police supposed to notify people in the case of a death?

"What is going on?" Yolanda asked wildly. "Is Barry OK?"

"I'm afraid not," I said.

She jumped up. "Is he sick? Is he hurt? I should go to him!"

"No, it's too late for that," I said. "He died! Last night."

Chapter 30

Jillian drained her gin and tonic in one draft, then went to work on the second drink that Jimmy G had placed in front of her.

"I just came from the scene of a shooting," she said.

Jimmy G was impressed. A dame who knew where to find some action.

"Who got shot?" he asked.

She shook her head. "Some dogs."

"Dogs? Here in Sequim?"

"Yeah," she said "Well, the dogs didn't actually get shot. Whoever did it missed them, but it was pretty nerve-racking."

"Always is when there's gunfire," he told her.

"Especially when some innocent guy gets shot," said Jillian, wrapping her hands around her glass like it was something she desperately needed to hold onto.

"Guy?" Jimmy G asked. "What guy?"

"Some farmhand," she said. "Guess he was trying to protect the dogs. Lucky he wasn't killed."

"Are you talking about Lucille Carpenter's dogs?" asked Jimmy G. "The ones at Carpenter Manor?"

Jillian locked eyes with him. "How do you know about them?" she asked.

"That's where this shooting was, huh?" he asked in return.

"I'll answer your question if you answer mine," Jillian told him.

"OK," he told her. "Jimmy G's a private investigator. We PIs know everything. Your turn, doll."

"Fine," she said. "Yes. Somebody shot at my mother's stupid dogs."

"What were you doing at Carpenter Manor?"

"I wasn't there. I was at the farm next door, helping them prepare for the lavender festival. Is there some reason I shouldn't have been there?" She finished off the last of her drink, her hands still shaking.

Jimmy G studied her for a moment. Aside from being more than good-looking, Jillian was obviously shook up. And who wouldn't be after seeing some joe get shot?

"Sorry," he told her. "We PIs are always asking questions—it's just part of our nature. Why don't we start again?"

"I'm ready to start again," she told him, holding up her empty glass.

Jimmy G liked a dame who could belt them down. He signaled the bartender for another round.

Jillian caught a glimpse of the .45 in Jimmy G's shoulder holster when he raised his arm to get the bartender's attention. She gave a wry smile and said, "You're packing, aren't you?"

Jimmy G opened his jacket further so she could better see his pistol. "Sure," he told her. "Wouldn't be without it."

"You're dangerous." She said it like she liked it. Jimmy G liked that she liked it.

"Sometimes," he said.

"Well, Mr. Dangerous," she said, "I've got a question for you."

"Shoot," said Jimmy G in his best Sam Spade/Philip Marlowe voice.

"You're the second PI who's asked me questions today. What's up with that?"

Jimmy G thought that honesty was the best policy. So he lied.

"Yeah, I've heard about her. A young woman with a little white rat-dog. She's working for the other side."

Jillian was impressed. Her eyes got wide. "What do you mean?" she asked as the fresh drinks arrived.

"She's working on behalf of the dogs," Jimmy G said. "Boswell hired her. But Jimmy G's on your side, kiddo." He raised his glass in a toast to her.

"My side?" Jillian asked.

"Natch," he told her. "Jimmy G's working for your brother, the judge, to prove that your mom was nuts when she willed all that dough to the dogs instead of her own children."

Jillian smiled—this time a genuinely warm smile. "That's awesome!" she said. "We need all the help we can get."

"Stick with Jimmy G, kid, you'll go far." He raised his glass again, saying, "Bottoms up!" and took a healthy slug of his bourbon.

Jillian followed suit. She studied him again—seemed to like what she saw.

"I don't think anybody's ever called me 'kid' or 'kiddo,' let alone 'doll.' I kind of like it."

"Just normal PI-speak," he told her, feeling much complimented.

Jillian moved closer to him—close enough that her hip was touching his.

"I like the way you dress, too," she said. "The fedora, the suspenders. You don't follow the crowd. You've got your own style."

"Don't forget 'dangerous,'" he told her.

"I won't," she said, moving even closer.

Jimmy G liked a dame who'd come on to him.

"Where are you staying tonight?" Jillian asked.

"Don't know exactly. Jimmy G figured he'd get a motel room."

"There won't be any rooms in town with the lavender festival starting tomorrow," she said, putting a hand on his shoulder. "I've already got a room reserved. Why don't you stay with me?"

She was undressing Jimmy G with her eyes. He tried undressing her with his eyes, but it didn't work. He figured he'd just have to see Jillian in the flesh.

"You bet," Jimmy G told her. "Let's blow this joint!"

Chapter 31

Yolanda looked stunned. "No!" she said. "No, that cannot be true." Her face was white. "What happened to him?"

"It's too soon to tell. But the police think he might have been murdered."

"Poisoned!" intoned Pepe in a solemn voice.

"I don't believe you!" said Yolanda. "How do you know this?"

"Pepe and I went to his home this morning to get a copy of the trust document. When we got there, we found him dead."

"And they think he was murdered?" She was horrified.

"Possibly poisoned, like Bickerstaff," I said.

"Why would anyone poison him?" Yolanda wanted to know.

"It is possible," Pepe suggested, "that Bickerstaff died accidentally when he drank the lemonade meant for Boswell. Then someone finished off the job."

"Why would anyone kill Boswell?" I asked. "Would it change the terms of the trust?"

"No, there should be an alternate trustee," Clara said.

"I really need to see a copy of the trust document!" I said.

"Didn't Mr. Boswell give you one?" Clara asked.

"It seems to be missing," I said. "And I think it's connected with Boswell's murder. Also, someone broke into Hugh's veterinary clinic and stole the trust document the same night someone broke in here."

"But no one broke into Boswell's house," pointed out Pepe.

"But they didn't get the trust document when they were here," said Yolanda.

"How would you know?" asked Clara. "The office is a mess."

"Because I keep it under my mattress," said Yolanda, looking a bit embarrassed.

"What?" Clara was shocked.

"Yes, I figured it was safer there than anywhere else in the house. And apparently that is so, as according to these two, I have the only existing copy of the trust document."

"It sounded like maybe Kevin Carpenter had a copy of it," I said. "At least he was talking about some important document when we were at the B&B."

"Why would he have a copy of the trust document?" Clara asked.

"Aren't they included in it?" I asked.

Yolanda shook her head. "Boswell advised me not to share my copy with any of the kids. He said since they were not parties of the trust, they were not entitled to copies, and if they ask me for a copy, I should send them to him."

I don't think she realized she was still speaking about Boswell as if he were alive.

Yolanda got up. "I'll get my copy and we can look at it together." All of her hysteria was gone. She seemed calm and capable.

Clara looked after her in amazement. "I really thought she would fall apart," she said, "after hearing about Boswell."

"They seemed very close," I observed.

Clara nodded. "I think he had a little crush on my aunt, but then again, I'm not so sure about his tastes. There were rumors in Port Townsend that he liked boys."

"Boys?" I asked, alarmed.

"I mean young men," Clara added hastily. "Much younger than him. Like maybe thirty years younger. He hung out at the—" She stopped abruptly as her aunt entered the room.

Yolanda was carrying a typed twenty-page document full of legalese. We flipped through it. One thing was clear: the beneficiaries of the trust were the dogs, and those who cared for them: Yolanda, Clara, and Hugh. Another thing was clear: Yolanda was the alternate trustee if anything should happen to Boswell.

"Did you know this?" I asked her.

She nodded. "Boswell told me I would never have to worry about it," she said, with tears in her eyes.

"Do you mind if I take it with me so I can read it more carefully?" I asked.

Yolanda reluctantly agreed.

"I promise to bring it back tomorrow," I said.

There was a knock on the door. It was one of the police officers. "We've finished our investigation," he said. "We're heading back to town."

"Did you find and arrest the villain who shot at the dogs?" Yolanda asked in a stern voice. She was standing tall and straight. She seemed like a different person.

"No, ma'am, we did not, but we did find the shotgun that was used. We're going to take it back to the station and dust it for fingerprints."

"I know whose fingerprints will be on it!" said Pepe indignantly. "I think we need to question the woman who likes to shoot at dogs."

Chapter 32

Clara went with us to Colleen's farm, showing us a place behind the back garden where a gate had been installed in the fence. Apparently she used this passageway frequently. Once on Colleen's property, we strolled through a kitchen garden and past several greenhouses and a metal utility shed that was locked with a rusty padlock. They hadn't cleaned up much. We saw the usual clutter of farm equipment: a propane tank, hoses and buckets, shovels and watering cans, stacks of dark-green plastic plant trays.

But on the other side of the big red barn and the old wooden farmhouse, we got a completely different picture. The whole place was abuzz with activity. The long driveway was full of pickups and small vans. The lawn area in front of the house was edged with temporary booths constructed of piping and white canvas, leaving an open rectangle of grass in the center. A guy was wrestling a huge, oil-barrel-style BBQ into place in the back of one booth. In other booths, people were setting up tables and display cases. Two men on ladders were hanging a banner that read LAVENDER DISTILLATION over the open door of the barn.

"Where are all the visitors going to park?" I asked. What with the lavender fields running right to the edge of the drive and all of the booths on the lawn, there wasn't room for more than eight or nine cars.

"Oh, Colleen's on the bus tour," Clara said. When she saw my puzzled look, she added, "People get on the buses at the fairgrounds and then get dropped off at the six farms that are part of the official tour. When they want to leave, they just jump on a bus and go on to the next farm. The buses make a big loop and end up back at the fairgrounds."

"That sounds like a great system," I said.

"Yeah," Clara shrugged. "Some of the smaller farms are open to the public and you can drive to them. But in that case, you have to reserve a lot of space for cars. And being on the bus tour is more prestigious."

"They are busy beavers," said Pepe, surveying the scene.

"I want you to be on your best behavior," I told him. "Don't chase the chickens again—remember what happened the last time."

"Geri," he said, "I will keep my instincts in check. I certainly do not want that *loca* woman with the shotgun after me again."

"Speaking of Colleen," I said, "I wonder where she is." I looked around. There were probably forty or fifty people on the premises, including people walking in from the lavender fields carrying bunches of lavender. But I didn't see Colleen anywhere.

"Let me ask in the house," said Clara, heading toward the open door of the two-story blue farmhouse. I wasn't sure I should follow her. After all, my last encounter with Colleen had involved a shotgun.

As I stood there in the middle of the driveway, a young man with a clipboard approached me. He was wearing a purple T-shirt that read LOST LAKES LAVENDER FARM.

"I'm Doug," he said. "Are you here for a shift?" he asked.

I shook my head.

"I'm just looking for Colleen," I said.

"I am looking for the beautiful Phoebe," said Pepe, his nose to the ground, sniffing the area near the entrance to the barn. "She was here not long ago." He trotted into the dark recesses of the barn.

"She went to the hospital to check on Jay," Doug said.

"The guy who got shot," I said. "Do you know how it happened?"

"Some maniac was trying to shoot at the dogs next door."

"Did anyone see who did it?"

"Not that I know of."

Pepe said, "Ask him if he saw any suspicious *hombres* around the farm."

"Were there any strangers—anybody suspicious here today?" I asked.

The guy laughed at that. "You've got to be kidding! Everyone is new, except for Jay and the other apprentices." He showed me his list. "You've got your choice of tasks. Cutting lavender in the fields, setting up booths, baking shortbread cookies, bottling lavender oil, making lavender wands, squeezing lemons for lavender lemonade . . ."

"No thanks," I said, shuddering, thinking of Bickerstaff's death by lemonade.

Clara came out of the farmhouse and headed over to us.

"Where was Colleen during all of this?" I asked Doug.

"She was supervising. It's hard to say where she was at any particular time."

"Was she in the barn at any time?" I asked.

Doug looked at his list. "It was closed until after the shooting. Colleen was doing the last distillation."

"So she was in the barn!" I said.

"What are you implying?" Clara asked.

"Well, isn't it obvious? Colleen was in the barn right before the shooting, and it was her gun that was used."

"Colleen would never shoot at the dogs!" Clara declared indignantly.

"Thanks for standing up for me, *chica!*" said Colleen. She had come up behind us as we were talking, and now gave Clara a big hug. She was wearing a blue bandanna over two tightly woven braids that brushed her shoulders, and her face was streaked with both tears and dirt.

"Is Jay OK?" Clara asked, returning the hug.

Colleen nodded. "He's fine. They just wanted to pick out the buckshot in a sterile environment. Nothing vital got hit." She winked at Clara.

Clara blushed.

Colleen turned her cold blue eyes on us. "What are you two doing here?"

"We came to find out who was shooting at the dogs," I said.

"The police think I did it!" she declared. "Have you ever heard anything so absurd?" She faced us all, her eyes flashing. No one said a word, except Pepe.

"It is not absurd at all. It is totally logical," he said.

Just then Phoebe came running over, and jumped up and put her forepaws on Colleen's denim-clad knees. The sight of his new crush seemed to stun Pepe into silence. He stood there with his pink tongue hanging out a little.

"And to make things worse!" Colleen pulled a crumpled piece of colored paper out of the pocket of her jeans. She slapped it on her hand. "I picked up this brochure while I was in town. They completely left Lost Lakes off the bus tour! What are we going to do?" She burst into tears.

"How could that happen?" Clara asked. "You've been on the tour for years."

"It must have been Julian!" said Colleen, swiping at her tears with her fists. "He told me there would be repercussions if I didn't cooperate with him. Well, he has no idea who he's messing with!" She dropped the brochure and ground it into the dirt beneath the heel of her dusty cowboy boot.

"Does that mean we should stop working?" Doug asked.

"Absolutely not!" said Colleen. "If Julian thinks he can threaten me, he doesn't know who he's messing with. We're definitely going to be on the bus tour." She stormed off toward the farmhouse.

Phoebe lifted her lovely neck and gave a howl, then trotted off after Colleen.

"Who's she talking about?" I asked Clara.

"Julian. Judge Julian. The oldest of Lucille's kids. He's the one who hired Bickerstaff to break the trust."

"She says she will bite him where it hurts the most," said Pepe. It took me a moment to realize he was translating for Phoebe.

Chapter 33

"You should have left me at the farm," said Pepe, "if all you were going to do was run off on a date."

"It's not a date," I said for the third time, while checking in the mirror to see if my efforts at brushing had tamed my curls, which had gone wild after the dunking. "I'm going to question Hugh about the trust."

I had been looking over the document once I got back to the room. It seemed pretty clear. The use of the property and a generous allowance were set aside for whoever lived in the house and cared for the dogs. Yolanda and Clara were both named as the recipients of this benefit. Hugh also received an allowance for being on call to provide medical services for the dogs, plus he was to be reimbursed for the cost of any medical procedures or services he performed. There were two witnesses to the trust: one was Bernie Bickerstaff, and the other was Lionel Talent. That seemed odd to me. Why would Bickerstaff witness a document that opposed his clients? And how did Boswell know Lionel Talent?

I had tried to call Jimmy G to tell him I had a copy of the trust, but he wasn't answering his phone.

"I could have protected the dogs and had a little chat with Phoebe," said Pepe, who was curled up on top of the pillows on the bed in the Rose Room.

"She didn't seem interested in talking to you," I pointed out.

"Playing hard to get," he said. "It is part of the dance of seduction. You might do well to remember it on your date tonight."

"It's not a date," I repeated, checking my watch. It was five minutes to ten, and I was supposed to meet Hugh at ten. I hoped the restaurant was nearby. "Now be good!"

"I will be investigating," said Pepe in a frosty tone, turning to his iPad, which was lying on the bed.

Kevin was in the lobby. I told him I was meeting someone at Chez Pierre, and he told me it was just two blocks down the hill and two blocks toward the water.

Chez Pierre occupied an old house on the waterfront in which several rooms had been redone to serve as dining areas. When I entered, a few diners lingered over coffee and dessert. They watched with curiosity as the maître d' whisked me into a secluded alcove, near the kitchen, just big enough for a small table for two in front of a window that looked out over the water. A candle flickered on the table. Out on the water, lights danced on choppy waves as they rocked boats at anchor.

Hugh was already seated at the table, looking over a menu. He was no longer in his pale-blue clinical coat but in a slate-blue silk shirt that brought out the blue in his eyes. He certainly knew how to complement his fair coloring and his piercing eyes.

He stood up and held out my chair for me, his eyes telling me how much he liked what I was wearing, as did the hand that he trailed down my bare arm. I had changed into one of my favorite dresses: a black-and-white printed cotton with a V-neck, which gave me the chance to show a little bit of cleavage, and a full skirt, which made my waist look slim.

"You dress up very nicely," he said.

I nodded my appreciation, suddenly shy.

"We'll take whatever is the chef's pleasure," said Hugh, handing the menu back to the waiter, who showed up promptly to ask us if we wanted a drink. "And let's start with some oyster shooters."

Ever since I was a kid and read the poem about the Walrus and the Carpenter in *Through the Looking-Glass* I had been squeamish about eating oysters. The waiter showed up with two shot glasses, each containing, according to Hugh, a shot of vodka, a splash of Tabasco sauce, and an oyster.

"Now tip your head back and toss it down!" Hugh coached me.

I tried, I really did, but the vodka burned, and the oyster seemed to get stuck in my throat. I swallowed hard, fighting the urge to bring it back up. I finally got it down, but I swear I could feel the oyster trying to swim in my stomach.

Hugh insisted that I try another one and coached me by demonstrating his oyster-swallowing prowess. Luckily, he was so absorbed in savoring the flavor that I was able to spit the oyster out of my mouth and into my napkin. Maybe I could smuggle it home to Pepe, who would no doubt appreciate it more than I did.

"Better?" Hugh asked, smiling at me with his twinkling blue eyes.

I nodded. "Much better," I agreed, although the two shots of vodka were making my head swim.

"So how was your day today?" I asked Hugh.

"Uneventful until now," he said, leaning close to me.

Oh, dear! I would really have to get him to back off.

"Mine was anything but," I said, launching into a description, starting with my unexpected plunge into the ocean (I didn't mention that I had been breaking and entering at the time) and ending with the shooting of the dogs. It seemed he already knew about that.

"Yes, Yolanda called me and wanted me to come out and inspect the dogs," he said, ordering two more oyster shooters.

"Did you go check out the dogs?" I asked.

"Yes, she insisted. It's one of the terms of the trust. I need to be available twenty-four seven for their medical needs, so I had no choice about it." He didn't sound happy. "Yolanda can be overly anxious."

"So were the dogs all right?"

"Yes, not a scratch on them." The oyster shooters arrived, and Hugh tossed back another one. "Yolanda told me you took her copy of the trust document," he said.

I nodded. "I'm going to make a copy of it and then return it to her," I said. "It looks pretty straightforward. Do you really feel the heirs have any chance of overturning it?"

"They'll try to say Lucille was crazy," Hugh said bitterly. "They will try to smear my name in the process."

"How would they do that?" I asked.

"They'll say I seduced her," he said. He looked at me, his eyes earnest. "Everyone thought we were having an affair. No one could imagine that a man and woman could spend time together without it being sexual." His voice lingered on that word.

"I know," I said. "How silly! Even my dog thought this was a date."

"Well, isn't it?" he asked.

"I hope not," I said. "I have a boyfriend in Seattle—"

He cut me off. "A boyfriend in Seattle doesn't count," he said. "He's not here, is he? And he doesn't need to know what you do. As far as he's concerned, you're just working a case."

"I am just working a case," I said. "Now that I've got a copy of the trust document, I need to find people who think Mrs. Carpenter was in her right mind when she left all her money to her dogs."

"Good luck," said Hugh. "I benefited from the trust, but I still thought she was crazy."

"What do you mean?" I asked.

"Well, she claimed her animals spoke to her," he said. "Are you sure you don't want this?" He pointed at the oyster shooter.

I shook my head. "Lots of people think their animals speak to them," I said cautiously.

"I mean she really believed they were speaking to

her," Hugh said, raising his eyebrows. "Like she could understand what they were saying."

"Well, dogs are very expressive," I started to say. "You must see that in your line of work."

"Why are we talking about dogs?" he asked. "We should be talking about what we are going to be doing after dessert. All of those oysters remind me of something else wet and briny that I would love to explore."

He lifted up my hand, turned it over and began licking my palm, working his tongue in between my fingers. I was so shocked, I couldn't move for a minute. And then a chill wind blew into the room. I looked up to see Felix in the doorway. He was dressed in his usual working clothes: just black jeans and a soft T-shirt, but he looked magnificent as usual, with his dark hair, just a little too long, framing his pale face, and his dark eyes glittering.

"Felix!" I said getting up. But I didn't get a chance to say more than that because he turned on his heel and stalked out of the restaurant.

Chapter 34

A loudly buzzing alarm went off. It was jarring and roused Jimmy G from a great dream he was having about being in bed with a knockout dame who thought he was the best thing since sliced bread. He'd had this type of dream more than once and always hated to wake up from it.

Still half asleep, Jimmy G reached over to turn off the alarm and was surprised when it shut off by itself. He was even more surprised when he fully opened his eyes and saw Jillian standing beside the bed. She wasn't wearing a stitch and, in the early morning light, was even more sexy and fetching than the dames in his dreams ever were.

Brother, he thought, it wasn't a dream, it was real! And she sure wasn't like those broads in the movies who sat up in bed after having sex, but for some ridiculous reason kept their chests covered demurely with a sheet while they talked to their lovers. Nope—Jillian just stood there before him naked as a jaybird, every mouthwatering curve exposed and a nice smile on her full lips.

He matched her smile as he thought, boy, did Jimmy G get lucky last night!

"Morning, Mr. Dangerous," Jillian told him. "I'm leaving."

With that, she whirled away from him, went into the bathroom, and shut the door.

Jimmy G was shocked and just lay there. He was being loved and left. It had happened before. Wasn't anything to do about it. He sure wasn't going to protest, let alone beg—it had never worked before anyway. He'd just have to take it like a man. Besides, it was better to be loved and left than never loved at all.

With that thought on his mind, he must have dozed off again, because the next thing he knew, Jillian was standing over him once more, this time fully dressed. She was wearing a short skirt and a halter top that really showed off her breasts.

"Hey, you," she told him. "I'll be working my booth at Lost Lakes Lavender Farm. Come and find me if you want to get together later."

Lucky, lucky, lucky, after all! Jimmy G had been loved but *wasn't* being left!

He propped himself up on an elbow and was about to reply when Jillian suddenly ripped the covers off of him, exposing his complete nakedness.

"That's better," she said with greedy eyes. "I want to see all of you."

She turned around and grabbed a little camera out of her open suitcase, which sat on the nearby stand. She stood over him, clicking pictures. Startled, Jimmy G quickly pulled the covers back up over his chest.

"Ah, Mr. Dangerous is bashful, too," said Jillian, tossing the camera back into the suitcase. She headed for the door, turned, blew him a kiss, said, "I like that in a tough guy," then went out the door with a wicked giggle.

Jimmy G wasn't bashful or shy or self-conscious about his body, he had just been . . . well . . . surprised. Guys were supposed to ogle naked dames, not the other way around. In any event, it seemed certain he and Jillian would be having a repeat love-session. He'd rise to the occasion, and she could ogle to her heart's content.

The alarm clock read 6:00 AM, but he was too excited to sleep with the day holding such promise. A smoke and some coffee would put him right, so he dragged himself out of the sack, found the little motel-sized coffee maker, and put two of the under-strength java pouches in it so it would have some kick. Then he took a leak, looked at himself in the mirror (he thought his physique was pretty buff for a guy in his early forties; no wonder she liked it), and poured a cup of the half-brewed java, which was extra strong, just like the java-juice he got in Iraq (so heavy-duty that he and the other troops called it knife-and-fork coffee).

As he was unwrapping a stogie, Jimmy G remembered that smoking wasn't allowed in the room, so he put on his pants and sport coat, no shirt, and stepped outside. It was going to be another hot day, he thought, lighting his cigar—nice and warm already, even at this time of the morning. Gonna be a busy one, too. The motel parking lot was full. The traffic was constant: cars on the road, pedestrians on the sidewalk. A couple of buses rumbled by,

bearing signs that read TOUR #1—FARMS A TO C and
TOUR #3—FARMS G TO J.

When he went back into the room, he noticed
that Jillian had left her large suitcase open on the
little folding stand by the TV set. Always one who'd
stoop to snoop, Jimmy G flipped on the nearby
floor lamp and had a look-see. On the right side of
her suitcase were a few pairs of the same style of
satin-smooth, bikini panties he'd come to appreciate last night, ditto for some silky bras, and a couple
of short shorts he'd like to see her in.

In one side pocket, he found the camera and a
pair of binoculars. The other side pocket was full
of envelopes. All of them were past-due notices
for bills: electric bill, cell phone bill, two credit
card bills that showed maxed-out balances, and a
notice from her mortgage company threatening
foreclosure if she missed another payment. She
had written across that one:

> *I will be coming into more than enough money*
> *after the lavender festival to guarantee full*
> *payment to you.*
>
> > *Thank you for your patience,*
> > *Jillian Valentine*

That's nice, thought Jimmy G. He understood financial troubles better than most since he'd had
plenty of his own over the years. He poured himself
more coffee, sat down in the small chair by the
front window, and smiled as he thought about his
new paramour. He was glad everything was going so
well for her, because it sure was for him.

Just then the motel phone rang. At first, Jimmy G wasn't going to answer it. Then he thought maybe it was the management giving him a wake-up call, not that he had scheduled it, but maybe Jillian had. And then his heart lifted a little as he thought maybe Jillian was calling him. Maybe she missed him so much already, she just had to talk to him. After all, she was the only one who knew he would be there.

He picked up the phone. "Loverman, at your service."

"I don't like it that you're messing with my sister," said a voice. With a sinking feeling, Jimmy G recognized the voice of Judge Julian Valentine. "And I don't like it," the judge went on, "that you promised to deliver the trust document to me and you haven't done it yet."

"Jimmy G got distracted," Jimmy G said.

"Don't you ever refer to my sister as a distraction," said the judge.

"Jimmy G meant she's mighty fetching," Jimmy G tried to explain.

"She's a wacko, is what she is," the judge said. "You have no idea who you're messing with."

Jimmy G wasn't sure if that referred to the judge or Jillian.

"I'm in Sequim, only about five blocks from the motel at the headquarters for the lavender festival. I'll be here for two hours. If the trust document is not delivered to me within that time, you will be very sorry."

Before Jimmy G could reply, the judge hung up.

Now what to do? Jimmy G couldn't afford to alienate his client. Especially since his client had such an attractive sister. He paced around and smoked another cigar and drank another cup of coffee, and then he had an idea. Maybe Geri had found the trust document. The last time he had talked to her, she was on her way to the vet's office to see if he had a copy of it.

He picked up his cell phone and dialed her number. It only rang once before she picked up.

"Felix!" she practically squealed. "I'm so glad you called. I'm so sorry about what happened."

"No need to be sorry, kiddo," said Jimmy G. "Since this is Jimmy G, not your boy toy."

"Jimmy G." Her voice went flat. There was a shuffling sound. Perhaps she had dropped the phone. Then she said, in a sharper tone: "Do you realize what time it is?" Then she told him what time it was: "It's seven o'clock in the morning." Jimmy G heard the rat-dog make some noise in the distance—sounded like he was protesting, too.

"Jimmy G is looking for the trust document, doll," he said. "Tell me you found it."

More rustling. "Well, to tell you the truth, I do have it," she said. She sounded kind of proud of herself. Well, she should be.

"Nice work!" he said. "Jimmy G needs you to deliver it. Judge Valentine is at the headquarters for the lavender festival in Sequim." He read off the address. "He needs it delivered to him by nine this morning. Can you do that for Jimmy G?"

"I guess," she said. He could tell she was starting to wake up. He heard the rat-dog barking in the background. "Why would we deliver it to the—"

Jimmy G cut her off before she could ask any more questions. "Jimmy G out!" he said, and hung up. The day was starting very well. With Geri taking care of his obligation to the judge, he could find some breakfast, then head over to the Lost Lakes Lavender Farm to check out Jillian.

As he was heading out the door, he thought about the camera. It really wasn't fair that she had naked photos of him. He'd have to even up the score. He picked it up and put it into the pocket of his sport coat.

Chapter 35

I went to bed crying, and I was still crying in the morning while I was driving toward Sequim. Felix had refused to answer any of my calls, either last night or in the morning after Jimmy G woke me up.

Pepe didn't help. He kept telling me "I told you so." But then I didn't really expect him to be very sympathetic. He's not a big fan of Felix and he definitely doesn't think too much of the vet.

"He has got only two stars on Yelp, Geri," he told me. "That is pathetic. People complain about his high prices and say he recommends procedures their pets do not need, like gum surgery."

"Isn't that what he's doing to Henry on Monday?" I asked.

"*Sí,* and according to the PetVet site, it is not recommended for senior dogs. Not without a series of lab tests."

"We'll have to check into that after I meet with the judge," I promised my pooch.

Traffic was already heavy as we headed toward Sequim and was projected to get heavier as the weekend went along. Luckily, because Jimmy G had called so early, I had a head start, and so although I hit a few bad patches, where the traffic was stop and go, I managed to pull into a spot in front of the lavender festival office just five minutes after the time we were supposed to meet the judge.

Downtown Sequim is only about five blocks long, with many little shops, all small, one-story buildings with no coherent architectural theme. But they have one thing in common: lavender. There were posters for the lavender festival in every window. Lavender paint on the doors and window frames. Lavender planted in barrels outside the front doors. Lavender flags waving in the breeze.

The building that served as the festival head-quarters was at the edge of town in an anonymous-looking cinder-block building that might have once been an auto repair shop. It was set back on a concrete pad that provided plenty of room for parking. The receptionist tried to turn me away at first, insisting that I wanted to be at the fair-grounds, but when I finally got across the name Julian Valentine, she changed her tune. She led us through a warren of cluttered desks to a back office where a man in a superbly tailored black suit was arguing with a woman seated at a desk. A nameplate on her desk read IVY MALONE, FESTIVAL DIRECTOR.

"Sorry to disturb you," the receptionist said, "but these two say they have an appointment with Judge Valentine."

The woman frowned and the man turned around. He wore a white shirt and a blue-and-red striped tie. The woman wore her gray hair in a pageboy and black-rimmed eyeglasses that made her look like a librarian. She did not seem pleased to see Pepe. "We provide a dog-care area at the fairgrounds," she said. "We don't allow dogs on the buses or at the farms."

"I'll keep that in mind," I said.

"As if I would ever deign to use public transportation," said Pepe.

"Let's adjourn to a more private setting," said the judge, putting his hand over my elbow and steering me into a temporary cubicle, constructed of movable beige walls. It contained a large metal desk, a few chairs, and some cardboard boxes.

I was glad to finally get a look at the fourth of Lucille Carpenter's children. Judge Valentine was in his midforties. He had dark brown hair, which he wore in a helmet. His lips were large and fleshy, and there were dark circles under his eyes. His eyes were a startling greenish-blue.

According to Jillian, he was the one who had hired Bickerstaff to break the trust. And according to Colleen, he was trying to bribe her into helping him build a case. But I didn't know much more than that about him.

"Geri Sullivan, of the Gerrard Agency," I said, holding out my hand.

"Yes, I've talked to your boss," he said. "Peculiar fellow."

"You have?" I was confused by that.

The judge hesitated a moment, then said, "Of course, who do you think recommended you to Boswell?"

"Why would you recommend any agency to

Boswell?" I asked. "I thought you were trying to break the trust?"

"Well, yes," Julian cleared his throat, "but, you know . . . No reason to be hostile about it."

"Ask him how he learned of us," Pepe suggested.

"How did you hear about us?" I asked.

"Well, I believe you are the only detective who works with a dog for a partner," he said, laughing at Pepe. He pulled out a chair and waved me to a seat at a small wooden table. He sat on the edge of the desk, looming over us.

"He is taking up the posture of a bad cop," said Pepe. "Take the initiative."

"Colleen said you were trying to coerce her into supporting your side," I said. Although, come to think of it, why wouldn't Colleen be on his side?

"I don't know what you're talking about," Julian replied.

"Something about the brochures and the tour," I said.

"A silly mistake with the printer, I believe," Julian said in a mild voice. "It's so like Colleen to blame it on me. I had nothing to do with it."

"What is Colleen's position on the trust?" I asked.

Juilian shrugged. "She would benefit if it was declared invalid. She'd have enough money to buy the farm, instead of having to lease the property and make payments to Boswell, who was just putting the money into his own pocket."

"You do know that Boswell is dead."

"Yes, that was very unfortunate," Julian said in a mild voice.

"Ask him how he heard of it!" Pepe asked.

"How did you learn of it?" I asked.

Julian smiled. "I have good friends on the Port Townsend police force."

"So you think Boswell was not handling the money properly?"

"A motive for murder!" said Pepe.

"It was one of the things we would find out if he was forced to provide a financial accounting for the trial," Julian said. "Instead, we'll have to hire a forensic accountant to go in and try to track the money."

"Suddenly Mr. Boswell is the *maleante* in the story," said Pepe.

"It certainly increases the number of suspects," I said, thinking of Yolanda, Clara, and Hugh, all of whom Boswell was defrauding, not to mention the children of Lucille Carpenter.

"I have it on good authority," said Julian, "that the police are narrowing in on a suspect. Someone was in the house with Boswell that night. As soon as they find that person, they'll be able to make an arrest."

"Funny, you didn't smell anyone in Boswell's home," I said to Pepe.

"What do you mean?" asked the judge.

"Good point," said Pepe. He went over and began sniffing at the cuffs of Julian's pants. Julian kicked out at Pepe, who ducked the blow.

"Aha!" said Pepe. "I begin to think I might train you yet, Geri. I do catch a whiff of Cohiba cigars, the same scent present in Boswell's office."

"Do you smoke Cohiba cigars?" I asked.

Julian shook his head. "Why would I do that? It could potentially damage my reputation. Those are illegal!" He stood up and held out his hand. "Now,

I understand your boss told me you have a copy of the trust document."

"Yes," I said, digging it out of my purse. "It seems like everyone is looking for a copy of it. I don't understand why you want it."

Julian practically yanked it out of my hands. "It should be obvious. We just want to verify that the copy is identical to the one we already have." He flipped through the pages quickly.

"And is it?" I asked, as he got to the end.

"No, we need to verify the validity of these witnesses," he said, examining the final pages.

"Surely, if you have a copy already you know who the witnesses are—" I started to say.

"Yes, we do," he said, "and, just as I suspected, the names are different. This document is clearly fraudulent. Boswell was trying to pull a fast one. Where did you get this?"

"From Yolanda."

"As I thought. She is part of the conspiracy!" He put his hands on the top of the pages and, with one powerful motion, ripped them in half.

"Hey!" I said, getting up. "You can't do that. I need that!"

"What for?" asked the judge, turning the papers sideways and ripping them again. "It's invalid."

Pepe growled.

"Maybe you shouldn't be the one making that decision," I said, trying to grab at the pages. "Wouldn't it be useful to prove there was a conspiracy?"

The judge actually hesitated at that. Then he blinked and said, "We already have enough evidence of that." And then he turned his back to me and fed the pages into a shredder that was partially concealed behind the boxes. I heard it grind away, and as I pushed forward, I saw the last few scraps of paper waving above the metal teeth before they were pulled into the machine.

"Thank you, Miss Sullivan, for your assistance," the judge said, turning around to face me. He had a big smile on his face. "It was indeed a pleasure to meet you." And then he strolled out the door.

Chapter 36

Pepe and I were sitting on the floor beside the shredder trying to reassemble the pieces of the trust document when we heard a big commotion. We went out into the big room and found Colleen Carpenter arguing with Ivy.

"Have you talked to the bus drivers and notified them to stop at my farm?" Colleen was asking.

"But Julian said—"

"I don't care what Julian said—"

"He said you weren't ready this year. That it would be an embarrassment if we transported people to your farm—"

"I told you already. That's an outright lie. I'm totally prepared for the festival."

"Well, I don't know," said Ivy. "We can't afford to tarnish the reputation of the lavender festival."

"Colleen is absolutely right," I said, stepping forward. "We were just at the farm yesterday. They've got booths, a stage, a sign . . ."

Ivy frowned. "Well, I guess we can do it—"

"I brought you a whole box of new brochures,"

Colleen was saying. "I paid for them myself. They show my farm on the bus tour."

Ivy turned to the receptionist and told her to get somebody named Sam to take Colleen's new brochures to the various spots around town where the literature on the festival had been distributed. She then replaced the festival brochures in the rack by the reception desk with a bunch of Colleen's new ones.

"There," Ivy told Colleen. "And I'll notify the bus drivers personally. Satisfied?"

"For now," said Colleen. "In future, though, you talk to *me* about anything regarding my farm, not Julian. He doesn't speak for me."

She headed for the door. Pepe and I followed her.

"Why would your brother do that to you?" I asked Colleen as we exited the building.

"*Stepbrother*," she said pointedly. "Julian's *Mr. High and Mighty.* He thinks just because he's a judge, he can be the judge of *all* things."

"Humans argue too much," said Pepe. "In the *perro* world, it is simple: one dog establishes dominance, the rest are then submissive, and all is well."

"Like you, huh?" I asked him. "You're always trying to be the alpha male."

"Of course," he told me. "*Pepe el Macho* is submissive to no *perro.*"

Just as Pepe said that, we saw that Colleen had brought Phoebe with her. The lovely white-and-black dog was on a long leash, tied to a newspaper stand directly in front of the building.

Pepe was overjoyed to see her and rushed up to Phoebe saying, "*Mi amor!*"

Phoebe responded by lunging at Pepe and giving a couple of loud, deep, menacing barks.

Pepe immediately rolled over on his back, showing his little white belly.

"So much for not being submissive," I told him.

Colleen thought I was talking to her. "Yes, you really have to be assertive if you want to succeed," she said.

"It is only an act," Pepe said, still on his back, gazing up at Phoebe. "And I must say, the view is *muy bueno* from this angle."

"Thanks for sticking up for me," Colleen said. "Can I buy you a coffee? Or breakfast? I didn't get a chance to eat this morning, I was so busy."

"Sure," I said, realizing that I was in the same situation. Colleen suggested a café just a block away called Wanda's Waffles.

"What about the dogs?" I asked.

"I think they're fine," said Colleen. "But you should probably tie your dog up with Phoebe while we're inside. Sequim has a leash law."

Poor Pepe, I thought, as I took his leash out of my purse. He hates leashes, just detests them. But as I hooked it to his collar, he didn't struggle or protest.

"I do not mind being tied up with Phoebe," he told me. "When it comes to *amor*, there are no bonds except love itself."

I had to chuckle. It was obvious that he was head over heels in love. (Or maybe I should say he was *heels* over *head* in love.)

"I'll bring you some bacon," I called to him as we walked next door to the restaurant. He didn't even respond, just kept his attention on Phoebe. It was the very first time my dog had ever ignored the promise of bacon.

We got seated quickly, even though Wanda's was pretty full. It wasn't terribly large, maybe twenty tables or so, all covered with blue-and-white-checked tablecloths, with assorted syrups displayed in small lazy Susans at the side of each table. The wonderful vanilla scent of waffles filled the air. The diners around us were eating everything from Belgian waffles heaped with whipped cream and strawberries, to sturdier waffles covered with berries and nuts and butter.

It was hard to choose, but I finally ordered the special of the day: a lavender waffle with lavender butter. Plus a side of crisp bacon for Pepe. Colleen ordered a raspberry waffle.

Savoring my cup of hot tea, I said, "I'm happy you got that business with your brochures straightened out. That could have been—"

"A disaster," she said, finishing the sentence for me. "I would've been ruined."

"Just from being left out of the festival brochure?"

"The festival gives me over half my annual revenue. Same for most of the lavender farms around here. None of us could afford to lose that income, least of all me."

"Well, I don't want to bring up a sore subject again," I said, very much wanting to bring it up, "but if that's the case, I really can't understand why Julian would try to sink you."

"Julian's determined to break the trust," she said, with a sigh. "I think he would do anything to get his hands on his mother's money. He wanted me to provide him with a statement saying my stepmother was crazy. He figured I'd be the most compelling witness since I lived right next to her all those years, when neither of her real kids came to visit. But I just couldn't do it."

The waitress showed up with our waffles, and Colleen paused a moment to pour some syrup over hers. But before she took a bite, she went on, "My stepmother was a lot of things. She was eccentric. She was narcissistic. She was manipulative. But she was not crazy. And I told Julian that."

"So he retaliated against you? That's cold."

"Cold describes Julian to a T," she said, pressing her fork into her waffle and taking a big bite.

Luckily the waffles were not cold. For a while, we ate in silence. The subtle flavor of the lavender was just right with the vanilla-flavored waffle, and the lavender butter added a nice touch. Colleen finished first, mopping up the last bits of raspberry juice on her plate with the last few bites of waffle.

Then I said, "I just gave Julian a copy of the trust document and he tore it up. He said it wasn't valid. Do you know anything about that?"

Colleen shook her head. "But Kevin might. He thought Boswell was up to something. He tried to tell me he was skimming money from the trust, but I didn't want to listen." She leaned across. "I think Julian got to Kevin. He was going to testify on his behalf."

"So Kevin has a completely different picture of your stepmother than you do?"

Colleen's eyes were sad. "She wasn't nice to either of us. But it was harder for Kevin. He was younger than me when our mother died and he was a Mama's boy. The idea that anyone could take her place—it was unthinkable to him. He resented our dad for marrying Lucille, and he tried to make her life miserable. No wonder she sent us both to boarding schools."

"Yikes!" I said. "That's terrible."

"Yes, we were separated at a time when we really needed to be together. Kevin had it worse. He went to an all-boy's school where he was bullied, I think. I hated my boarding school, but I was there for only two years before I was out and came back to Sequim. My dad had moved in with Lucille in the new house she built, and I asked if I could stay at the farmhouse and learn to run the farm."

She took a last sip of her coffee. "Speaking of that, I've got to go! So much to do there. I hope you'll drop by later!"

As she stood up, I stuffed the last of my waffle into my mouth, quickly wrapped Pepe's bacon in a napkin, and said, "I'll take care of the bill." But she wouldn't let me. She insisted that I had done her a big favor by standing up for her.

Outside, the dogs were still tied to the newspaper box, but Pepe was now on his feet. It seemed that he was on better terms with Phoebe.

I knelt down and gave Pepe a piece of his bacon. He took the long rasher in his little mouth, then turned and gave it to Phoebe, laying it gently in front of her. Phoebe snarfed it right up.

"Was it good for you?" Pepe asked her. "I know it will be good for me."

Colleen untied Phoebe and took the lead in her hand. "Thanks for being on my side," said Colleen, giving me an unexpected hug, then walking off with Phoebe.

"My bacon, *por favor,*" said Pepe.

"Here." I set it down in front of him.

"Ah," he said, munching on it ecstatically. "Bacon and Phoebe, what else can Heaven hold?"

"Did Phoebe tell you anything?"

He glanced up at me, his big brown eyes sparkling. "She said she wanted to see me again. Is that not *grande? Aye yi-yi!*"

"Anything else, Romeo? Something that might help us, maybe?"

"She said that Colleen called her brother yesterday, and they had a big fight. Something to do with Boswell and the trust."

"That's all?"

"Is that not enough?" he said. He went back to his bacon with gusto.

"You're supposed to be helping me investigate," I said. "While you were mooning over Phoebe, I was interviewing Colleen. I learned a lot, but I still don't know why the judge tore up the trust document. Maybe Jimmy G will know what's up. He's the one who told me to take it to him."

Chapter 37

Jimmy G had just settled onto a stool at the bar where he had met Jillian the night before when his phone started ringing. It was Geri.

"What's shakin', doll?" Jimmy G asked. "Whole lot of shakin' going on around here, that's for sure. Give your boss some good news."

"I don't think it is good news," Geri said. "We gave the trust document to the judge, like you said, and he shredded it!" He heard her little rat-dog barking in the background, probably adding his two cents.

Jimmy G thought about that for a while. It was not what he expected.

"Why would he do a thing like that?" he asked, more to himself than Geri.

But she had a quick answer: "Maybe he's trying to destroy all the copies of the trust document. What would happen then?"

Jimmy G snorted. "Does Jimmy G look like a lawyer?"

"No," she said, in a snappy voice, "and now all the lawyers are dead."

"Then it's a good time to not be one," Jimmy G pointed out, pretty proud of himself for coming up with that quip.

"It doesn't make sense," Geri said. "We're supposed to be helping the dogs, and if the trust disappears, so do their home and their income."

"Don't know what to tell you, doll. Jimmy G is just doing as he's told."

"But who is paying us now that Boswell is dead? And did you hear that Boswell was skimming funds? Should we investigate that?"

Darn, she was insistent. How was Jimmy G going to get her off his back? "Look, doll," he said. "You did a great job so far. Take the weekend off. We'll regroup on Monday and figure out what to do next." That would give him plenty of time to hang out with Jillian at the lavender festival, then head back to Seattle.

She didn't sound happy, but she hung up the phone. Satisfied he had done his job and done it superbly, Jimmy G ordered a farmer's breakfast with a Bloody Mary. The place was packed, but luckily there was room at the counter, where he was sandwiched between a couple from Seattle and an elderly woman who rattled on about all the things to do at the lavender festival: hayrides, art shows, concerts.

Jimmy G could barely think, but he knew there was something bothering him. He just couldn't figure out what it was as she yapped in his ear, like Geri's little yappy dog. Was it that he had double-crossed his own operatives and thrown the evidence they had so assiduously collected into the arms of the other side? Nah, he decided that didn't really bother him. A client is a client, and a client is the one who pays you. The judge was their client now. Boswell was dead.

Then what was it? It wasn't until he was out in the parking lot, lighting up a cigar, that he realized it. He reached in his pocket for his lighter and came up with the camera. That naked photo! What was Jillian going to do with it? Was she one of those dames who posted photos on the Internet? Would Jimmy G's naked bod be exposed for all to see? It made him nervous. She had no right to take a photo of Jimmy G without his permission.

He pulled the camera out of his pocket and fumbled with the buttons. He finally figured out which one turned the camera on, and after some more poking around, during which he took several photos of the asphalt surface of the parking lot, he found the back button.

The first photo that came up was of Jimmy G sprawled on the sheets.

"Not bad!" he thought, checking himself out. No wonder Jillian wanted a photo of him. Sort of a trophy, he assumed. Let her relive those glorious moments when he wasn't around. Well, he could get into that. As long as she didn't post it on the Internet.

He scrolled back through several photos of himself, admiring the artistic angles she had used, which made everything look bigger.

Then he was looking at a photo of another man, a fair-haired guy, with a smooth, bare chest. The guy had a huge smile on his face. He was shown only from the waist up, but Jimmy G had a pretty good idea that he was naked from the waist down. Unable to stop himself, he clicked back, and sure enough, the camera angle widened, and he took in the whole scene. The man was tall and well-endowed. He was standing, nude, in some kind of exam room, with a stainless-steel table in the middle and glass-fronted steel cabinets in the background. A little farther back in the sequence of shots, the man was sprawled on the table.

Jimmy G stopped there. He didn't want to see any more. This dame that he thought was in love with Jimmy G, or at least hot for his body, was just some kind of heartless femme fatale who used men and then discarded them. No way was he going to spend the weekend with her or visit her at Lost Lakes Lavender Farm. No way was he going to give her the camera back.

Jimmy G was going to go straight to the casino, halfway between Sequim and Port Townsend, and drown his sorrows.

Chapter 38

"Pepe," I said, when I got back in the car, "Jimmy G said we should take the weekend off."

Pepe shook his little head, then his whole body. "We are Sullivan and Sullivan. We never give up when we are on a case."

"Yes, but what case?" I asked. "Are we protecting the dogs? Collecting statements to be used in the lawsuit?"

"Finding the murderer of Mr. Boswell," said Pepe.

"Yes, what about that?"

"I have been thinking about that," he said, "when I am not thinking about Phoebe."

"Not Siren Song?" I was teasing him.

He ignored me. "There was a witness to Boswell's murder."

"Well, we know that," I said. "The judge said there was someone in the house with Boswell that night. But how do we figure out who that was?"

"There was indeed someone in Boswell's house that night, someone who saw the whole crime go down," said Pepe in his most portentous true crime-show-narrator voice. "Someone who watched from the shadows as his beloved companion died an agonizing death. Someone who was unable to help because of the tragic fact that he was a cat."

"The cat!" I said. "That's brilliant! Of course, the cat was there."

But then I looked at Pepe. "But we can't talk to a cat. At least, I can't. Can you?"

"Not most cats," he said, "but I have established a sort of simple pidgin language I use with your cat. Perhaps Albert could interview the cat of Boswell and then communicate what he has learned to me."

"You are going to invite Albert to be on our detective team?" I asked, incredulous. Pepe and Albert were always competing, like two siblings, for a higher ranking in my affections.

"Of course not," said Pepe quickly. "We would be simply requesting his services as a translator. One time only. Very minor position."

"We would need to find the cat first," I said.

"Yes," said Pepe. "He is no doubt in one of those horrid animal prisons."

"The animal shelter," I murmured. "Probably in Port Townsend, which is good, since then we can talk to Kevin."

Traffic was light leaving Sequim since everyone was going the other way. In fact, the cars were lined up bumper to bumper, starting at the Indian casino. I was glad I already had a room for the night in Port Townsend, though sad that I wouldn't be sharing it with Felix. I would have to try to call him again as soon as I got to Port Townsend.

By now, I was getting angry instead of sad. How dare he assume that I would cheat on him with someone like Hugh? Of course, I was perfectly willing to let Hugh think I was interested in order to get some information for our case, but that was an entirely different matter. Or was it?

I suddenly turned and looked at the sleeping Chihuahua on the passenger seat. Was he courting Phoebe just to get information? Or was he truly in love, as he claimed? For a talking Chihuahua, Pepe was not as easy to read as you would think.

My first stop was at the Port Townsend animal shelter. Sure enough, Boswell's cat had been taken there by the police, and no one had come to pick him up. Pepe wasn't allowed inside the facility, but he insisted on coming along, so I concealed him in my purse.

Once inside the cat room, he poked his little head out and looked around. The small room was lined with crates from floor to ceiling, and almost every one had a feline occupant. Big cats, little cats, black cats, calico cats, ginger cats, tabby cats, fluffy cats, skinny cat, fat cats. Pepe started shivering and disappeared into the depths of the purse.

I finally found the huge Maine coon in the corner of the room. He had turned his back to me, and all I could see was his fluffy tail, but the card identified him by name. Apparently his name was Precious Boswell.

"Precious!" I said, putting my fingers up to the bars of the cage. The magnificent animal lifted his head, turned around, looked at me with golden eyes, and then settled his head back on his paws, facing the back of the cage. I was not the person he wanted to see. His whole posture reeked of despair.

"Poor thing!" I said. "He must be in mourning for Boswell." I thought I saw the cat's ears twitch at the mention of his master's name.

"But, Pepe," I said, "do you really think we can talk to this cat?"

Pepe mumbled something I couldn't hear, but it sounded like he thought we should try. And I agreed. Just seeing this animal, so sunk in dejection, made me realize that we had to do something. His label said he was not available for adoption.

I went out to talk to the woman at the front desk. "What's the story with . . . um, Precious Boswell?" I asked.

"Oh, such a sad story," she said. "His owner died, and we have to hold the cat until the heir comes to pick him up."

"Oh, so they found Boswell's family?" I asked.

"I don't know if the gentleman is a member of his family," she said, looking down at some papers on her desk. "The name we have on file is Lionel Talent."

"That's weird," I said. "Isn't he the owner of the Floral Fantasy B&B?"

"You know him?" she asked.

"We must rescue this poor prisoner," insisted Pepe.

"Yes, he's the owner of a bed-and-breakfast just down the road."

"Well, that's good news," she said. "Let him know we are happy to turn the cat over to him if he brings proof of identity. The sooner you get the cat out of here, the better. Cats just do not do well under these conditions."

"I wonder why Boswell left the cat to Lionel," Pepe asked, as we headed out to the car.

"Well, we can ask him," I said. "We're headed there right now."

When we arrived at the Floral Fantasy B&B, Kevin and Lionel were busy at the front desk checking in an older couple. Pepe sniffed the air, trying to identify what we might have missed since we had left too early for breakfast.

"Overripe cantaloupe and salmon quiche," he declared. "You did much better at the waffle place, Geri!"

"But Albert would have loved it here," I said as we headed down the hall to the Rose Room. Albert, for some weird reason, loves cantaloupe. I was beginning to worry about my own cat. Although I knew Albert had plenty to eat—I always leave his bowl full of dry food, which he rarely deigns to devour—he had been alone for almost a day now. And although he pretends not to care if I am around, I know he does like company, if only to boss me around. "Maybe I can get Felix to go over and check on him."

"An excellent idea," said Pepe, as we entered the Rose Room. He began sniffing around the edges of the wall. "I wish they would not use a vacuum cleaner. It muddles up the scents."

I dialed Felix's number again, and to my surprise, he answered the phone. I was so startled, I didn't know what to say.

"Geri?" he asked. "Is that you, Geri?"

"I'm so sorry," I said when I found my voice.

"No, I'm the one who should be sorry," he said. "I made assumptions."

"I was questioning a suspect," I said.

There was a long pause. "Why don't you explain to me how his licking your hand was part of your investigation?" he finally said.

"He thought it was a date," I said.

"It certainly looked like a date," he said. "The two of you alone in the restaurant. The candles. The table overlooking the harbor."

"That was part of my strategy," I said, though it was actually Hugh's strategy.

"Someone was in here," Pepe said.

"Of course someone was in here," I said. "Someone made the bed and brought us new towels."

"Are you talking to your dog?" Felix asked.

"He's talking to me," I said.

There was another long pause. "Did your strategy work?" Felix asked at last.

"Not really," I confessed. "And if it made you unhappy, it wasn't worth it. I was so looking forward to spending a nice relaxing weekend with you at the B&B. I have a lovely queen-size bed and a claw-foot bathtub big enough for two!"

"Geri, please!" said Pepe. "A bath is bad enough. To share it with another would be twice as horrible."

But what sounded so unattractive to Pepe sounded appealing to Felix. "I like the idea," he said. "But don't you still have to work?"

"My boss gave me the weekend off," I said. "And you know how rare that is!"

Felix hesitated for a moment. "OK," he said at last.

"OK?" I could hardly believe it.

"Do not forget the cat!" Pepe commanded.

"But there is one favor," I added.

"What is it?"

"Well, we're sort of worried about Albert. Do you think you could stop by my house and check on him?" I had just given Felix a key to my house the previous week so he could take Pepe to the groomer to have his nails trimmed while I was working.

"Sure. Do you need anything else from your house?"

"We need the cat!" said Pepe.

"Do you think you could bring Albert here?"

"Bring your cat? In the car?" Felix sounded puzzled.

"You can put him in his carrying case," I said. "It's on the top shelf in the hall closet."

"But why do you want Albert?" Felix asked.

I looked at Pepe. No way I could tell him we needed the cat to question a suspect. Even though Felix had reluctantly agreed that maybe I thought my dog talked to me, he would never believe that my dog could talk to a cat.

"Pepe's lonely," I said. "He misses Albert."

Chapter 39

Pepe practically fell over when he heard that line.

"I had to come up with something plausible," I told him after I hung up.

"That is hardly plausible," said Pepe, shaking his head.

"What do we do now?" I asked.

"I think we need to question Lionel," Pepe said. "Did you not say that his name was on the list for the cat?"

"Yes!" I said. "And I want to talk to Kevin, too."

No one was at the front desk when we approached, but we could hear them in the back office, arguing.

"I can't believe you never told me!" Kevin was saying.

"Believe me, I didn't know either!" Lionel was saying. "He must have drawn it up while we were still together."

"But you told me that was over years ago!"

"It was!"

"So why would he leave you everything?"

Lionel laughed, a bitter laugh. "I suppose he never changed his will. Pretty ironic! A probate lawyer who doesn't update his will."

"Then we don't really need the money from the trust," Kevin said. "I can tell that bully Julian what to do with this stupid document." I could hear paper rustling.

"Geri, ring the bell!" said Pepe.

I slapped my hand down on the bell on the front desk. The next moment, Kevin poked his head out of the office. He did have a sheaf of papers in his hand.

"I heard you talking," I said. "I'm looking for a copy of the trust document. Do you have one?"

Kevin looked back over his shoulder, and the next moment Lionel appeared beside him in the doorway.

"You heard everything we said?" he asked.

I nodded.

"Let's talk," said Lionel, waving me into the office. It was actually a charming space, the walls painted mauve and covered with gilt-framed oil paintings of seascapes. There was a delicate French provincial desk with curvy legs and a small Victorian sofa covered in olive-green velvet against the wall. Across from a coffee table covered with lifestyle magazines were two comfy armchairs, with a fringed floor lamp between them.

"Very nice!" I said, looking around.

"Thanks to Kevin," said Lionel. "He has a great eye."

"Thank God, you can cook!" said Kevin.

The two smiled at each other, in mutual admiration, a distinct change from the acrimonious conversation I had interrupted. Was it all an act?

"Do you have a copy of the trust document?" I asked Kevin. He was still holding a sheaf of papers. Kevin looked at Lionel. Lionel looked back. Then he nodded.

"Yeah, we found it in one of the rooms," he said. "Julian, that's—"

"I know who he is," I said.

"He hired a private detective, and the guy left it behind."

"Can I see it?" I asked.

Kevin handed it over, reluctantly. I flipped through the pages. It seemed to be the same as the document I had obtained from Yolanda, although I hadn't studied every clause. I flipped to the back to see the names of the witnesses: Bernie Bickerstaff and Lionel Talent. The same names that had been on the other copy.

"I'm surprised Bickerstaff was a witness to the trust," I said.

Lionel nodded. "You know, Barry grabbed whoever was nearby, and Bickerstaff was right across the hall from him."

"But surely, given the subject matter . . ."

"Bickerstaff probably didn't even glance at the document. He was just there to witness the signature of the old lady. Anyway, he wasn't hired to represent the other side until much later."

"So is it possible," Pepe asked, "that Bickerstaff was killed because he was a witness?"

"Good question!" I said. "Is it possible Bickerstaff was killed because he was a witness?"

Lionel and Kevin looked at each other. "I don't see how," Lionel said.

"Well, he would have known something about Mrs. Carpenter's state of mind."

"If that's true, then you're in danger," Kevin said to Lionel.

"Yes," I said, "and how come you were a witness?"

Lionel blushed. "I was dating Barry at the time."

"And how could he sign it," Pepe asked, "if he had a stake in the outcome?"

"Well, he didn't have a stake in the outcome until now," I said.

"Yes, that's true," said Kevin, with a sigh, sliding one arm around Lionel's waist. "No one would have known that you would benefit from Boswell's estate."

"Except Boswell," Pepe pointed out.

"Except Boswell," I said.

Lionel cringed, then got thoughtful. "Well, if that's true, then that would make the trust invalid, wouldn't it?"

My heart sank. We had just scored a point for the other side.

"Yes, but now we don't need Lucille's money," Kevin pointed out. "You've got all the money from Boswell, plus his house."

"And his cat," I said.

"What?"

"Yes, his cat is at the pound with your name on

his cage. They're expecting you to come by and pick him up."

Lionel groaned. "But Kevin's allergic to cats."

"Maybe you can take him back to Boswell's house temporarily, until you figure out what to do with him," I suggested. "Or, better yet, why don't you put him in my room. I'm not allergic to cats. I have one at home." Albert should be arriving, along with Felix, in a few hours.

"Good idea," said Kevin.

"Your sister mentioned that she had a big fight with you," I said to Kevin. "Can you tell me about that?"

He looked embarrassed. "It was no big deal. We just have different opinions about Lucille. She's entitled to her opinion. I have mine. She didn't want me helping Julian. And I thought that if I helped Julian overturn the trust, that would help her." He looked at Lionel. "And us, of course."

"So you were willing to say Lucille Carpenter was crazy?"

"Well, she was crazy," said Kevin harshly. "She left all her money to her dogs!" He looked at Pepe. "No offense, little fellow. I like dogs!"

"No offense taken," said Pepe, "as long as you never call me 'little fellow' again!"

"And you?" I asked Lionel. "Did you think she was crazy?"

"She was a bit eccentric," he said. "She would come to visit Boswell and bring all of her dogs. Then she would spend all her time talking to the dogs instead of to Boswell. It was almost like she believed they were actually speaking to her."

"Like what?" I asked.

"You know, stuff like," he imitated the higher register of an old lady's voice, "Henry says he wants another bite of that delicious pâté!"

"Did her dogs ever say anything more intelligent?" I asked.

"That's pretty intelligent," said Pepe.

"No," said Lionel. "Just mostly requests for creature comforts. The sort of things people pretend their dogs are saying."

"If only they could handle the reality of our opinions," said Pepe.

Chapter 40

Jimmy G woke up feeling like he could hardly move. His mouth was dry, the light was too bright, and something was making an irritating thumping sound. He tried to roll over and go back to sleep, but was met by some kind of wall that hemmed him in. Only then did he realize that he was in the backseat of his car. The "wall" was the white leather upholstery that was now smack in his face. And of course he felt cramped—his six-foot frame was wedged into a space less than five feet long.

He rolled back over and tried to stretch, but his feet just ran into the armrest of the rear passenger door. "What a bunch of BS," he thought, grabbing the back of the front seat and pulling himself up to a sitting position. The blaze of light intensified as he got level with the car windows. Slowly, he recognized that his sensitivity to the light and his dry mouth and the thumping in his head were the signs of a hangover.

What the devil was Jimmy G doing last night, he asked himself as he dragged himself out of the car and took his bearings. He was standing in a huge parking lot, full of cars, the metal sparkling in the sun. Far off was a large building he recognized as the casino. That's when it came back to him: he had spent the night drinking and gambling, stumbling out of the casino just as the sun was coming up, too wasted to get in his car and drive.

And drive where? He remembered now he had been staying with a good-looking hippie chick in a motel the night before. But she had betrayed him. Taking naked photos of other men.

He looked at his watch. It read 9:30. It was a beautiful sunny morning, but Jimmy G didn't feel sunny at all. Wasn't the first time he'd slept in his car. Neither was it the first hangover he'd had. Or the first dame who had betrayed him.

But maybe she hadn't betrayed him, he thought. Maybe she just liked to take photos of naked men. After all, she was an artist. Artists did that kind of thing all the time.

Jimmy G climbed into the front seat and poked around in the ashtray until he found a stogie. He fired it up and puffed on it like mad. His next move would have to involve gallons of caffeine. And perhaps a little hair of the dog. He could find both at the casino.

But what was his next move with the dame? He figured he hadn't really given her a chance. Maybe she could explain those photos to Jimmy G. He pulled the camera out of the glove compartment and manipulated the buttons to look at the photos.

He winced when he got to the photos of the other guy. Who was this naked, blond-haired, bronze-bodied, pearly-toothed Adonis, anyway? But this time, he kept on going back. And sure enough, the photos that preceded the male model, for that's how Jimmy G now thought of him, were innocent enough: an old red barn in a field of lavender, a black-and-white dog sitting poised by a sign that read LOST LAKES LAVENDER FARM, a plate of cookies beside a white picket fence. Nice angles, he thought. She clearly had the artistic eye. Which must be why she had fallen for Jimmy G.

And he had blown it. Made off with her camera. Stood her up. He needed to make it up to her. Give her a second chance. And he knew where to find her. He would head off to Lost Lakes Lavender Farm just as soon as he was presentable. He got out of the car, tucking the camera in his pocket, and ambled off toward the casino.

Chapter 41

I woke up from a wonderful dream and realized that my dream had actually come true. I was gazing at the sleeping form of my handsome boyfriend. Felix lay sprawled on his back, one arm flung over my side. Pepe was curled up against my back, and I could hear Albert purring from above my head. The sun was shining, and the room smelled like roses.

Pepe can always tell when I wake up. I don't know how he knows, but he does. I wanted to prolong the moment, but as soon as he sensed I was awake, he jumped down from the bed and ran to the door and started scratching on it. Next thing I knew, Felix's dog, Fuzzy, had joined him, whining softly.

Felix opened his warm, dark eyes and asked, "Is this what it would be like to have kids?"

"Probably," I told him.

"No!" blurted Pepe. "*Niño*s would have already peed their diapers when you awoke, unlike yours truly, who waits to pee outside like a civilized being."

Felix sat up and rubbed at his eyes. "OK, you two, calm down, I'll take you out."

I smiled. Felix didn't even ask me if I'd do it. My ex would've given me a shove out the door and *told* me to do it. (We never had a dog, or kids, but that's beside the point.)

"Be quiet as you can," I called after him. "We don't want Kevin or Lionel to know about the extra animals." We had smuggled in Felix's dog, Fuzzy, and my cat, Albert, when Felix arrived the night before. He had to wake me up, as I had fallen asleep trying to read the legalese in the trust document.

Felix had thoughtfully brought a picnic: a French baguette, some grapes, a delicious cheese, and a bottle of white wine, which meant we could eat in the room with the animals. After the dinner, we took a stroll along the waterfront, with the two dogs, before returning to the room to try out the fabulously huge bathtub, which was a nice prelude to several hours of satisfying sex, with the animals locked in the bathroom so they wouldn't disturb us.

"We didn't get much sleep last night," complained Pepe as they went out the door.

"Well, neither did we, but we aren't complaining," I said, smiling at Felix.

"What do you have planned for today?" Felix asked, when he came back into the room with the dogs. He hadn't bothered to put on a shirt, just pulled on a pair of worn jeans. He was barefoot.

"What about coming back to bed?" I asked.

"As you wish," Felix said, wrapping his arms around me and pulling me down onto the bed. I was still just wearing the flimsy nightie I had packed

for my romantic weekend, a little black silk number
that revealed more than it concealed.

"Hey, Geri," said Pepe, "we have work to do!"

"Ha!" I said.

"You're pleased to have me under your control?"
asked Felix, who I had just pinned underneath me.

"Yes," I said, determined to ignore Pepe and
bending down to kiss Felix.

"And it is breakfast time!" said Pepe, hopping up
onto the bed.

Pepe never misses a meal. And he was right. It was
9:30, and breakfast was served only until 10:00 AM.

"Do you think you and Fuzzy could leave us
alone for just a few minutes?" I asked.

"Only a few minutes?" Felix asked. "I think we
can do better than that!" He pulled me down for
another kiss.

"Geri, you forget our mission!" Pepe said. "Boswell's
cat is in the building."

"The cat is in the building?" I sat up abruptly.

"Is that some kind of code?" Felix asked. "Are we
playing spies?"

"Sort of," I said. "We've been assigned to reconnoiter the dining room." I climbed off Felix, shaking
back my hair.

"OK, Agent Sullivan," said Felix. It is one of the
things that I love about him: he likes to play games.
"Agent Navarro, at your service."

I put on more suitable clothes—a pair of shorts
and an embroidered cotton top—without much
help from Felix, who kept trying to take them off
again, and without much help from Pepe, who kept
nagging me to hurry up. But finally Felix and I
arrived at the dining room, leaving the dogs in the

bedroom, just fifteen minutes before the end of breakfast.

Lionel poured us some coffee in painted china cups, then left to get the morning's offerings: lavender-crusted roasted red potatoes and a scramble with fresh tomatoes and spinach and a dash of parmesan, the plate garnished with a sprig of lavender. Apparently all the other guests had already left, headed for the lavender festival.

"So what are we reconnoitering?" Felix asked, after Lionel left the room.

"Breakfast for now!" I said, filling my fork with the roasted potatoes.

We talked about what we wanted to do during our weekend while we polished off the breakfast and drained the pot of coffee. Felix was fascinated by the idea of walking out to the end of Dungeness Spit, a five-and-a-half-mile-long sand spit that projects out into the bay near Sequim, while I wanted to drop by Carpenter Manor and check on the cocker spaniels.

"I have a favor to ask," Lionel said, as he cleared our plates.

"Yes?" I asked.

"We just picked up the cat from the pound and Kevin's already wheezing. You said you could keep him in your room. Is that OK with you?"

I nodded.

"I'll take him in there," he offered.

"Oh, no, let me do it!" I said, knowing how Lionel would feel if he saw the menagerie in our room: not just Pepe, but Felix's dog, Fuzzy, and my cat, Albert. I jumped up and followed Lionel into the cozy room behind the office. The cat was in a large crate in the center of the carpet.

I staggered under the weight of the huge cat and the heavy crate, but luckily Felix had come in behind me, and he got a firm grasp on the carrier and hauled the crate and the occupant out the door. I followed him.

Having four animals in a tiny bedroom is not ideal. Having four animals who don't know or like each other in a tiny bedroom is a disaster. Fuzzy and Pepe have developed a cordial relationship—after all, they helped each other take down a gangster in a previous case. But my cat Albert doesn't like Pepe, whom he considers a usurper, and Precious didn't like any of them. Poor cat. He was probably still in mourning for his person.

Albert took one sniff at the crate of the big cat, eliciting a hiss and an outstretched claw from Precious, and then stalked off to one corner of the bedroom.

"Why did you ask me to bring the cat?" Felix asked.

"I'm trying an experiment," I said.

"Really, what?"

"Interspecies communication."

"I don't understand."

"You know how Pepe speaks to me."

"And you speak to him!"

"Yes, and Pepe claims he can speak to Albert."

I saw the worry in Felix's brown eyes. "OK."

"And if Albert can speak to the cat who was in

the house when Boswell was killed, then we can find out who killed Boswell."

Felix pondered this for a moment. "So you are working still," he pointed out.

"It's just a good opportunity to try this out," I said. "Since the cat is in our possession."

Felix crossed his arms and looked glum.

"It could be a huge step for mankind," I said.

"Or catkind," said Pepe. "They are not known for their services to humanity. Unlike dogs."

"Even if you could get this cat to tell you what it saw . . ."

I knew it! Felix was coming around!

"How could you possibly use that evidence in a court of law?" Felix asked.

"We do not need a court of law," said Pepe. "We are judge, jury, and fury."

"Pepe and I will think of something," I said. "We always do."

"Well, it's worth trying," said Felix. "What do you want me to do?"

"Maybe you can take notes," I said. There was a pad of pink paper on the desk, embossed with the Floral Fantasy emblem. I handed it to Felix, along with a pen bearing the same logo.

"Pepe!" I said. "Tell Albert what we need."

Pepe approached Albert in the corner. Albert gave a few yowls. Pepe muttered. To my surprise, after a few minutes, Albert reluctantly sidled up to the crate containing the Maine coon. He sat and looked through the bars. The cat inside the crate hissed at him again.

"He is reassuring him that we mean him no harm," said Pepe.

"It doesn't sound that way," I said.

"Am I supposed to write that down?" Felix asked.

"Not yet!"

There was more yowling and hissing at the cat cage. Then Pepe, who was seated to the side of Albert but out of view of the cat in the crate, turned to me. "Precious is willing to help us if it means we find the person who killed his servant."

"Someone killed a servant?" I asked, confused.

"The person who fed him. I assume he means Boswell."

"Oh, of course!"

"What's going on?" asked Felix, his pen poised.

"The cat's going to help us!" I said. "Tell Precious that is our goal."

More muttering between Pepe and Albert, more yowling between Precious and Albert.

"What are they saying?" I asked Pepe.

Pepe shivered. "The cat is describing what he will do to the person when he is caught. It involves rending and tearing at the throat with sharp teeth. You do not want to hear it, Geri."

"OK," I said.

"What now?" asked Felix.

"Cat threats," I said. "Tell Albert to ask for a description."

Pepe muttered in Albert's ear, and another round of yowling and hissing ensued.

"What are they saying?" I asked.

"I don't understand cat," said Pepe. "I just caught a few words. Stranger. Hat." He conferred with Albert, then turned to me. "Apparently there was a stranger in the house that night. A man who treated the cat roughly. A man who stole some papers from Boswell's desk."

"Oh, that's great!" I said.

I turned to Felix: "Stranger in the house on the night of the murder. Treated the cat badly. No skip that. We don't need that. The man stole papers from Boswell's desk."

Felix looked confused. "Just write it down," I said.

"It's not going to stand up in a court of law," Felix said. "You're just pretending to talk to a dog, and then telling me to write it down."

"I'm actually translating from cat to pidgin to English," said Pepe. "And that is more than you can do!"

"It's just for our use," I said. "Go on!" I told my dog. "Ask him to describe the man."

There was more hissing and muttering. Then Pepe said to me: "The cat describes a man who wore a funny hat on his head and had brown eyes that bulged like an English bulldog's."

"That sounds almost like our boss," I said.

"That's what I thought," said Pepe. "I told you Jimmy G was there that night."

"What would Jimmy G be doing in Port Townsend?" I asked. "And did he murder Boswell?"

"What?" That was Felix. "What does this have to do with Jimmy G?"

"Just thinking out loud," I said.

Pepe turned back to Albert, who resumed his hissing and spitting dialogue. Pepe seemed to be able to get every other word. "Papers," he muttered.

"Rough man leaves. Boswell goes to kitchen. Returns. Sits at desk. Drinks yellow water. Falls over on floor. Hacking like he had a fur ball."

I repeated those words to Felix, who wrote them down. "The stranger leaves. Boswell goes to the kitchen. Returns to his desk. Sits down, drinks his lemonade and then falls to the floor, hacking and coughing like he had a fur ball."

"Poisoned!" said Pepe.

"Yes, we already knew that," I said.

"You already knew how Boswell died?" Felix asked.

"Well, he looked just like Bickerstaff, and the one thing they have in common is they both drank lemonade before they died," I said. "The question is, did the man in the hat put the poison in the lemonade?" I didn't want to use Jimmy G's name. I still didn't really believe our boss would murder someone.

Pepe had another consultation with the cat. "The man never went into the kitchen," he said. "In fact, the man was with Boswell the whole time he was in the house. The cat said he smelled like wet, rotting leaves."

"A cigar!" I said. That's exactly what Jimmy G's nasty cigars smelled like.

"You want me to write down cigar?" Felix asked. I nodded.

"The cat thinks the man put a spell on his servant that took effect after he left." Pepe turned to me. "Apparently cats believe in witchcraft."

"The cat thinks Boswell was killed by a witch," I said to Felix.

"A witch who wears a hat and smokes cigars," said Felix, looking at his notes.

He held my gaze for a long time. I could practically guess what was going on behind those big, soulful eyes. He was thinking, "My girlfriend is as crazy as a loon."

Chapter 42

A knock on the door broke the trance.

"Geri, it's Lionel!" said the voice on the other side. "I've got to get the cat up to Boswell's house before we leave for the lavender festival."

"Oh, don't come in!" I shouted out quickly. "I'm just getting dressed."

"Geri, we should offer to take the cat," Pepe said. "We could examine the crime scene."

"Great idea!" I told him. "Do you want us to take the cat for you?" I called out.

"Oh, that would be fabulous!" said Lionel. "We're in a hurry to get to Lost Lakes. Kevin promised to help his sister in the gift shop, and I've got to deliver the lavender cheesecakes I made."

"Just leave the keys on the front desk," I said. "We'll deliver the cat, and then return the keys to you. We're going to Lost Lakes, too!"

And that's how it turned out that less than half an hour later, we were tiptoeing up the steps of

Boswell's gorgeous Victorian mansion. Precious seemed to get more upset the closer we got. Albert doesn't like car rides either, but Precious wailed constantly from the moment the car started—maybe it was because we took Felix's old beater of a car, as it was set up for carrying animals, but surely smelled like a lot of dogs. I thought Precious would stop wailing when the car stopped, but he howled even louder, heart-breaking cries that reminded me of how he sounded on the morning we found Boswell dead. Felix carried the heavy cat crate up the front steps as I struggled to turn the key in the lock. Finally I applied the right pressure and the ponderous door swung open slowly.

The air in the house was warm and stale. We set the crate down in the hallway, with its welter of Victorian objects, and lifted the latch on the door. Precious sprang out and ran up and down the hall, galloping, like a wild thing, like a cat on a rampage.

"What's that about?" I asked Pepe.

"I have never understood that behavior," said Pepe. "In a dog, it would mean he was full of glee, but in a cat?" He shook his head.

"Probably he's just releasing pent-up energy," said Felix. "He has been cooped up in a crate."

Then Precious stopped in midgallop and dashed into a door at the end of the hall.

"That's the study," I said to Felix, "that's where Boswell died." I was reluctant to reenter the crime scene, but Pepe was not.

"Let us investigate," he said. "We will, no doubt, turn up something the police did not." And he ran down the hall and disappeared into the room as well.

I tiptoed down the dim hall with Felix close on my heels.

"Why is there so much stuff in here?" Felix asked, as he sidled sideways past an unopened box and ducked under a carved wooden hanging lantern.

"I don't know," I said. "I think Boswell was a bit of a pack rat." I almost knocked over a Japanese screen. "I heard a rumor that Boswell was skimming money from the trust. The judge was threatening to hire a forensic accountant."

"The judge?"

"One of the heirs," I said, as we reached the doorway.

The window blinds were rolled up, and the room was flooded with sunlight. I felt I could smell the death in the room. I knew that Pepe could.

Precious had jumped up on the desk and was looking around, puzzled. So was I. The top of the desk, a nice dark mahogany, was completely bare. The police must have taken away all the papers to sort through them for clues.

Precious jumped down from the desk with a thump and headed for the kitchen.

It looked quite different as well, with black fingerprint dust all over the granite counters and the back door. The pitcher of lemonade was gone, which made sense as that was probably the way the poison was administered.

With one mighty bound, the cat jumped up onto the granite counter, paced back and forth along its surface, then clawed at the closest cupboard.

Thinking that Precious was hungry and was asking for treats, I opened the cupboard to find Boswell's liquor cabinet. It contained a few dusty bottles of useless liqueurs like crème de menthe and obscure syrups like grenadine, probably secured for some recipe once and never used again, and a big plastic gallon bottle of vodka in the front.

"Well, that's weird," I said. "Why would the cat want something from the liquor cabinet?" But before I could answer that question, Precious jumped down, ran over to his water bowl, lapped at the water, then fell over, writhing and hacking and coughing.

"Oh my God!" I said, "The cat is dying, too!"

But Pepe stopped me. "Bravo! Senor Precious," he said. "Bravo! That was the sort of performance that could land you a starring role on *Paraíso Perdido!*"

Precious, as if understanding Pepe, got up, did a long feline stretch, and then began meowing plaintively. It was the cry of a hungry cat.

"He's hungry!" said Pepe.

"Yes, I know," I said, a little grumpy. "I can speak a little cat, too."

I followed Precious into the pantry area and poured some kibble into his bowl. Of course, he refused to eat it in front of us—that is, Pepe, Fuzzy, Felix, and me.

"What am I missing?" I said. "Precious was acting out the murder scene. He was trying to tell us something." I looked at the counter, where the lemonade pitcher had been. "But we knew all that before: the poison was in the lemonade. Boswell drank it when he sat down at his desk and died."

"But how did it get in the lemonade?" asked Felix.

"Yes, that's puzzling, because presumably Boswell

came home and either bought the lemonade at the store or made it from frozen." I opened up the refrigerator. More wails from Precious. I could see why: there was a can of wet cat food on the top shelf. I got it down, pried the lid off, and spooned it onto a plate, which I set on the floor in the pantry. Precious turned his fluffy butt to us and began chowing down. I returned to the refrigerator.

"There's no lemonade in here," I said, looking at the contents. Some pâté. A jar of caviar. A deli container of mushrooms.

"Probably the police would have taken it to test," Felix observed.

I opened up the side door of the freezer and noticed several cans of frozen lemonade. "Or he made a fresh batch from frozen when he got home from work." I looked at the brand: one of the big manufacturers. "It doesn't seem like Boswell. He seemed to have had gourmet tastes."

"Probably doesn't matter what kind of lemonade you drink, if what you're really doing is trying to cover up the flavor of cheap vodka," said Felix, wryly.

"Could it be that the vodka was poisoned?" I asked. "Rather than the lemonade?"

"That is what the cat was trying to tell us!" Pepe said.

"Good work, Geri!" said Felix, looking at me with admiration. "You should share that theory with the police."

So I did. Neither of the homicide detectives was in, but I was able to leave a voice message. Then

we were finally on our way to the lavender festival.
Unfortunately, we weren't moving very fast. Traffic
was stop-and-go all along the main highway.

"What about Jimmy G?" Felix asked. He was driving because we decided his dog-mobile would be
better for the dogs. They were both confined in
crates in the back, because Felix is very strict about
letting dogs ride loose in the car. Pepe, to his indignation, was in Albert's cat carrier

"It stinks like a cat!" he declared.

"What about him?" I wasn't sure I wanted to talk
about my boss.

"Didn't you mention his name as having something to do with all this?"

"If the man with the hat was Jimmy G, and the
man with the hat stole papers from Boswell's office,
then Jimmy G stole papers from Boswell," Pepe
said. "That is logic!"

"Why would he steal papers from Boswell?" I
asked.

"It seems like Jimmy G is capable of anything,"
said Felix grimly. He did not have a great deal of respect for my boss. Neither did Pepe, actually.

"Do you recall that Lionel said the judge had
hired a private detective who left behind the trust
document you have in your purse?" Pepe asked.

"Yes, and he said the judge hired the private
detective," I pointed out. "But we were hired by
Boswell."

"This is a mystery," said Pepe. "And one we can
solve only by confronting Jimmy G."

"Good idea!" I said, looking at the bumper of the
car in front of us. "And I have plenty of time to talk
to him." I dug my cell phone out of my purse and

dialed Jimmy G's number. It rang a few times, and then Jimmy G picked up. His voice sounded shaky. I could hear the sound of slot machines in the background and some soft jazz.

"Where are you?" I asked.

"Casino," he said. "What's up, doll?"

"I've got a question to ask you, and it's important!"

"Fire away!" he said. "Jimmy G's had two cups of joe and is starting to get back in the swing of things."

"Then good, you'll be able to tell me what you were doing at Boswell's house on the night he died!" I said.

There was a long silence. I heard chinging sounds and the canned music. "Are you there?" I asked.

"Sure! Jimmy G is just impressed by your detecting abilities." He gave a little laugh. "How did you figure that out?"

"I'm good at what I do!" I said.

"And do not forget who really broke the case open!" insisted Pepe.

"Well, to tell you the truth, Jimmy G did call upon Boswell." He paused. "Do the police know this?"

"Not yet," I said. "I wanted to confirm it with you first.'

"Jimmy G can explain everything, doll," he said quickly.

"Well, explain away. I'm listening."

"Look, Jimmy G is about to wrap up this case. That's why you got the weekend off. Jimmy G has everything under control."

"I want to know what you were doing at Boswell's house," I repeated. "Otherwise, I am calling the police."

"Jimmy G didn't want to tell you this," he said. "But Boswell called up Jimmy G. Was concerned about how the case was going. Thought he needed a more experienced operative. Wanted Jimmy G to take over. Jimmy G couldn't say no. Important client and all that."

"Boswell was unhappy working with me and Pepe?" I was indignant.

"Let's just say he was not overly fond of dogs," said Jimmy G.

"But he represented them . . ." I realized I was getting sidetracked. That happens all the time when talking with Jimmy G. "Never mind. So what were you doing there?"

"Boswell gave Jimmy G a copy of the trust document."

"But you wanted me to find it."

"Um, unfortunately, Jimmy G lost that copy."

"At the Floral Fantasy B&B!" I said. "You were there! But Lionel said the private detective who stayed with them was hired by Julian, the judge."

Another long pause. I thought I heard a gulp. "Now you see how Jimmy G works," he said, finally. "All a ruse to get the situation squared away. Jimmy G plays one side against the other. The double double cross. A Jimmy G specialty."

"I don't know what side you're on now," I said, frustrated by his double talk.

"Jimmy G is always looking out for Jimmy G," he said. "So if you stick with Jimmy G, you'll be fine."

And then he hung up.

I relayed the results of my unsatisfying conversation to Pepe and Felix. And I suppose Fuzzy was listening, too, although we had never had any indication that Fuzzy was capable of communicating the way Pepe could. She was extremely loyal, though. A trait I really admire. And a quality that seemed to be missing in Jimmy G.

Chapter 43

The phone call from Geri sobered Jimmy G. His darn girl Friday was starting to show some aptitude for the private detecting business. Too much, as far as Jimmy G was concerned. He wanted someone to type, answer phones, look at him adoringly, and say things like "Wow, I could never do what you do! It's so dangerous." Not some dame who was going to call him up, all accusing, "What were you doing and with whom?" None of her business. She worked for him, not the other way around.

And really, when he thought about it, and he had a lot of time to think, as the traffic was terrible, he had managed to deliver what the judge wanted, so the job was done. No harm, no foul. Jimmy G just needed to collect some moola from the judge and let the police catch the killers and hook up again with Jillian.

By the time he arrived at Lost Lakes Lavender Farm and found a place to park, miles back along the edge of the road, behind some buses, the festival was in full swing. As he trudged down the highway, another bus passed him and disgorged a load of passengers. He followed them up the long driveway, past the lavender fields.

The place was swarming with people. In the barn, he saw a crowd gathered around the still. Colleen, in overalls and cowboy boots, was demonstrating how it was used. On the stage at one end of the yard, a guitarist and an accordionist were playing a polka. Some toddlers were turning in circles on the lawn in front of the musicians while their mothers applauded. Under a tent alongside the house, women in yellow aprons were serving cookies and slices of cheesecake and glasses of lavender lemonade. One of the young men who worked at the Floral Fantasy B&B came out the side door of the house, wearing a frilly purple apron and carrying a cake, decorated with purple frosting.

Jimmy G surveyed the booths that lined the lawn. Smoke rose from a grill in a booth on the end, which advertised Lavender Rubbed Ribs. The smell was tantalizing. Other booths offered jewelry, T-shirts, lavender wreaths, lavender jelly, and pastel art prints of lavender fields.

With a start, Jimmy G recognized Jillian talking with an older couple who were pawing through a box of the prints on the table at the front of her booth. She looked delectable in a cropped lilac halter top and a pair of tight pink shorts. She also looked tired. He wondered if she had spent the night worrying about where he was. A sudden feeling of guilt swept over him. This lovely broad was probably pining over him, and he had carelessly toyed with her affections.

He bounded up to her, suddenly eager to make amends, certain she would welcome him with open arms.

"That will be forty-four ninety-five," she was saying to the old man, who handed over some crumpled bills. Jillian turned to a metal box on the table, rooted through it, and pulled out a few ones, which she pressed into his hand.

"Thank you so much, dear," said the old woman, clutching a plastic-wrapped print to her bosom. "You are truly an artist."

As the couple wandered off, Jillian turned her attention to Jimmy G. To his dismay, her eyes went cold.

"What are you doing here?" she said.

"You invited me," he replied, suddenly unsure of his status. He pretended to look down at the prints on the table. Most were landscapes of lavender fields and farmhouses and old barns. In the back of the booth, he saw that she was at work on something new. An easel was set up, and a cloth was draped across the canvas.

"That was yesterday, Mr. Dangerous," she said. Her voice was flat.

"Jimmy G got a little bent out of shape when he saw the photos you took," he said, pulling the camera out of his pocket and holding it out to her.

"So that's where my camera went," said Jillian. "I had to paint your picture from memory. I did pretty well, too."

She whisked the cover off the easel in the back, and Jimmy G was shocked to see a nude portrait of himself, sprawled on the bed at the motel. She

had done a fairly good job of capturing the right
proportions.

"Hey! Cover that up!" he said, glancing around.
"Wouldn't want to give any other dames the idea
Jimmy G is available."

Jillian complied with a pretty smile. "So where
did you spend the night last night?" she asked.

Jimmy G had an idea. "Jimmy G got called away
on a case," he said.

"Really? Did you have to use your weapon?" Her
eyes got bright.

"Natch," he said. "Jimmy G! Big gun for hire.
What is your desire?"

"Well, to be frank," Jillian looked around, to one
side and then the other, as if she were afraid someone was listening, "there is something you could do
for me."

Chapter 44

When we finally arrived at Carpenter Manor, the entrance to the driveway was blocked with a chain. Someone had painted NO PARKING in bright red letters on a piece of wood and propped it up against the chain. I got out of the car to release the chain and move the board so Felix could drive through and up the driveway to the house. I followed him more slowly, looking over at all the merriment happening next door. It seemed Colleen had been able to attract a good crowd to her farm. I counted four buses parked below the lavender fields, so she must have been able to get back on the bus tour.

Felix was releasing Pepe and Fuzzy from their confinement when I reached the car, which was parked in back of a little scooter and an old Chevy. Pepe ran over to the door, his tail wagging furiously.

"Happy to see the cocker spaniels?" I asked him.

"No, it is Phoebe! My love is here!" he declared, turning around in circles of joy.

"That doesn't make any sense," I said, but, sure

enough, when Yolanda welcomed us into the living room, I saw the sleek and slender Phoebe towering above the churning pack of cocker spaniels. She was the only one who did not seem excited to see us, although she did let Pepe go up and sniff her. Perhaps the gift of the bacon had helped him win a little favor. Fuzzy dove right in and started nipping at the cockers playfully. Felix had to call her off, which was difficult as I was trying to introduce him to Yolanda.

"I brought back the trust document," I said, digging it out of my purse. I hoped it looked enough like the one Yolanda had loaned us that she wouldn't realize I had lost that one. She took it in her hands and began examining the pages.

Clara came in, dressed in a purple T-shirt that read LOST LAKES LAVENDER FARM. She greeted us and explained she had just come over to borrow some masking tape.

"How are you two doing?" I asked, expecting to hear a tale of woe.

"Actually, great!" said Clara.

"Yes, I've already hired a new lawyer," said Yolanda. "She comes highly recommended, and she lives in Sequim, so it's more convenient than working with Barry." A cloud passed over her face. "Have the police figured out who killed him?"

"No, but we have figured out how it happened!" Pepe said.

I shook my head. "I don't think so. But we have a new theory. We think someone might have poisoned Boswell's vodka."

Yolanda and Clara looked at each other.

"He did like his drinks. What did he call that?" Yolanda asked Clara.

"A lemon drop?" she suggested.

"He even kept a bottle of vodka here," she said.

Pepe and I looked at each other.

"Do you suppose someone has tampered with that, too?" I asked.

"I'll fetch it," said Clara.

"No! Don't do that," I said. "It might have fingerprints on it. Let my dog sniff it."

Yolanda and Clara looked at each other again. Then they looked at Felix. He just smiled and shrugged his shoulders. I carried Pepe into the kitchen, where Caroline was whisking some cream in a stainless-steel bowl. Little slices of pound cake were set out in china bowls and covered with fresh strawberries.

The vodka was up in a cupboard on top of the refrigerator. Caroline said she hadn't touched it since it was put up there. I set Pepe on top of the refrigerator, and he sniffed the bottle from a cautious distance.

"I smell nothing but Mr. Boswell," he said, "and also the yummy grease from a steak that was cooked in this kitchen last night."

"Did you have steak last night?" I asked Yolanda. She nodded. "How did you know that?"

"Detecting skill!" I said.

"My detecting skill!" said Pepe.

Pepe sat down on top of refrigerator and nodded his head with a regal air. "I can see why cats like being up so high," he said. "You feel superior!"

"I don't think this bottle is contaminated, but I

don't know," I said. "Don't touch it until we find out from the police if the poison is in the other bottle."

"But I am too far from Phoebe," said Pepe. "Take me down, Geri, *por favor.*"

I lifted him down and carried him into the living room. Phoebe had stayed behind and was standing, gazing out the window at the scene next door.

"Why is Phoebe here?" I asked.

"Colleen asked if we could keep her during the weekend," Yolanda said. "She thought it would be too chaotic to have a dog running around the farm. The festival organizers really frown on that. Some people are afraid of dogs."

"But Phoebe is worried. She senses an evil force at work," said Pepe. "She cannot relax while she is over here. She needs to be protecting her property and her person."

"Poor dog!" I said, rubbing the top of her velvety head. She turned and gazed at me with soulful dark eyes. Believe me, I could almost hear her saying, "Take me back home where I belong."

"I wish I could take you over there," I said.

"She'll be fine here," said Yolanda firmly.

"Oh, I have one other thing I need to tell you," I said. "I don't think you should take Henry to the vet on Monday. I think Hugh is doing unnecessary surgeries on the dogs."

"Why would he do that?" asked Clara.

"Well, he gets paid, doesn't he, for any services he performs? And that kind of surgery can be dangerous, especially in an older dog."

"Sure, I'll cancel it," said Yolanda. "I never really liked him. I thought he was a bit sleazy, to tell you the truth."

"Yes, sleazy is the word," said Felix.

I ignored him.

"Thanks for bringing me the trust document," said Yolanda. "Now I can give it to Sheila and she can get started." She flipped through the pages.

"Oh, this is interesting," she said, stopping at a page near the front. Her eyes narrowed as she read the sentences over again and again. "Look at this, Clara!" She passed the papers to her niece.

Clara studied the line Yolanda was pointing out. "It looks all right to me."

"But it says that the trust applies to all the dogs living on the property at the time of Lucille's death and their issue."

"Yes."

"That would include the farm."

"How do you figure that?" Clara asked.

"Well, the farm is owned by Mrs. Carpenter's estate. Colleen is just leasing it."

"A good point!" Clara said. "You'll have to ask Sheila her opinion, but I don't see how it makes much difference."

"Phoebe," said Yolanda, looking over at the graceful black-and-white dog. Phoebe looked up briefly, then returned to her vigilant posture.

"Was Phoebe living on the property when Mrs. C died?" Clara asked.

"I think so," said Yolanda. "We'd have to ask Colleen."

"Surely if that was true, Colleen would have noticed it sooner," Clara said.

"Well, I don't think she's ever seen a copy of the trust document," I said. "I don't think any of the heirs have." Except for the judge, and he had torn it up. And Kevin, and he had stolen it from Jimmy G.

"Does this mean what I think it means?" asked Pepe, his voice full of wonder.

"What do you think it means?" I asked.

"I think it means Colleen doesn't have any more money troubles," said Clara, reading a little farther down the page. "Because anyone who is caring for one of the dogs or one of their issue receives an allowance, plus expenses."

"I think it means Phoebe is exactly my favorite type of bitch!" said Pepe. "Beautiful and rich!"

Chapter 45

"So you're heading over to the farm for the lavender festival?" Clara asked. "You can come with me the back way, if you want."

"That would be great," I said.

"But you can't bring the dogs," she said.

I looked at Fuzzy and Pepe. Fuzzy was wrestling with one of the younger cockers. I think it was Victoria, the chocolate-colored one. Pepe was gazing dreamily at Phoebe, who was still glued to the window.

"Could we leave them here?" I asked Yolanda.

"Absolutely," she said. "It's good for the dogs to have some company."

As Felix and I followed Clara out the door, I commented on the change in her aunt. "She seems like a different person," I said. "So take charge. So confident."

"I know," said Clara. "It's amazing. She's always had other people bossing her around—Boswell, most recently. But having the full responsibility for the dogs, and defending the trust—that's really

energized her. She's already cleaned up the office
and turned it into her command center. And she's
organizing a memorial service for Boswell. It turns
out she just needed something more fulfilling to do
than take care of a pack of yapping dogs."

We followed Clara through the gate in the chain-
link fence and approached Colleen's farm from the
back. The chickens squawked at us as we passed
their pen. We picked our way over some hoses that
were lying in the garden rows.

"Have you heard anything more about who shot
at the dogs?" I asked.

"No, not a word. I think the police department
is just swamped making arrangements for the festival."

"And how's Jay?"

"Oh, no problems there," said Clara. "He'll be
fine."

"It was very brave of him to run straight at the
shooter," I said.

"He is very brave," she said, with a blush.

"So have you been over here today?"

"Oh, yeah, I've been here since six this morning."
Clara led us in the back door of the farmhouse. It
was hot and humid inside. The ovens were going
full blast, I guess, and the house was full of people:
women in yellow aprons, volunteers in purple
T-shirts, vendors wearing lilac-colored baseball
caps. Clara handed off the masking tape to Jay, who
was sitting at a table in the living room, ticking off
the names of volunteers who were coming in to
sign up for various tasks.

I looked around—I studied interior design,
and I'm always curious about how people deco-

rate their homes. It seemed like Colleen might have inherited the furniture from her father: a nubbly beige sofa, a dark brown Barcalounger, a boxy old TV on a wooden table, a rag rug on the scuffed hardwood floor. The wallpaper was a faded yellow-brown with vertical maroon stripes.

She could really use her new fortune, I thought. Maybe she would hire me to redecorate the place. Just then, Colleen breezed in the door, smelling intensely of lavender, and rushed past us.

"We have the best news for you, Colleen," Clara sung out. But Colleen said, "Just a minute," and hurried down the hall.

"Should we really tell her?" I asked Clara.

"Tell her what?" Jay asked.

"We haven't had a lawyer look at it," I pointed out.

"What are you guys talking about?" Jay wanted to know.

"Colleen might inherit a whole bunch of money, just because of Phoebe," Clara said.

"What?" That was Kevin, coming out of the kitchen.

"Oh, hi, Kevin," Clara said. "Yes, the trust document says that whoever is taking care of a dog that lives on Mrs. C's property gets an allowance and the use of the property for as long as the dog—and its issue—lives."

"I didn't see that clause in the trust document," Kevin said.

"When did you have a copy of the trust document?" Colleen asked him, coming out of the hallway and giving him a hug. She still smelled like lavender, but it wasn't as strong.

Kevin looked a bit embarrassed. "A guest left a

copy behind," he said. "Actually, a private detective that Julian hired."

"What did this private detective look like?" I asked.

Kevin narrowed his eyes. "He dressed like a forties cartoon of a detective," he said.

"Fedora, suspenders, narrow moustache, bulging eyes," I said.

"Yes! How did you know?" Kevin asked. "In fact, he's here. I saw him just a minute ago at Jillian's booth."

"Jillian is here?"

"Yes, I told her she could have a booth here," Colleen said. "I felt sorry for her. She didn't have enough money to pay the deposit for a booth at the fairgrounds or in town."

"I need to talk to that guy," I said.

"How do you know him?" Colleen asked.

"He's my boss," I said.

"But he's working for Julian," Kevin said. "I thought you were working for Boswell and the dogs."

"That's what I need to figure out," I said.

I went storming out the front door and plunged right into the crowd, with Felix close behind me.

The front yard was awash with people. They were forming lines outside the booth that sold the specialty cocktail of the day; they were standing and swaying in front of the stage, where a guitar player and accordionist played rancheras and polkas; they were thronging the aisles of the gift shop; they were gathering around the still as the brownish liquid gushed out of the copper tubing and squirted into a plastic bucket; they were sitting at picnic tables with plates of food purchased from the kitchen booth, where Lionel was dishing up skewers of lavender-marinated chicken and green salad dressed with lavender-honey dressing; they were wandering through the fields of fragrant bushes that stretched out in long purple rows and scented with air with their sweet perfume.

It took a while, but I finally found Jillian's booth, at the end of the line of booths. But it was empty. She had boxes full of the plastic-covered prints we had seen at her gallery lined up on a table in front. A few larger pictures were propped on stands on a side table, and there was a large easel in the back that was covered with a cloth.

"Where's the artist?" I asked the young woman who was selling lavender wands and lavender wreaths at the next booth over.

"Oh, she went on an errand. She asked me to watch it for her," she said. "Do you want to buy something?"

"No, I'm just looking," I said, shuffling through the prints right in front of me.

"This looks like Phoebe!" said Felix, pulling out a copy of the print that Pepe had wanted, showing the farm dog sitting by the Lost Lakes sign.

"I think it is Phoebe," I said. "Don't let Pepe know there are copies of it. He thinks he has the original."

Something about the print bugged me, and then I realized what it was. For Jillian to have captured the scene so well, she must have been on the property earlier. And that meant she had been near the cocker spaniels. That, combined with the suspicious chocolate-chip cookie and her disturbing paintings, made me wonder if she was the one who was trying to harm the dogs.

"Is it OK if I look at these others more closely?" I asked the neighboring vendor, inching my way behind the table.

"Sure," she said. "I don't think Jillian would mind."

I slipped between the poles of the booth and studied the pastels propped on the table. There was no way to tell exactly when they had been painted, but there was a little camera sitting next to them. I picked it up and found the buttons that would allow me to view the photos.

To my horror, the first photo that came up was one of my boss, completely nude and lying on a rumpled bed, with a silly grin on his face. The date stamp said it had been taken only the previous day. I rapidly paged back past that, only to be even more horrified by the sight of Hugh the Handsome, sprawled out nude on one of the steel exam tables in his vet clinic. And the date stamp on that one was the previous night, in fact, the evening of the day when I had first visited Hugh, the evening when his clinic was supposedly burglarized. Clicking back, I finally came to the photos that confirmed my suspicions: one of Phoebe outside the sign for Lost Lakes on the day when the chocolate-chip cookies were left for the dogs, and then, even more damning, a photo of a plate of chocolate-chip cookies, lying by the driveway of Carpenter Manor.

"It was Jillian!" I said, turning to Felix and waving the camera around. "She's the one who's trying to kill the dogs!" But in my enthusiasm I knocked against the picture on the easel, and it went flying.

I set the camera down as I bent to pick the painting up.

"Ack!" I was really sorry I did. I was staring at a large oil painting of my boss. The painter had established a point of view near his feet and painted him as he lay in a rumpled bed, every detail of his anatomy displayed in great detail. Except for the fedora on his head, he was completely nude.

"Oh my God!" I said, turning my head away and groping for the cloth on the ground to cover it up. I wanted to erase the image from my brain, but I feared it would stay with me forever.

"Is that who I think it is?" Felix asked.

"Please just let me forget I ever saw this," I mumbled.

In my haste to cover up the painting, I knocked it off the stand. It landed facedown in the dirt. When I picked it up, some dirt and grass clung to the wet paint. I tried to brush it off and got flesh-colored paint all over my hands and my polka-dotted navy sundress.

And just as I was holding it, paint side out, to avoid further contamination to the painting, I looked up and saw Jimmy G looking at me from the other side of the booth, a look of horror on his face.

Chapter 46

Jimmy G had been flattered when Jillian took him by the hand and led him away from the booth, after asking the vendor next door to keep an eye on her merchandise. He was keeping his eye on her as she threaded her way through the crowds, through the barn, and through the garden behind it, looking back over her shoulder frequently as if she was afraid they were being followed. He assumed she was interested in a roll in the hay, but he didn't see how they were going to manage that with all the people around. Even behind the barn, a few tourists had gotten separated from the hordes in front and were wandering around, like lost ants off the trail, poking their noses into the greenhouse and peering into the henhouse.

"Where are we going, doll?" Jimmy G asked.

"Shhh! It's a secret," said Jillian, putting one finger to her lips.

Well, fine. Jimmy G didn't have anything to do except be led around by a gorgeous dame. He saw they were heading toward the back of the property along the fence line, which was planted on the other side with bamboo. But then they reached a little gate, which swung open and permitted them entry into the yard next door. He could see the back of a big house, designed to look like an English cottage, only on a grand scale, and a formal garden bordered by trimmed hedges.

"I just discovered the gate today," Jillian said, "while watching Clara."

That didn't mean anything to Jimmy G, but he could see the logic: why not sneak into the next-door neighbor's yard for a romantic rendezvous. This was one bold chick, but Jimmy G liked that! He probably wouldn't admit it, if anyone asked, but Jimmy G liked dames who took charge.

Jillian ducked down behind a hedge and motioned for Jimmy G to join her.

"Here goes!" thought Jimmy G, sliding in beside her and tumbling her down into the soft grass. He tried to kiss her but, to his surprise, she hauled off and punched him in the nose

"What?" he sat up, holding his schnoz, which was bleeding.

"What do you think you're doing?" she asked, re-arranging her top. Jimmy G's enthusiastic embrace had caused a wardrobe malfunction.

"I thought that's what you wanted," he said, wiping at his nose with his handkerchief.

"No, stupid. I just want your weapon!" And Jillian made a lunge for the gun in his shoulder holster.

Jimmy G pushed her back. "No one touches Jimmy G's weapon!" he said.

"Fine!" she said, with a pretty pout. "Then you will have to shoot the dogs!"

"What are you talking about?"

"Those stupid dogs. They'll be coming out the door any minute now. Yolanda has them trained like clockwork. They go out right after lunch. And I want you to shoot them!"

Jimmy G worked that out in his mind. "So you're the one who's been trying to attack the dogs," he said.

"Yes, and it hasn't worked. I tried putting poison in some cookies, and the stupid dog walker noticed the cookies and wouldn't let the dogs eat them. How was I supposed to know that chocolate is dangerous for dogs?"

"Jimmy G wouldn't have known that either," he said, trying to be sympathetic.

"And then I tried shooting them with a rifle, but I missed." She shrugged her shoulders. "I'm not very good with guns."

Jimmy G remembered the conversation in the bar the night he met Jillian. "That was you? You told me someone got shot."

"Yes, some stupid farmworker got in the way while I was trying to shoot the dogs." Jillian tossed her hair back. "So you can see why I need you, Mr. Dangerous." She looked at him coquettishly. "When I get the fortune, I'll pay you. I'll pay you a lot." She ran her hand along his arm.

Jimmy G hesitated, trying to buy time.

"Why are you so angry at the dogs?"

"First, they got all my mother's love. Then they got all her money. It's not fair!"

Jimmy G tried to think. He was aware of the clock ticking down. The dogs would be coming out any minute, and Jillian expected him to do something.

Jimmy G was willing to do a lot of things, but shooting dogs was not one of them.

He came up with an idea. "Well, Jimmy G can handle this assignment," he said. "But you shouldn't be anywhere around. So how about you go back to your booth to establish an alibi, and Jimmy G will meet you there."

Jillian sulked but finally agreed when Jimmy G pointed out that the fortune would not do her much good if she ended up in jail. He was shaking by the time she wandered off. What now? He couldn't shoot dogs. He had to get out of there. He waited for three minutes, five minutes, ten minutes. Then he figured enough time had passed. He would make up a story, tell Jillian that he had taken care of the dogs, and then figure out what to do next.

He tiptoed out of the yard—the dogs still had not made their postprandial appearance—and made his way back to Jillian's booth. And to his shock, Jillian wasn't there. Instead he saw his girl Friday holding a huge nude portrait of him. He had to admit, just for a second, that he looked pretty darn hot.

Then he ordered her to put it down and cover it up! "What are you doing here?" he asked. "Where's Jillian?"

"We haven't seen her," said Geri, nodding at Felix, who nodded at Jimmy G. It was weird to see his operative without her little dog.

"Where's the rat-dog?" he said.

"Over at the house next door, with the other dogs," she said.

Jimmy G got a sinking feeling in his stomach.

"Jillian is trying to kill the dogs," he said. "She wanted me to shoot them."

"I know!" said Geri. "I just figured that out. We've got to call the police."

"What we have to do is find her!" said Felix. "Before something happens to the dogs!"

Chapter 47

Felix and I looked at each other. We both realized at the same moment that our dogs were with the cocker spaniels Jillian was trying to kill.

"Where was she the last time you saw her?" I asked Jimmy G.

"By the gate," he said, pointing toward the back of the property.

"We've got to find her!" I told him.

And Felix and I took off running. But we were a bit late. Before we had even pushed our way through the crowds on the lawn, we started hearing screaming and barking, and we caught glimpses of cocker spaniels running by, their ears flapping, their tails wagging. They seemed to be having a marvelous time.

The confusion they caused was mammoth. People were dropping plates of food, and cocker spaniels were stopping to chow down. Mothers were snatching up children, who were being licked in the face by the rogue dogs.

"Geri! Geri! Geri!" Pepe came running up to me,

doing jumping jacks against my shins. "The dogs are loose!"

"I know!" I said. "How did it happen?"

"Well, Yolanda let the dogs out after lunch," Pepe said. "And I took Phoebe aside for a little romantic interlude. Suddenly we heard all this barking, and when we untangled ourselves, we saw that Jillian had opened the gate and was luring the cocker spaniels through it with strips of chicken. We went running at them, telling them to stay put, but they didn't listen."

"Where is Phoebe now?" I asked.

"She is trying to round them up. And so must we!" he yelled. "They are going off like popcorn in all directions! They might get hurt—there is no time to lose!"

It was hard to get a good idea of what was going on because of all the people in the way. You could get a glimpse of the havoc only by the way it rippled through the crowd, in a wave of yelling or people scattering.

When I ran out onto the driveway, I finally had a better understanding of what was going on. The cocker spaniels were now loose in the lavender fields, being chased by various people and various dogs.

I saw the golden cocker, Queen Mary, cornered by Phoebe in the U-Pick section of the lavender fields, but only momentarily, because Queen Mary suddenly changed direction and almost tripped a woman and her kid who were in the way. The kid, no more than three, dropped his ice cream cone and started crying. But he cried even louder when his mom's ice cream cone also went airborne and landed splat on top of his head.

Making matters worse, every one of the dogs suddenly came tearing up out of the fields and went pell-mell through the line of booths, zigzagging as they darted in and out of them. One booth, constructed like an open tent, came crashing down, causing a few choice epithets from its occupant, a guy selling different colored bottles of lavender oil that went caroming around like so many loose marbles.

Even worse, Jay chased one of the dogs—it looked like James, the black cocker spaniel— toward the chicken coop, only James ducked under it at the last minute. This caused the coop's door to fly open, and a dozen or more chickens got loose and joined the wild scene, all clucking and squawking and flapping as they dodged people and dogs. That's when we noticed Fuzzy; she was almost nose to beak with a big rooster and had an "I'm hungry for KFC" look in her eyes.

"Fuzzy!" screamed Felix, striding toward her. "Leave that chicken alone! Come!"

The rooster changed Fuzzy's mind by giving her a couple quick pecks to the snout. She yelped and made a beeline to Felix.

Meanwhile, Pepe and Phoebe had managed to get all the dogs headed in the same direction. The problem was that said direction was straight out toward the road. To make matters worse, Jillian had joined Pepe and Phoebe as they went after the cockers. She was red in the face and screaming as she waved her arms at them.

"Stupid dogs!" she hollered. "I'm going to get you!"

"Do something!" Pepe told me as he and Phoebe

went running past me. "She is making them head for the highway."

"Jillian!" I yelled, almost catching up with her. "Stop! They'll go into traffic and get hurt!"

"Yes, stop!" It was Felix. He and Fuzzy were just behind me now.

Over to my right, I saw Clara and Jay chasing after the dogs. Lionel and Kevin were not far behind them.

"That's my plan!" shrieked Jillian as the cockers neared the road and began to spread out, no longer in a tight pack.

Everything was utterly frenzied. Barking, yipping, and screaming—the long fur of the cockers flying as they ran—not to mention my leaping heart, since it looked like the dogs would surely run into the cars that were speeding by the long line of buses.

Speaking of the buses, all four of them were starting their engines and had both their front and back doors still open.

"Get the dogs on the buses!" I yelled at Pepe. They would be safer there than running in the street.

He must have conveyed the message to Phoebe and Fuzzy because suddenly each of them singled out one of the dogs and herded it toward a bus. James jumped on the first bus and Queen Mary got into the second bus. That left just two dogs on their own. Jillian made a beeline for one of them, trying to scare it into the street. The first two buses closed their doors and pulled out onto the highway.

"Can you stop her?" I asked Jimmy G as he went galloping by.

"Jimmy G will try!" he said.

In my haste, I tripped and almost fell down, but Felix caught me. As I looked up, Jillian followed Henry onto the second-to-last bus. The driver closed the doors and drove off.

"Oh, no," I said as the last of the cocker spaniels, Victoria, jumped through the rear door of the one bus still there. "We've got to get her off the bus!" I told Felix and Jimmy G.

"*No problema,*" Pepe told me. He hopped aboard the bus. I could hear the bus driver yelling something. He got up, and I could see him heading toward the back of the bus. He must have been trying to shoo the dogs off the bus.

And he was successful. Pepe and Victoria ran off the bus through its back door, the driver right behind them. But Victoria ran straightaway to the bus's front door and reboarded it, Pepe following her right back aboard, yelling, "No! *Perro estupido!*"

As the driver stood scratching his head at the rear of the bus, I said, "We've got to catch up with those buses!"

"Follow Jimmy G!" said my boss. "He drove bigger than this in Iraq." Moving faster than I thought he could, Jimmy G jumped in and took a seat behind the steering wheel. "Come on!" he told me.

There was no time to think, and Pepe and I got in with him. But Jimmy G closed the doors just as Felix tried to join us.

"Hey!" said Felix, looking in at us and pounding on the closed door.

"Hey!" yelled the bus driver, also looking in and pounding on the door. "That's my bus!"

Jimmy G was waiting for no one. As he pulled

out, Felix yelled, "We'll take my car and be right behind you!" He and Fuzzy ran off as we merged into traffic.

Jimmy G gunned it, and we picked up speed.

"Follow that bus!" Pepe yelled at our boss, the bus that left before us barely visible far ahead. Then my dog turned to me. "I have always wanted to say that, Geri," he said. "I know the phrase is really 'Follow that car,' but it is close enough."

Chapter 48

I sat in the jump seat across from Jimmy G, holding Pepe up so he could see the road ahead. Victoria sat in the seat behind us, looking out the window as the scenery went by, her ears flapping in the breeze.

"Love this automatic transmission," said the boss. "Wish Jimmy G had had one during the war."

"*Vamonos! Vamonos!*" Pepe told him.

"He wants you to go faster," I said.

"Who? The rat-dog? Tell him this tub's going fast as it can."

"There are three buses that left ahead of us," I said. "I wonder where they're all going."

"And those crazy dogs are on all of them," said the boss. "Well, all we can do is follow our noses. Right now, Jimmy G's nose is glued to the one ahead."

The road we were on was a little curvy and had a few up and downs. At one of the rises, we saw two buses ahead of us, and the one in the lead turned off when it came to a Y in the road.

"Which one to follow?" asked Pepe.

"We've got to follow the one with Jillian on it. She's dangerous to dogs!"

"She called Jimmy G Mr. Dangerous," said Jimmy G. He sounded wistful.

"What were you doing with her anyway?" I asked.

"Some investigation," said Jimmy G. "Just trying to get the lay of the land."

"Everyone tells me you're working for the judge," I said.

"That's what Jimmy G wanted them to think," he said.

Another lavender farm came into view. A crowd of people stood at the edge of the road, waiting to be picked up to continue their tour.

The bus we were following just passed them by. When we also passed them by, I looked behind us and saw a few people shaking their fists at us.

We came to another Y in the road, and the bus we were after turned off to the left, just as the other bus had done. We took the turn with too much speed—I could feel the bus hunker down on the driver's side tires and was afraid we were going to roll over. Thank goodness we righted ourselves just in time.

"Ah," said Pepe. "That was *muy* exciting! I had a chase like this when I worked with the *federales* going after the drug cartel."

I took a deep breath and looked out the rear window. I'd almost forgotten that Felix said he'd follow us in his car, and I hoped I'd see him. When I spotted his car a couple hundred yards back, I felt much better.

"We are heading back toward town," said Pepe.

"How do you know?" I asked, looking around at the rolling, straw-colored fields.

"We *perros* have a keen sense of direction," my dog told me. "How else do you think my wolfy ancestors tracked bison across the Great Plains?"

I had no answer for that but was soon relieved to see that Pepe was right. Hot on the tail of the bus in front of us, we took another hard turn, then looped around through a stand of trees, and the fairgrounds came into sight. There were banners everywhere and crowds of people walking toward the center of activity.

The bus we followed pulled up onto the grassy field in front of the fairgrounds and came to a stop. The other three buses were already there. We rolled to a stop beside them. As we all got out, we could hear the various bus drivers cajoling their canine stowaways to get off their buses.

"We must round those cockers up, *pronto*," Pepe told me.

People started disembarking from the buses. I saw that Kevin had managed to get on one of the buses, and was clutching James, the black cocker spaniel. Queen Mary, the golden cocker spaniel, went running off another bus, pursued by a little girl who was crying, "Mommy, I want that doggie."

Felix drove up just then and got out with Fuzzy.

"What a wild ride," he told me.

"What now?" asked Jimmy G, poking a cigar in his mouth.

Jillian got off one of the buses, dragging Henry by the scruff of his neck.

"Hey!" said Pepe. "Unhand that dog!"

Chapter 49

Jimmy G figured he should be the one to handle Jillian. After all, he had the best rapport with her. He swaggered over toward her.

"Hey, babe!" he said.

"Back off!" she said. "You let me down, Mr. Dangerous!"

"You didn't give Jimmy G a chance," he said, strolling nearer, his hands extended.

"*Mr. Dangerous?*" said Felix.

Jillian held the struggling cocker by the scruff of the neck. "If you come any closer, I'm going to hurt this dog." She shook it a little. "Since you're not man enough to do it."

"We got the evidence on you!" his girl Friday shouted out, waving the little camera. "We know what you've been doing. We've got the photos on your camera that show the chocolate chip cookies where you left them."

"Hey, you've got no right to do that!" Jillian said. "That's my property." She grabbed for the camera and, in doing so, dropped the dog. Henry hit the ground with a yelp and went running off into the crowd.

Jillian whirled around and took off running after the dog, and Jimmy G followed her. But he didn't get too far. Just a few yards into the crowd, he ran into a tall, fair-haired man with blue eyes. Jimmy G recognized him immediately. The mook. From the camera.

"Hey, you!" Jimmy G yelled. "You've been messing with Jimmy G's lady."

"Who's Jimmy G?" asked Hugh.

"Right here," said Jimmy G, pointing at himself. "And Jimmy G is going to whip your butt."

"I don't think so," Hugh said. "I was a wrestling champion in college."

"And Jimmy G's got a black belt in *pissed off!*"

"Stop acting like an idiot, boss!" yelled Geri.

Too late. Jimmy G hit Hugh like a freight train and landed a right hook to his noggin. This shook Hugh, but he stayed on his feet and knocked Jimmy G off balance with a hard shove to his shoulder. Next thing Jimmy G knew, the guy had grappled with him and put him in a vise-like headlock. He was trying to take him down to the ground! But being the bigger man, Jimmy G held on for all he was worth. He gave Hugh a shot to the ribs with his left elbow, which caused him to grunt in pain, but the guy still managed to tighten up on the headlock, and Jimmy G started seeing stars.

"Gimme a hand!" he called to Felix. "This guy's tougher than he looks!"

"Gladly!" said Felix, jumping into the fray.

Chapter 50

I couldn't believe Jimmy G and Felix were fighting with Hugh. Felix had stepped in and smacked Hugh in the nose, which was now bleeding. Even so, Hugh still had my boss in a headlock and they were all on the ground, rolling around and grunting like pigs as Felix struggled to loosen Hugh's grip on Jimmy G.

"It is a real battle royal!" said Pepe. "It is like the *lucha libre,* but without masks, and much more realistic."

"It *is* real," I told my dog. "Can't we stop them?"

"You may wade in if you like," he said. "But for myself, I have no wish to be made into a tortilla."

Fuzzy joined in, barking like crazy, evidently not happy to see her master involved in a fight.

I couldn't believe the childishness of the men in my life. Felix and Jimmy G were so proud of themselves for taking down Hugh when all the poor guy had done was hit on me and maybe get a little frisky with Jillian.

"Geri?" It was the voice of my counselor. I turned

around and saw Suzanna behind me. She was with two other women who looked at me and then looked at each other.

"Suzanna!" I said, trying to sound happy to see her.

"What's going on?" she asked, looking at the men who were rolling over each other on the grass, punching and grunting.

"That's my boss," I said, trying to point out Jimmy G. He had lost his fedora. His nose was starting to bleed again. "And over there, that one is my boyfriend, Felix." Felix was trying to pry Hugh's arm off Jimmy G's throat.

"And the other guy?" Suzanna asked.

"Uh, that's a veterinarian who forced me to eat oysters," I said.

"And subjects dogs to unnecessary surgeries," said Pepe indignantly.

Suzanna looked worried.

Just then, two of the escaped cockers raced by, one pursued by Kevin and the other by Lionel. The other two must be out there somewhere, and Jillian was after them. I could track their progress by watching the crowds, some tripping, some swearing, parting like the Red Sea as the dogs went running through.

Felix finally managed to break Hugh's grip on Jimmy G, and the three of them got to their feet.

A security guard came running up. "Break it up, folks!" he said. "This is a family venue."

"We're trying to rescue some dogs!" I said to the guard. "They got loose at one of the farms. There's a woman: red hair, very thin, wearing pink shorts and a purple top. She's trying to kill them!"

"Well, the dogs can't be running around loose," he said. He stared at Pepe and Fuzzy. "Dogs aren't allowed on the festival grounds. You're going to have to take them to the dog-sitting area. It's located on the other side of the amphitheater."

"I have not needed a dog-sitter since I was a pup," said Pepe.

"What'll we do?" Felix asked me.

"I'll tell you what *I'm* going to do," said Hugh, staring bullets at Jimmy G. "I'm going to talk to my attorney."

"Go for it," Jimmy G told him.

As Hugh stalked off, still dabbing at his nose, I said, "We need to find the cockers ourselves. We can't risk them getting hurt."

"Good plan," Felix told me, then added, "Boy, that felt good."

"What?"

"Smacking that smarmy Hugh," he said.

"Yeah," Jimmy G told him. "Thanks for the help."

"*De nada*," said Pepe, who had wisely only watched. "Say, Geri," he asked me. "You are not going to put Fuzzy and me in that *stupido* dog-sitting area, are you?"

"No time," I told him. "Come on, everybody, we need to find the dogs."

"Let me know what I can do to help," Suzanna said.

We all split up and went in separate directions through the fairgrounds. You'd think it would have been easy to locate a bunch of dogs, but there were so many tourists packed in and around all the different booths that all we heard from time to time was some distant barking and yelling. Every time we thought we had a bead on a cocker, we hit a dead end: just crowds of happy festival-goers enjoying the scents and flavors of lavender. I was getting pretty worried. It was clear that Jillian was willing to do almost anything to punish the dogs she perceived were her enemies.

After about fifteen minutes of fruitless searching, Pepe said, "This is reminding me *muy* much of a snipe hunt."

Good grief, I thought, maybe the cockers had left the fairgrounds, or maybe someone had found them and taken them to the dog area.

"Let's see if they're in the dog area," I said to Pepe. We bumped into Felix and Fuzzy on our way over there.

"Anything?" Felix asked me.

"*Nada*," said Pepe.

"Nothing," I told Felix. "We're going to see if anyone turned them in." As we headed toward the dog-sitting area, we had to pass the amphitheater. When we first arrived, a band had been playing some cowboy ballads. But now a podium was set up in the center of the stage, and a man bent over the microphone prepared to make an announcement.

"And now it is my great honor to introduce Judge Julian Valentine," said the voice. "As we all know, he has been instrumental in organizing our lavender festival for years, and he is currently running for reelection as Clallam County's Judge of the Superior Court. Let's give him a big hand!"

The people sitting in plastic chairs and sprawled

on picnic blankets on the grass in front of the stage responded with a light spattering of applause.

Judge Valentine was wearing a white linen suit and a red, white, and blue striped tie. He nodded, acknowledging the applause with a faint smile on his lips. He looked like a movie star. And that impression was enhanced by the inclusion of a bodyguard, a heavyset man in a gray T-shirt and mirror sunglasses, who stood with his arms crossed in back of the stage, scanning the crowd. I noticed he had a bandage wrapped around one wrist.

"I'm happy to say," the judge announced, "that this is the most successful festival in the history of Sequim. This festival, which was conceived as a way to celebrate our reputation as one of the premier lavender-growing regions in the country, has become another source of pride and income for our community—"

"Blah! Blah! Blah!" said Pepe. "A typical political speech. More dog bones for everyone!"

I had to agree, but as the judge droned on about jobs created and plans for future expansion, things got more interesting. The golden cocker, Queen Mary, appeared to the right and ran through the crowds on the grass, zigzagging back and forth, with Jillian in hot pursuit. And in her hand, she carried a butcher knife. She looked completely crazy. People began screaming and scrambling to their feet, moving off to the side.

Queen Mary scurried toward the stage, perhaps hoping it would be safe, but Jillian was close behind, swinging at her with the wicked-looking knife.

The golden dog scrambled up the stairs to the

stage, and Julian bent down and scooped her up, holding her close against his chest. Jillian followed.

"Stop!" he said, holding out his hand. It was a dramatic picture, as Jillian—her red hair flying, her mouth mumbling threats, and her arm upraised with the sun glinting off the edge of the knife—confronted her brother.

"I will not allow you to harm this innocent animal!" said Julian.

Everybody stood frozen in horror—everyone except Pepe and Fuzzy. They took one look at each other and headed for the stage. They leaped onto the platform just as Jillian took a swipe at the dog in her brother's arms.

The judge took a defensive step back, and she missed and raised the knife for another try. Too late: Pepe and Fuzzy chomped onto the back of her ankles, one on each side. She gave a shriek and staggered forward. At the same time, the bodyguard grabbed her arm and wrestled the knife free. It fell to the stage with a thud.

The crowd erupted in applause. Felix and I rushed onto the platform and picked up our dogs. We gazed out at the applauding crowd and saw Jimmy G standing in the back of the crowd, holding the black cocker spaniel. Kevin was there, too, holding the silvery-colored Henry, with Lionel beside him. And Clara was next to him, with Jay by her side, cradling Victoria. They couldn't applaud, with their arms full of dogs, but their happy smiles said it all.

Chapter 51

A month later we were all back in Port Townsend for the memorial for Barrett Boswell. Felix and I drove up with Pepe and Fuzzy. I still wasn't talking to Jimmy G and didn't even know if he was going. As far as I was concerned, we could have solved the case and protected the dogs much sooner if he hadn't gotten in the way. I didn't know if I could ever trust him again. I also didn't know what I would do for a job if I stopped working for him.

Lionel and Kevin had opened up Boswell's house for the occasion. Kevin was already working his magic with the decorations. The heavy Victorian furniture was still in place, but all the clutter was gone. The beautiful wood pieces gleamed, and the sun shone through the lace-covered windows, illuminating the gorgeous Aubusson carpet on the floor of the living room.

Kevin saw me admiring it. "It's the real thing!" he said.

"Nice!" I replied, knowing that carpets like that were worth a small fortune.

"And the best news is that we get to keep it! Julian has dropped the suit now that he's decided to adopt a dog and collect his share of the fortune that way."

"Julian adopted a dog?"

"Yes, the one that Jillian was going to kill," Kevin said. "I think her name is Queen Mary. It seems he fell in love with her after saving her life." He leaned in and whispered in my ear. "I think it really helps his image. You should see the old ladies in Sequim cooing over him whenever he takes her out with him. He's a shoo-in to win the election."

Lionel came into the room, bearing a silver plate of stuffed mushrooms.

"Bacon!" said Pepe.

"Is that bacon?" I asked, staring at the fragrant morsels.

"Of course," said Lionel. I picked one up and held it out to Pepe. He gathered it up in his little teeth and took it over to a corner to eat. Despite his greedy nature, he is a fastidious eater and likes to take his time with his food.

"I thought you ate light! Egg whites and vegetables and all that."

"We're still eating light at the Floral Fantasy," Lionel said, "but we decided on an entirely different feel for Boswell Abbey. We're going for an elegant, decadent period feel. Cream sauces. Beef roasts. Yorkshire pudding. Crumpets with butter." He beamed. "It's such a pleasure to get to create an entirely new cuisine."

The big Maine coon cat strolled into the room and went walking up to Pepe. Pepe stood his ground but began to shiver.

"I see that Precious seems to be adapting to life without Boswell," I said.

Kevin sneezed. "I forgot to take my allergy pills," he said, giving Lionel a wry look. He turned to me. "I spend most of my time at the Floral Fantasy with James."

"James?"

Kevin smiled. "We adopted one of the cocker spaniels, too."

"But the pet policy?"

"We changed it. Floral Fantasy now accepts dogs as guests, and Boswell Abbey will welcome guests with cats."

"Guess we'll be staying at the Floral Fantasy," said Felix, drawing me close. I smiled, thinking about how much I had enjoyed the rest of my romantic weekend with Felix after we had rescued the dogs and returned them to Carpenter Manor.

The doorbell rang, and Kevin rushed to answer it. Yolanda and Colleen came in together. They seemed to be best friends now, instead of enemies. Yolanda was wearing a flowery dress, and she looked lovely with her dark hair pinned back in a French braid. This was the first time I had ever seen Colleen out of her overalls, and she dressed up nicely in a jade-green silk blouse, a pair of gray linen slacks, and strappy black sandals. When Yolanda sent the invitations to the memorial, she indicated that, as this was a celebration of Boswell's life, we should wear colors, not black. I had chosen to wear one of my favorite vintage dresses, which had little pink flowers on a dusty-green background.

Yolanda hugged me. "It's so good to see you,

Geri. We really owe so much to you. You saved the dogs, and you reunited a broken family."

"Thank you!" I glowed. It was nice to know someone appreciated my efforts. Jimmy G had not called me since that dreadful day at the fairgrounds when I had discovered that he had double-crossed me. And I refused to call him, I was not going anywhere near him unless he apologized for his behavior.

"Where is Phoebe?" Pepe asked, running in circles around Colleen and sniffing her ankles.

Colleen looked at him with amusement. "Turns out that Phoebe is pregnant!"

"What?" I said.

"What?" said Pepe.

"Yes, I noticed she was acting differently and I took her to the vet. Not Hugh, of course—the rumor is he's closing up shop—but our old vet. Anyway, he said she's pregnant. Probably four weeks along." She wagged her finger at Pepe. "Wonder how that happened?"

"I'm going to be a father?" Pepe said, turning around in circles.

"How did that happen?" I asked. I thought Pepe was fixed.

"I suppose the usual way," Colleen said.

"When are the puppies due?" I asked.

"Another five weeks," Colleen said. "You'll have to come up and visit. Maybe you'll take one? They come with a little fortune of their own."

"That's right," I said. "The trust applies to the issue of the dogs."

"Sure," she said, "so the farm is safe for a long time."

"This is amazing!" I said.

"¡Es una noticia asombrosa!" Pepe said.

Pepe wanted to hang around in hopes of hearing more about his lady love, so I followed Yolanda and Lionel into the kitchen. Every surface was covered with platters, all beautifully arranged. There were little puff pastries, decorated with orange nasturtium flowers. A platter of Camembert cheese and grapes. A beautiful yellow-and-blue pottery bowl full of sliced tomatoes, mozzarella, and basil leaves.

I noticed two large pitchers of lemonade sitting on the sideboard with stalks of lavender floating in them. I shuddered. "Really? Lavender lemonade?"

Lionel looked surprised.

"Oh, I never thought about it that way. Just that it was Boswell's favorite drink."

"As long as it had vodka in it," Yolanda observed wryly. She turned to me. "The police finally let us know that was how the poison was administered. It was in the vodka."

"But we still don't know how it got in there?" I asked.

"Actually," said Yolanda, "they think it was Bickerstaff. They found a bottle of potassium cyanide in his home."

"But that doesn't make any sense," said Lionel. "Who poisoned Bickerstaff?"

"They think that Bickerstaff put the poison in Boswell's vodka bottle. But he didn't know that Boswell spiked his lemonade. So when he was in Boswell's office, looking for a copy of the trust document, he took a sip of the lemonade."

"And died of his own poison! A sad story!" said Lionel.

"Then Boswell took the vodka home—the bottle

was probably in his briefcase, so the police wouldn't have found it during their investigation—and poured himself his usual nightcap."

"What a relief!" I said, because I still had been wondering about Jimmy G and his late-night visit to Boswell.

Yolanda gave me a funny look.

"Knowing the true story," I said.

As we headed back to the living room, we passed the office. I saw that it was full of flowers. A large photo of Boswell sat on the desk, along with a glass of lemonade.

"I thought he would appreciate it," said Yolanda, a little smile on her lips.

There was a fancy cat tree beside the desk, made of plush maroon velvet and trimmed with gold fringe. Precious, despite his size, leaped into its higher branches, as light as a bird, and sat there glaring at me with his golden eyes. I don't think the cat would ever like me, despite the fact that we had helped him figure out how his servant had died.

"Nice cat tree!" I said.

"Yes, Lionel bought it for the cat," Yolanda said. "He's crazy about the animal. I'm glad because I couldn't have a cat with Victoria."

"So you only have one dog left?" I asked.

"Yes," she said, "and I'm so grateful. My life is so much more flexible now that I don't have to coordinate all those different caretakers for the dog. I'm thinking of going back home to visit my family."

The scratchy front doorbell sounded, and we went down the hall to find Clara and Jay entering. They were bringing flowers as well. Yolanda went off to arrange them in a vase.

"So how are things at Carpenter Manor?" I asked.

"So peaceful without all those crazy dogs," said Clara.

"We're going to take care of Victoria while Yolanda travels," Jay said.

"Jay moved in," said Clara, giving him a big squeeze. Her face turned pink as she looked up at him, but he just gazed down at her with adoration. "He's still working for Colleen, but we're talking about using some of the Carpenter Manor property to grow cut flowers to sell to florists. We've got to think about the future, when the dogs won't be here anymore. Of course, we hope to adopt one of Phoebe's puppies."

"So how did it all work out with the dogs?" I asked.

"Julian got us all together in a room and negotiated an agreement," Clara said. "Everyone who takes care of one of the dogs gets an allowance from the trust. It's being split up rather than all going to one person, but that's fine with Yolanda. She didn't want the responsibility for all the dogs, plus she gets to live rent free as long as she stays at Carpenter Manor. Same for Colleen with Lost Lakes Lavender Farm."

"So if Kevin has James and Yolanda has Victoria and the judge has Queen Mary, then who has Henry?" I asked.

"We're taking care of him right now," Clara said. "The judge insists that Jillian should get a chance to adopt one of the dogs if she wants, but no one trusts her."

"She would be better off with a cat!" said Pepe, who had coming running up to join us.

"What happened to her?" I asked.

"Well, Julian arranged for her to go away to a private clinic for a complete mental evaluation. There wasn't really any crime she could be charged with—"

"Except for shooting me," said Jay, "and that was an accident! So I didn't want to press charges."

The doorbell rang again, and the judge strolled in, carrying the beautiful golden cocker spaniel under his arm. He certainly seemed happier and more relaxed than I had seen him in the past. He wasn't even wearing a suit: just a Hawaiian shirt in shades of peach, coral, and gold that matched the fur of his canine companion. His bodyguard was at his side, carrying a pillow for the dog and a gold water bowl.

Pepe glared at the man.

The bodyguard glared back. It had become very obvious, when we saw the bandage wrapped around his wrist, that it was Judge Julian's bodyguard whom Pepe had bitten. He had broken into the veterinary clinic and Carpenter Manor and Jillian's home looking for copies of the trust document, under orders from the judge. Pepe wanted to file charges, but I told him that he was not going to be allowed to sign the paperwork.

The house started to fill up with other citizens of Port Townsend. We saw Flynn, the bartender from the Windjammer, who told us that he just had to come to honor the memory of his best customer. We also met many of Boswell's friends from the various charitable and artistic enterprises he sponsored. It was a congenial group, and it was a lovely way to honor Boswell's memory as people exchanged their favorite stories about him.

Just as the judge had gathered us in the living room to raise our glasses in a toast to "our dear departed friend, Barrett Boswell," the scratchy front doorbell sounded again. Whoever it was, was about one hour late. Since I was closest to the door, I went to answer it. To my shock, Jimmy G stood on the doorstep, dressed in his usual sport coat and fedora, with a big bunch of Gerbera daisies in his hand.

"Sorry to be late," he mumbled holding them out. "I just wanted to pay my respects."

"We have no respect for you!" said Pepe, who had come to the door with me. "Without your so-called help, we would have solved this case on the first day."

I just turned away without saying anything.

"Oh, come on, Geri," said my boss, following me into the hallway. I was a bit shocked. I don't think I ever heard him use my first name before. "I'm sorry. I've learned my lesson. I'll never hold out on you again."

"That's because you won't have the chance," said Pepe. "We are going into business for ourselves. Sullivan and Sullivan!"

"I can't trust you," I said. "And if I can't trust you, I can't work with you. From now on, I'm working with the only partner I can count on."

"And that partner is me!" said Pepe.

Recipes

Floral Fantasy Lavender Vodka Tonics

Make lavender-infused simple syrup by combining 1 cup of sugar and 1 cup of water in a pan. Stir over low heat until the sugar is completely dissolved. Sprinkle in 2 to 4 heaping tablespoons of lavender buds (depending on how much you like the flavor of lavender) and stir. Turn off the heat and let the lavender infuse into the simple syrup for 5 to 15 minutes. Strain and store in glass in the refrigerator until ready to use. Lionel loves lavender, so he usually leaves the lavender buds in the simple syrup and doesn't strain them out until he's making the drinks.

Combine 1 tablespoon of lavender-infused simple syrup with 2 ounces of vodka and 6 ounces of tonic water. Serve over ice. Adjust proportions of ingredients to your taste. Lionel's preference: 1 shot of lavender-infused simple syrup, 2 shots of vodka, and a splash of tonic.

Lost Lakes Lavender Shortbread

¼ cup lavender buds
½ cup sugar
2 sticks unsalted butter
2 cups flour

In a food processor, process ¼ cup of sugar with the lavender buds. Add another ¼ cup of sugar and 2 sticks of unsalted butter. Cream together. Add the flour. Press the crumbly dough firmly into a round pie pan. Pierce the dough with a fork in a decorative design and flute the edges. Bake at 350 for 30 to 35 minutes.

Acknowledgments

Seattle is a great place to live if you are a writer. We're thankful for all the folks around us who like to talk about and celebrate the writing life. Several members of our local writing community deserve a special thank-you: Kevin O'Brien, our fellow Kensington writer, for career advice. Tracy Weber, author of the Downward Dog mysteries, for shepherding us through conferences. Judith Gille, author of *The View from Casa Chepitos,* for reviewing Pepe's Spanish (any mistakes that remain are ours). Shayla Simuel and Monte Hakola, Pepe wranglers, for prepping the real Pepe for his personal appearances. And our friends, the booksellers at our local independent bookstores who welcome us: Karen, Casey, Justus, and Brandi at Elliot Bay Book Company, Wendy at Third Place Books, Olivia at University Bookstore, and Fran, Adel, and J.B. at the Seattle Mystery Book Shop.

We also thank the members of our writing group—Linda Anderson, Rachel Bukey, and Janis Wildy—who listen when we read and chuckle in the right places. In addition, we thank the Shipping

Group members, who help us with our social media strategy and website design, as well as the members of the local chapter of Sisters in Crime, who provide camaraderie, education, and a great holiday party.

Special thanks and affection to Faizel Kahn, the owner of the coffee shop where we meet every Tuesday afternoon. Faizel keeps us well supplied with food and coffee while we argue over whom and how to kill. If you ever want to see the best Yelp reviews in the world, look up Café Argento in Seattle. Better yet, go visit.

We add a special thank-you to our agent, Stephany Evans, whose initials SE also stand for Super Editor. She always makes our first sentence (and many subsequent ones) better. Our editor at Kensington, Michaela Hamilton tempers her gentle reminders of our deadlines with encouragement and enthusiasm.

Finally, we are most grateful to our families: Curt's wife, Stephanie, and Waverly's daughter, Shaw, who make our writing lives possible.

Don't miss the next delightful entry in the
Barking Detective mystery series—

THE SILENCE OF THE CHIHUAHUAS

Coming from Kensington in 2015!

Keep reading to enjoy a sample excerpt . . .

Chapter 1

The veterinarian was a short man shaped like an egg, with a rounded torso that narrowed at either end to a bald head on top and tiny feet at the bottom. He wore rimless glasses and a white lab coat.

"Hello, I'm Norman Dodd," he said, holding out his hand. It was small and clammy. Nonetheless, I clung to it as he pumped mine up and down. I had never consulted a vet before about my new Chihuahua, Pepe, but now I was really worried.

Pepe was one of a group of Chihuahuas who had been flown up to Seattle from L.A., where they were being abandoned in record numbers. I had adopted him six months earlier, and he had become my best friend and partner in my work as a private detective.

"Why are you here today?" Dr. Dodd asked, consulting the clipboard the receptionist had placed on the counter in the exam room at the Lake Union Animal Clinic. Pepe sat on the metal table, his long ears perked forward, his dark eyes fixed on me. I wished I could tell what he was thinking. That was the problem.

"My dog stopped talking to me," I said. "About four days ago."

The vet had been running his pudgy fingers along the sides of Pepe's white flanks.

"What do you mean?" he asked. "He used to bark a lot, and now he's stopped?" He chuckled. "Some Chihuahua owners would celebrate!"

"No, it's not that," I said.

"Then what do you mean?"

"I mean he used to talk to me, and then four days ago he mysteriously stopped talking."

The vet's eyes narrowed. "Define talking!"

"He spoke," I said. "Words strung together into complete sentences. He has a great vocabulary. A bit of Spanish. Mostly English."

Pepe sat on the table, smiling up at me with those big dark eyes.

"What's wrong with you?" I asked, addressing him as I had many times during the last four days. "Why don't you speak?"

Dr. Dodd shook his head. "I think you've come to the wrong place, miss," he said. "You don't need a vet. You need a shrink."

I didn't tell him I had already consulted with my counselor. Suzanna already knows about my talking dog, and when I told her he had stopped talking, she congratulated me.

"So what do you think caused you to own your thoughts and feelings instead of projecting them onto your dog?" she asked with a happy smile.

"You don't understand," I said. "He was really helping me. I don't think I could have solved any of those cases without him." Pepe and I had been responsible for catching several murderers, kidnappers, and bad dogs, while working for the private investigation agency run by Jimmy Gerrard.

"Geri, it has always puzzled me that you want to give credit to your dog. Why not acknowledge and celebrate your own accomplishments?"

"But that's wrong!" I said. Meanwhile, Pepe just sat there, on top of one of the many pillows in Suzanna's office, seeming quite pleased with himself without saying a word.

"What's wrong with you?" I asked him. "You always want to take credit for everything we do." My dog is a bit of an attention hound.

"Geri," said Suzanna, "if I didn't think this was just a metaphor, I'd be very concerned about your mental state. If you persist in this delusion, I think you should consider in-patient treatment."

I saw Pepe flinch at that. Thank God, he was still registering his reactions, if not actually expressing his opinion. And like many dog owners, I could read my dog fairly accurately. "You don't want that," I said to him. "You don't want me to go away. They won't let you come with me."

"Do you want me to check into some possibilities for you?" said Suzanna. "Or perhaps I should refer you to a psychiatrist?" Suzanna had been licensed as a counselor in the state of Washington after she earned her MA, but she can't prescribe medication. It takes someone with an MD to diagnose and write prescriptions.

"I don't need a psychiatrist," I said. "My dog does!"

I glared at Pepe. He looked a little worried. One ear quirked forward.

"Do you have referrals to dog shrinks?" I asked a little loudly and defiantly, directing the words at Pepe, not at Suzanna.

"I actually know several," said Suzanna. "Dr. Mallard was very helpful when my cat started hiding under the furniture. He gave her some antianxiety medication, and that cleared up her symptoms." She got up, went over to her desk, and flipped through her Rolodex. She picked out a card and handed it to me.

"Thanks," I said, getting up, "I think I will look into that." I could tell by Pepe's expression that he was upset. Good! I was upset, too. Maybe it would upset him enough that he would start talking.

I couldn't understand why he had stopped.

The irony is that I had spent the past six months trying to convince people, including my boss, Jimmy Gerrard, and my boyfriend, Felix Navarro, that my dog talked. They were just starting to entertain that possibility when he stopped. Now what? They would think I was crazy. Apparently everyone did.

The vet was talking again. "I'll check his vocal cords. See if there's anything causing problems in his throat. Perhaps he ate something . . ." He pried open Pepe's jaws and peered inside, waving around a little flashlight. "Nope. That all looks normal." He patted Pepe on the head. "I can't see anything that would cause him to stop barking. Of course, if you want, we can take some blood and do some tests . . ."

I saw the fright in Pepe's eyes, but I nodded. "Yes, I think that's a good idea!" If he wasn't going to tell me what was going on, I would do everything in my power to figure it out on my own. But, really, mostly I was terribly hurt. I don't know if this has ever happened to you: your best friend suddenly stops speaking to you, won't return your calls, won't answer your questions about what's going on.

It had happened to me just a few months earlier, and it was still painful. I had been working with Brad for over five years, ever since we both graduated from interior design school. He opened a small shop where he refinished furniture he picked up at auction sales and then sold it to his clients. He let me use the back of the shop for my own thrift-store finds and loaned me pieces I needed for my short-lived career as a stager.

Then suddenly I couldn't get in contact with him. When I went by the shop, it was closed. When I called him, my calls went straight to voice mail. I was desperately worried about him and also confused. Had I done something wrong? I kept going back over the last conversation I had with him. We had been in the back of the shop, surrounded by pieces of furniture in various stages of refurbishing. A stuffed owl looked over the scene from a perch on a grandfather clock. The skeletal remains of a Victorian sofa occupied one corner. A cracked blue-and-white Chinese vase sat on top of a mahogany drop-leaf table. Brad was at his sewing machine, stitching pink piping around an olive-drab velvet pillow. It seemed like an ordinary conversation. We talked about his volatile relationship with his partner, Jay.

We discussed whether or not he should agree to the color scheme his client Mrs. Fairchild demanded for her kitchen.

"Lemon yellow is such a harsh color to live with," I had said. And that was the last thing I remembered from that day. Surely my opinion about paint colors had not been so outrageous as to cause the rift in our friendship.

I came back to the present. Dr. Dodd was staring at me, waiting for my answer.

"Yes, let's go ahead and do some blood work!" I said.

Pepe just stared at me with his big eyes. He wasn't talking, but his message was clear: "Please don't do this to me!" But I was desperate. I needed to know what was going on. If anything was going to get him to talk, it would be getting poked with a needle. He hates it. He began to tremble, but still he didn't speak. When the vet sunk the needle into his little flank, he merely squeaked.

"We'll call you if anything unusual shows up in the results," the vet said.

We left the vet's office and went out into a typical September day in Seattle. Sunny but with a hint of coolness in the air. I had one more place to go. Since Pepe wasn't talking to me, I thought I would go visit Brad and see if I could get him to talk to me.

The clinic was on Eastlake Boulevard, just a few blocks from my condo. And Brad's shop was also on Eastlake, in the other direction, down near the University Bridge, a drawbridge that spans the manmade canal connecting Lake Washington to the east with Lake Union, Seattle's most urban lake, surrounded, as it is, by houseboats and restaurants.

Pepe trotted ahead of me, wearing his little turquoise harness, his white tail wagging from side to side, held high and curving over his back like a comma. He seemed like just a happy little normal Chihuahua, if a Chihuahua can ever be normal. Maybe I would have to get used to the fact that my dog was no longer extraordinary. Maybe that was what was truly bothering me. Either that or the distinct possibility that I was crazy.

We were still a block from the shop when I began to realize something was definitely wrong. The little sign that hung above the door was missing. And as we got closer, I could see that the big front window was dark. Usually Brad has a striking tableau in the window, designed to catch the eye of motorists driving by: maybe a tiger-striped chair next to a red ceramic vase full of pampas grass on top of a black lacquered table edged with gold. Or a Victorian sofa upholstered in buttercup yellow underneath a chandelier made of orange pill bottles.

Now, as we approached the front door, I saw that the interior was completely empty. I cupped my hands and peered through the window. The concrete floor was cleared, except for a pile of trash in the corner, and the walls were bare. I dug my key out of my purse and tried it in the lock, but it didn't work. I tried to turn the doorknob, but it didn't move.

"What happened to my stuff?" I asked Pepe, but

he didn't answer me, just lifted his leg and peed on the corner of the building. I walked around the corner and through the tiny parking lot. The windows on the side were up too high for me to see inside the back room, which is where I kept my current projects and my tools. But when I got to the back door and peered through its window, the room looked empty as well, although it was hard to tell as the cavernous space was full of shadows.

The telephone was ringing as we walked in through the front door of my condo. For a moment, I thought it might be Brad, calling to tell me what was going on. But that would be crazy, right?

I looked at the caller ID, and it wasn't a number I recognized. The cryptic ID ended with the word **Hospital**. I grabbed it up and said, "Hello?"

"Is that you, Geri?" said the female voice on the other end of the line. She sounded familiar.

"Who is this?" I asked.

"You've got to help me!" said the woman on the other end. Her voice was rising in pitch and intensity. "They're holding me captive."

And then there was a brief scuffle on the other end, and I heard the dial tone.

"That's weird," I said to Pepe, as he poked his head out from the kitchen door, clearly curious about what I was doing. "I think that was my sister."

GREAT BOOKS,
GREAT SAVINGS!

When You Visit Our Website:
www.kensingtonbooks.com
You Can Save Money Off The Retail Price
Of Any Book You Purchase!

- All Your Favorite Kensington Authors
- New Releases & Timeless Classics
- Overnight Shipping Available
- eBooks Available For Many Titles
- All Major Credit Cards Accepted

Visit Us Today To Start Saving!
www.kensingtonbooks.com

All Orders Are Subject To Availability.
Shipping and Handling Charges Apply.
Offers and Prices Subject To Change Without Notice.

Grab These Cozy Mysteries
from
Kensington Books

Forget Me Knot Mary Marks	978-0-7582-9205-6	$7.99US/$8.99CAN
Death of a Chocoholic Lee Hollis	978-0-7582-9449-4	$7.99US/$8.99CAN
Green Living Can Be Deadly Staci McLaughlin	978-0-7582-7502-8	$7.99US/$8.99CAN
Death of an Irish Diva Mollie Cox Bryan	978-0-7582-6633-0	$7.99US/$8.99CAN
Board Stiff Annelise Ryan	978-0-7582-7276-8	$7.99US/$8.99CAN
A Biscuit, A Casket Liz Mugavero	978-0-7582-8480-8	$7.99US/$8.99CAN
Boiled Over Barbara Ross	978-0-7582-8687-1	$7.99US/$8.99CAN
Scene of the Climb Kate Dyer-Seeley	978-0-7582-9531-6	$7.99US/$8.99CAN
Deadly Decor Karen Rose Smith	978-0-7582-8486-0	$7.99US/$8.99CAN
To Kill a Matzo Ball Delia Rosen	978-0-7582-8201-9	$7.99US/$8.99CAN

Available Wherever Books Are Sold!

All available as e-books, too!

Visit our website at **www.kensingtonbooks.com**

Catering and Capers with
Isis Crawford!